SEA SONG

DEPTHS OF MAGIC
BOOK TWO

EMMA SHELFORD

This is a work of fiction. Names, characters, places, and incidents either are the product of the author's imagination or are used factitiously, and any resemblance to any persons, living or dead, business establishments, events, or locales is entirely coincidental.

SEA SONG

Kinglet Books
Victoria BC, Canada

Cover design by MiblArt

ISBN: 978-1989677452 (print)
ISBN: 978-1989677469 (ebook)

www.emmashelford.com

First edition: May 2022

CHAPTER 1

One day, I wouldn't have to come when he called. But that day was not today.

I ground my teeth and waited with crossed arms outside the warehouse door. Gulls yowled and circled in the darkening sky overhead, a portent of stormy seas to come. Wind tossed my long, white-blond hair and fluttered the surface of the Fraser River which flowed wide and slow at its mouth.

I could have ducked out of the breeze and taken shelter within the warehouse. The entryway was warm and welcoming, with a cozy couch and a cheery greeter willing to help with anything—for a price. I hunched my shoulders, unwilling to enter. The warehouse had been the first place I'd come to after escaping my former home under the sea. The Seamount had been controlling, but Branc and his warehouse's façade of comfort were worse.

Besides, I wasn't cold. My siren blood took care of that.

A car roared into an adjacent parking lot, and I glanced its way. I recognized the vehicle as Branc's. My stomach flopped. What assignment had he called me here for? He'd been silent for weeks, and I was desperate to pay off my debts to him. He didn't know how close I was to paying him off—a stack of cash under my bed was waiting for the day when I could pass him the entire amount I owed him—but without Branc's assignments, my ability to earn extra money was limited.

Branc slammed the door and sauntered over to me. Some might find him attractive, with his smooth black hair and defined features, but I couldn't see past his stranglehold over my life.

"You're here," he said when close enough to speak without shouting. "Good."

"You called, I came." I dipped a mocking curtsy, something I'd picked up from a movie my friend Byssa and I had watched last week.

Branc narrowed his eyes at me but didn't comment on my antics. "I need something from a colleague, but he's proving less than helpful. You're the distraction while I fetch it."

I played with my lip between my teeth while I searched Branc's face. The mission didn't sound too bad, as far as Branc's assignments went. My stomach squirmed with unease.

"We're stealing something," I said. "What is it?"

"It doesn't matter to you." Branc crossed his arms with an affected expression of nonchalance. His tense shoulders told a different story. Whatever we were going to steal mattered a great deal to Branc, and he was worried about something. "Will you do it?"

I stared at him for a moment.

Branc huffed a sigh. "Do I need to remind you of the sizable debt you still owe me? For tonight's work, I won't make you pay for your next four packages of Grace. I don't mind collecting your interest payments, but you might see it differently."

I scowled. I hated his hold on me, but I couldn't see that being party to stealing whatever Branc wanted was so terrible. And four packets of Grace? The slices of sea anemone endemic to the Seamount gave sirens the ability to be so much more underwater. The promise of four packages for free was a powerful incentive, whether I gave it right back to Branc to further pay off my debt or ate it myself.

"Yeah, I'll do it." I pushed off the warehouse wall and stalked to Branc's black sedan. "You'll need to drive me, though. I don't have wheels."

We were silent in the car. Branc drove with a preoccupied expression, his fingers tapping the steering wheel sporadically. I had nothing I wanted to say to Branc—nothing that was wise, anyway—so I stared out the passenger window and watched streetlights in the darkness.

Finally, Branc turned the car into a dimly lit parking lot next to a large marina filled with yachts. I turned to him and raised my eyebrow.

"Tell me again what the plan is?" I asked.

Branc cut the engine and pulled a backpack from the backseat. He dropped it in my lap.

"Put those clothes on," he said. "You're crashing a party. The clothes will help you fit in before you sing."

I pulled out a glittery top short enough to expose my midriff and a tight skirt that would barely cover my backside. I tightened my lips but didn't argue. Branc was right. If I fit in from the start, my targets would already be lulled into a sense of security. My siren song would ensnare them easily after that.

I peeled off my top and slithered into the new clothes. After I pulled on a terribly uncomfortable pair of bright red strappy high heels that made my feet hurt just to look at them, Branc checked his phone.

"The yacht is on dock five," he said. "When you get on board, siren the whole group. Snap your fingers for a signal, and I'll sneak on board. I won't need long, maybe two minutes. Once I'm off the boat, you'll leave when you can."

"You forgot something." I held out my hand. "I can't siren a whole group without Grace. My body is depleted."

Every bit of extra money I earned went straight back to Branc, with hardly enough left over to buy the Grace I needed to survive. Well, I had ingested a whole handful of Grace a few weeks ago—my new friend Levi had been in danger, and it had been the only way to save him— but its effects had worn off long before now.

"Of course." Branc pulled a waxed envelope from his pocket and shook its contents into my open palm. "Eat it all up. I need this to work tonight."

I blinked at Branc. He hadn't accompanied the Grace with a reminder that it would be added to my debt, which was a first for him. A muscle twitched along his jawline. Branc was seriously worried about something.

Well, good. I wouldn't lose sleep over Branc's unease. Before he could snatch away the Grace, I threw it into my mouth and chewed.

Flavor exploded on my tongue. I closed my eyes and

groaned at the phantom sensations of succulent salmon, whale songs, and the touch of a lover caressing my skin. When the feeling had abated somewhat, I opened my eyes. Branc watched me with an odd expression.

"Are you ready?" he asked. When I nodded, he opened his door. "Let's go."

I strutted behind him across the parking lot in my hated heels. I didn't need the height, but humans liked the look of the odd footwear, and they would help me fit in. Branc's shoulders were tense, and again I wondered what he was so worked up about. Now that I thought about it, I'd never heard of Branc handling an assignment personally. Involving himself in this mission meant either that it was so important that he needed to supervise it to make sure it was done properly, or that he didn't trust others with it. The latter sounded like Branc, but then here I was. Did he trust me? The thought made my lip curl. He shouldn't. As soon as I paid off my debt, he wouldn't see me again.

It wasn't difficult to find our destination. Dock five was lined with massive luxury yachts, but only one was filled with a chattering, laughing crowd of scantily dressed women and open-shirted men in defiance of the worsening weather. Lights twinkled from the bridge, and champagne glasses clinked together. Despite the cool breeze, the September night was not yet cold with the chill of approaching autumn, and the partygoers were kept warm by alcohol and the exertions of flirtation.

Branc stopped in the shadow of a nearby boat and nodded me forward. I tossed my hair back, took a deep breath, then walked slowly along the swaying dock.

A gangplank connected the yacht's aft deck to the dock. A man poured beer down his throat while a couple kissed next to him. I stepped onto the gangplank.

"Rocking party," I said in a low voice.

The man glanced at my face and then at the rest of me. I let him—he would be under my control soon enough—and when his eyes returned to mine, I gave him a slow smile.

"What's a girl got to do to get a drink around here?" I said.

"Whatever she wants," he replied. "I'd never turn away someone like you. Not that it's my party, but I know Jin wouldn't mind."

He waved a beleaguered-looking server forward who carried a tray of champagne glasses in one hand and appetizers in another. I accepted a tall flute and sipped it. Grace slid through my veins, hot and strong, and the promise of a champagne buzz paled in comparison. Why was I waiting? This whole boat could be under my command as soon as I wished it.

A thread of unease rippled through me—I disliked sirening others after my many years of subjugation at the Seamount—but I pushed the betraying sensation away. I was a siren, and I wouldn't hide it anymore. I wanted to embrace my heritage, and what better way than to exercise my greatest skill?

A hum built deep in my chest. I reached out to touch the man with my tanned fingers. Although he would feel my song through vibrations traveling from me to the boat and up from his feet, the signal was far stronger if I touched him directly. He stared at me, his eyes dilating with desire, and I pressed my front against his for maximal effect.

Within seconds, he was mine. His eyes glazed over, and his hand dropped listlessly to the railing. I stepped back and approached the couple making out beside us. I ran one hand across the man's back and leaned into the woman. They broke apart with exclamations of surprise which quickly faded.

With a slight modulation of my song, I sent them back into their embrace. It was a great distraction for them, and a cover for those who were not yet sirened. I didn't want anyone to think something was wrong.

I slid from group to group, leaving controlled partygoers in my wake. The bartender and server were last. I snapped my fingers, and when Branc stepped onto the gangplank, I was eating bacon-wrapped scallops and finishing my champagne.

"Better hurry," I said. "I don't know how long the effects will last."

Branc nodded, his gaze sweeping over my handiwork of muted partygoers, then he disappeared into the yacht's cabin. I grabbed another scallop. Both scallop and bacon were delicious, and the combination confused and delighted me. They were an odd fusion of ocean and land that melded together so well on my tastebuds.

The server blinked next to me. "I feel strange," she said in a drowsy voice. "Is it time for my break yet?"

I glanced at the rest of the crowd, my heart pounding. All around us people were stirring, touching their heads, and shuffling their feet. Branc wasn't out yet, and I needed this assignment to succeed if I wanted payment.

I bent and pressed my hands to the deck. With the most powerful hum I could conjure, I passed a song of calm through my hands. One by one, the partygoers quieted. I kept up my song, my patience wearing thin with every second I waited. Where was Branc? How long did it take to grab something?

Feet in polished black leather shoes stepped into my view. I craned my neck to look at Branc.

"Give me twenty seconds to get away," he said quietly. "Then follow."

He disappeared without another word, and I counted twenty ways I wanted to get even with Branc. I stopped humming and stood straight. The group started to shuffle again, but I sauntered as casually as I could to the gangplank.

The first man I'd sirened blinked at me.

"Thanks for the drink." I ran my hand over his chest with light fingers. He glanced down at my touch, but I was already on the dock by the time he managed a strangled call after me.

Branc waited at the end of dock five. Water lapped against a piling, and the sea called to me. Grace flowed in my veins, and it seemed a terrible shame to eat so much and not use it underwater. I rubbed my arms and tried to focus on Branc's words.

"That was perfect." He swung a net bag filled with glistening green blobs over his shoulder and tucked a box under his arm that thudded with the sound of bone tablets clunking against each other. "I got exactly what I needed."

"What is it?" I peered around his back, but Branc

turned so I couldn't examine the green blobs. "Is it Grace? Don't you have proper channels for buying it? I didn't realize you stole what you sold."

"I don't—" Branc stopped and took a breath. "Don't worry about it. It's important, that's all. You did well. There aren't many women I'd trust to siren a whole party full of people, but you're one of them."

It was a compliment, but my mouth twisted. I didn't like how Branc valued my abilities. The more he appreciated what I could do for him, the less likely he would let me go when the time came to pay off my debt.

The water lapped at a piling again, and the smell of salt made my eyelids close briefly.

"Yeah, well, I'm itching to get in the water after all that Grace," I replied. "You're going to have to leave me here."

"I'm in no rush," he said. "Come to the parking lot when you're done. I'll drive you home."

I blinked at Branc—had he just offered to wait for me to swim before giving me a ride home?—then I stripped off my shirt. I wasn't going to waste an opportunity when it drifted into my open hands. My underwear and bra served as a bathing suit, and I dived into the sloshing seas without a backward glance.

It was only after the cool water surrounded me in waves of bliss that I thought to wonder why he hadn't joined me. Not that I wanted to swim with Branc, but he was half-siren like me. Why wait on land when he could be in his element?

CHAPTER 2

Branc drove me home after my swim, as silent as on our drive to the marina. I sank into a tranced state, too content to pay much attention to Branc's tight hands on the wheel and his contracted brow. If he didn't want to confide in one of the few women he trusted to siren a boatful of people, he could keep his secrets. Whatever ate at Branc could continue eating away, for all I cared.

My dreams that night were filled with the feel of currents over my skin and the joy of being underwater, fueled in part by the Grace still pulsing through my body. The next day was Sunday, the start of my weekend, and I luxuriated in bed when I awoke, still relishing the remains of Grace.

Mid-morning, I finally floated out of bed, ate breakfast to the pounding of a neighbor's music through the thin walls of my shoddy apartment, then hopped on a bus. Byssa would finish teaching swimming lessons soon, and we had plans to go for a swim. I presented myself in the lobby of the swimming pool to wait.

Byssa emerged from a private door that led to the lifeguards' changeroom. Her straight black hair was carefully pulled into a neat ponytail except for a fringe that didn't hide her startling green eyes nor her pale, petite features. She chatted with another young woman with black curls in a messy bun.

"Lune," Byssa greeted me. "You remember Eris, right?"

"Nice to see you again," Eris said warmly. Her bright

gray eyes crinkled with her smile. "Byssa said I could tag along for your swim. I hope you don't mind."

"Not at all," I said.

Eris was another half-siren, although gray eyes were the only outward sign. Her black curls and dusky skin were human through and through. We'd met once at a get-together at Byssa's apartment, and she'd struck me as warm and pleasant. She and Byssa had met as swimming instructors.

"I'll drive," Byssa said.

"I'm starving," Eris declared. Her eyes fell on a café attached to the pool. "I'll meet you at your car."

After Byssa and I settled into her car, Eris yanked the back door open and slid inside. She passed up two bags with a muffin each inside.

"Dig in," she said in a muffled voice around a mouthful of muffin. "Fuel for our swim."

"Thanks," Byssa said.

"You didn't have to get me anything," I said, half appreciative and half annoyed. I never had spare cash to treat anyone, so I could never repay her. *One day*, I told myself fiercely. One day, that person would be me.

"I know." Eris grinned at me and swallowed her bite. "But it feels nice to share, so I get something out of it, too." She leaned back and looked at her muffin contemplatively. "I'm happy I have enough to share. Some don't. If I'd arrived in Vancouver when I left the Seamount, who knows how I'd be doing? My mother dropped me off at a Grace distribution center in the States when I was sixteen, and the people there were great. Set me up, cared for me until I could leave, checked in on me until I didn't need it anymore. Vancouver's not the same at all."

"What do you mean?" Byssa started the car and pulled into traffic. "I don't know the state of things here, since my mother took Hades and I to my aunt's place on Vancouver Island, and she raised us."

"Oh, it's terrible," Eris said with horror. "The organization here lures sirens in and gives them everything they need."

"That doesn't sound so bad," Byssa said with a half-glance at me. I continued to stare out the windscreen, my stomach twisting at Eris's words. The story she told was my story, although the others didn't know it.

"That's because you don't know the rest of it. The newcomers have to pay back everything they get. And the interest is ridiculous, I've heard. Most people take years to earn their way free, if they ever do."

"That's horrible," Byssa gasped. "Why is it allowed?"

"Who's going to stop it?" I couldn't entirely mask the bitterness that seeped through my words. "Human authorities don't know anything, and nobody governs sirens on land."

"It is a bit of a free-for-all up here." Eris bit her muffin, her gaze contemplative. "It's okay if you land on your feet, but it's easy to slip through the cracks."

"I guess it's not all bad." Byssa flicked on her turn signal and took the next exit off the highway. "What would the new pale folk do if nobody greeted them? No money, no way to speak to anyone, no understanding of how life works among dry folk—at least someone is there, even if they are unscrupulous."

I gazed out the window, not seeing the cars that whipped past. Trust Byssa to find the tiniest whisper of a silver lining. As much as I hated to admit it, she had a point. The warehouse had been a beacon of hope during the most desperate, terrifying day of my life. What would I have done if I hadn't seen the nautilus shell sign on the bus stop leading me to the bank of the Fraser River and people who spoke my language?

It still didn't give Branc the right to own me, but the new perspective gave me something to consider.

I shook my head. Branc's invisible shackles chafed relentlessly, and I promised myself with fierce intent that I would be counted among those who broke free.

I laid my hand on Squirter's backpack on the floor between my legs and hummed a soothing tone to him. My octopus friend hummed back in his special watertight container, content for now. I tuned back into Byssa and Eris's conversation.

"I've been meaning to tell you." Eris fidgeted with the wrapping of her eaten muffin. She sighed and squared her shoulders. "I'm planning to move back to the Seamount."

Byssa's hands spasmed, and the car jerked in its lane. I twisted around to stare at Eris.

"What the vents for?" I blurted.

"Haven't you heard the news?" Eris leaned forward to see us better. Her eyes were bright with hope. "The Seamount Protectors are offering incentives for lost sirens to come home, and they sound amazing."

"Lost sirens," I muttered. "Is that what they're calling us?"

Byssa turned into a parking lot at a seaside park near the town of White Rock, turned off the engine, then stared at her friend. Seagulls yowled outside on the edge of the tidal flats covered by the high tide.

"What kind of incentive would possibly convince you to go back?" Byssa asked. "You left because you couldn't stand living in the ghetto anymore."

"But that's just it." Eris waved her hand. "They've changed all that. No more ghetto. They're promising new homes in the upper heights for those returning from land. And an escort to the Seamount for protection during the journey." Eris looked down at her clasped hands. "I really miss it down there. My mother and half-sister, they're still at the Seamount. This is my chance to get everything I want."

Byssa was quiet for a moment.

"How do you know they're telling the truth?" I said into the silence. "If something is too good to be true, it usually is."

Eris shrugged. "It's worth the risk to me."

Byssa grabbed Eris's hand and squeezed it. "If that's what you want, then I'm happy for you." Her voice was tight with strain, but she smiled at Eris.

Even if Byssa believed the Seamount's promises, she could never take advantage of them. She'd left the Seamount at age five with her twin brother Hades because she couldn't breathe properly underwater. She was stuck on land, no matter how much she missed the Seamount or her barely remembered mother.

"If I were you, I would have a plan to get out again," I said to Eris. "I trust the Seamount council as far as I can push them."

Byssa heaved a sigh, then she hitched a smile on her face and said brightly, "Are you ready for our swim? I haven't jumped in from White Rock in ages. I wonder if that old rowboat is still there." She held up her camera in its underwater housing. "I'm hoping to see a nice specimen of iridescent red algae growing on it because it's so shallow."

"I'm ready." I pushed open the door and swung Squirter's backpack onto my back. "So is Squirter."

Byssa's strain was clear to me, but Eris chatted without notice, clearly relieved to have told Byssa her big news. Byssa needed a distraction, and I wracked my brain to find one as we wandered over the grassy sand that led to the shore. A great blue heron gazed at us impassively from its stance in the shallow waters.

"How's your sexy new protégé these days?" I said when Byssa put her towel down on a driftwood log. "Jules, is it? Still working hard at the Crispy Prawn and providing you with eye candy?"

Byssa flushed a vibrant pink, and Eris raised a curious eyebrow.

"Byssa, what haven't you been telling me? Who's the new guy?"

"Nobody," she choked out with a half-hearted kick in my direction. "Just a culinary student that I helped with finding a part-time job at the Japanese restaurant I work at. He has a girlfriend, remember?"

I shrugged and threw her a coy look. "So? Girlfriends come and girlfriends go. It's not like they're pledged to each other." I held up a wagging finger to her in play.

"And I'm totally allowed to bug you about your love life, since you rarely leave mine alone."

Eris laughed. "Mine, too. You're the busiest matchmaker I know."

"Come on," Byssa said with a huff of laughter, her former unease forgotten. "Are you ready for this swim or not?"

CHAPTER 3

I poured Squirter into the tub when I got home and tossed in his favorite bath toy. Then, contented and feeling at peace with the world, I grabbed a towel and started drying my hair. I'd picked up the habit from Byssa, who insisted it looked better dry. After seeing my lank locks flat against my scalp in the mirror a few times, not to mention my soggy shirts, I agreed with her.

When dry, my locks were the palest ash blond now, dyed with Byssa's help in my bathroom last week. The color allowed me to avoid stares and fit in while still feeling true to my natural coloration. I'd ditched my temporary green stripes after Hades had teased me once too often.

My phone rang with an incoming video chat. Who would be calling me? When I picked up the phone, my heart squeezed with anticipation at the sight of Levi Storm's handsome face on the tiny screen.

He looked to be in his office at the Lodge, given the bookshelf of papers behind him and his dark hair glinting with mahogany highlights from the window on his left.

"Hi there, stranger." I smiled at Levi after propping the phone on my bathroom shelf. "How are things?"

"Better now that I'm talking to you," he said.

I rolled my eyes. "Have you been working on that line, or does the smooth talking naturally drip off your tongue?"

Levi grinned. "That information is on a need-to-know basis, and you don't need to know."

I grabbed my hairbrush and pulled it through my hair. "So, how's the Lodge? It feels like a long time since I was there. How are your plans for the grand re-opening?"

"Great, actually. It's going to happen September twenty-eighth, so hopefully that works for you. We have a party planned, music, all that."

"I'll make it work." I smiled at Levi, my stomach tight at the thought of seeing him in person again. I don't know what we had—friendship, at the least—but I wanted to explore our relationship further. I wanted to explore him further.

I schooled my thoughts before they could show on my face and cursed my blush-prone skin inherited from my unknown father. With the way my thoughts were going, they would soon be obvious.

"And the Grace-house construction?" I said to distract myself. "Last time you were in Vancouver, you were picking up supplies."

"We've made three different Grace-houses for redundancy. I don't want to fall prey to the same mistakes as last time." Levi scowled, the Grace-house arson from the summer clearly on his mind. "And they're built with concrete and metal. Nothing to burn here."

I put my brush down and fluffed my hair with my fingers. Levi's eyes tracked the motion, and I repeated it for longer than necessary. Suddenly, I wished he'd caught me in a more revealing outfit than my tee shirt that read "let's get kraken," accompanied by a drawing of a grumpy-looking octopus. I wanted his eyes on me.

"What about your brother Austin?" I said to diffuse my thoughts. "Any word from him?"

Levi sighed and leaned back in his chair. "Unfortunately, no. I'm really worried about him after that dagger someone left as a warning to me. What did he get himself into? And why hasn't he at least contacted our parents? Surely he would have sent word that he was still alive to them, even if he were ashamed of what he'd done. Mom took it hard, and Dad's health is suffering because of it, I'm sure. I don't know, I really think he saw the light at the end, then that pale woman sirened him."

I didn't know what to say. I wasn't as forgiving of Austin as Levi was—he wasn't my brother, after all—but he had been forced to get in the water and leave his brother in danger, of that I was certain.

"What would the pale folk want with him, though?" I asked without expecting an answer. Squirter knocked his toy against the bathtub wall, and I passed him a new one absently.

"I don't know, but it must have something to do with Grace distribution." Levi picked up a pen from his desk and twirled it in his fingers with a mesmerizing motion. "And I've heard rumors from visiting pale folk that a rogue coalition has formed at the Seamount. No one is quite sure what they want, or even if they truly exist, but the uncertainty is causing unrest down there."

"You know more than I do." I ran a hand through my drying hair, frustrated that I couldn't be much help. I had no information on the Seamount that Levi could use.

"It's rough right now," he continued. "Grace shipments are coming in late and half-filled, or sometimes not at all. I have a lot of sirens waiting for their promised Grace and nothing to give them until ages after they expect it. Not much point in my new Grace-houses. Maybe it's this unrest causing the shortage, but I wonder if Driftwood has something to do with it."

"Who's Driftwood again? I don't know the name." I did know—I'd heard the name from the siren I'd compelled during my time at the Lodge in the summer, but I wanted to hear what Levi knew.

"I don't know much about him, beyond that he's a distributor based in Vancouver. From what I've heard, he's shady enough that he could be behind the hiccups in the Grace supply chain." Levi scowled. "I wouldn't put it past him. Too many rumors of his ruthlessness must be backed by something."

I'd had my suspicions before, but Levi's words confirmed it. Branc must be the elusive Driftwood. I wondered if that were his last name since I'd never heard him referred to as anything other than Branc.

But as convinced as I was that Branc was Driftwood, I was almost as certain that he wasn't behind the Grace disruptions. Branc's actions the other night, the strain he appeared to be under, his reliance on me to steal with him, none of it pointed toward a satisfied smuggler. Branc would ooze smugness if he had successfully funneled extra Grace into his empire, I was sure of it.

But I couldn't tell this to Levi without revealing my own relationship with the Vancouver distributor. I didn't want to face Levi's consternation, his disgust, or his pity. Soon enough I would be free of Branc, then no one would have to know anything about our connection.

"I hope your brother contacts you soon," I said. We needed to change topics, so I leaned forward to get closer to the screen. If the position gave Levi a better view of my chest, well, maybe that was on purpose. "Hey, guess what Squirter did this morning during our swim?"

I showed up at the Crispy Prawn on time for my late dinner the next night with Byssa and Hades. When I peeked my head into the kitchen, the staff looked frazzled, although a slower pace had fallen over them. The tables that were filled in the restaurant had customers lazily sipping tea and picking at the remainders of their meals. Byssa would be able to take her break soon.

Byssa didn't see me—too intent on chopping tuna to notice—but a lanky young man with shaggy brown hair tied back with a headband passed by me.

"You're probably not supposed to be here," he mock-whispered at me. "Food safety and all that jazz. Do you need help finding a table?"

He took a second glance at me, and his eyes widened. Did he recognize me from somewhere, or were my white roots showing at the base of my too-blond hair? I raised my eyebrow at him.

"I know exactly where I'm sitting," I said. "I wanted to say hello to Byssa, that's all. Wait." I reached out my hand to touch his arm. "Are you Jules, by any chance?"

Jules nodded, his eyes narrowed in question.

"Byssa mentioned you once or twice," I said in a casual manner. My hand was still on his arm, and inspiration struck. This was a chance to find out more about Jules, for Byssa's sake. I could use my siren power to help her out. Just a little—nothing that would harm him—but enough to find answers.

I hesitated—I used to hate compelling others—but my spine stiffened. I was a siren, and I didn't want to reject any part of myself. That meant embracing all my abilities. And if it helped my friend? Double bonus.

"Do you have a girlfriend?" I said quietly, infusing my question with a low hum that would make Jules speak openly to me.

He nodded with a glazed look in his eyes. "Yes, her name is Trip. She's amazing. We've been dating for a month. She doesn't live here, though, so that's hard."

One month and long distance? That relationship wouldn't be difficult to end. Byssa might not have to even do anything to hurry its demise.

"What do you think of Byssa?" I purred.

"She's great," he answered quickly. "So helpful, and kind, and beautiful, too. It was great of her to find me this job."

Hmm. That answer had potential, but Byssa needed more to work with. I opened my mouth to find out more about Jules—his hobbies, his passions, something that Byssa could use—but a harshly cleared throat paused my words.

Byssa stood next to Jules, glaring with as much anger as I had ever seen her show.

"Lune," she said in a sweet voice. Only I could hear the venom behind the words. "I'll be out soon, okay? You can tell Hades I'm coming."

She glanced pointedly at my hand on Jules's arm. I let go and stepped back.

"It was nice to meet you, Jules," I said.

He nodded absently, and I retreated before Byssa could carve a hole in my head from her stare. I walked to the back of the restaurant, pondering Byssa's reaction. My stomach squirmed. Byssa clearly hadn't liked me compelling Jules, and I scrambled to understand why. She adored everything pale folk, and sirening was part of that. Was she embarrassed by my meddling? Jealous because her sirening skills were weaker than mine? Worried that I would give her identity away?

"Hi, Hades." I flopped onto the bench seat across from my friend. He'd given up his black and white dye job in favor of short green spikes tipped with black. The colors turned his cheeks sallow with an unhealthy tinge. "Are you trying to look like a pufferfish, or is that a happy coincidence?"

Hades crossed his arms as if offended, then he laughed. "Yeah, you got me. I couldn't resist. White hair is like an artist's palate. It's almost criminal to not dye it. You understand, finally." He waved at my blond locks.

I twirled a strand around my finger. "It's taking some getting used to, not wearing a wig. The paleness still draws a lot of attention, but I'm starting not to mind. The stares are more appreciative and less concerned about my prematurely graying hair."

"Embrace the glances." Hades spread his arms wide. "Soak them up. Sometimes they will grant you your wishes."

"Like Rachel?" Hades had recently started dating a

coworker at the aquarium, and he was always willing to expound on her virtues. She'd taken a while to say yes to his invitations, but now that she had, Hades was smugger than ever.

"Like Rachel." He nodded sagely. "She likes the spikes, by the way. Thinks they're hot."

My mouth puckered with my suppressed smile, but my mirth faded when Byssa dropped a sushi platter on our table with a thud. Her eyes blazed with anger.

"What the hell was that about?" she hissed. "Why were you sirening Jules?"

Hades shot a confused glance at me.

I shrugged. "I wanted to find out more about him. For you."

"I don't need your help." Byssa sank onto the bench next to Hades and pushed plates and chopsticks roughly at us. "And I don't need you sirening him to do it. Why did you do it, anyway? I thought you hated sirening others."

I snapped my chopsticks apart, my lips tight from Byssa's question. Sirening used to remind me of the countless times I'd been under the influence of others at the Seamount. Control was something I couldn't stand, not when it was exerted on me. But now that I wanted to accept my siren side, using my abilities felt like the right thing to do.

"It wasn't a big deal." I transferred sushi to my plate without meeting Byssa's gaze. "Just getting him to tell the truth. I'm pale folk. I might as well embrace my heritage."

Byssa snatched the soy sauce from the center of the

table. "Don't do it to Jules. End of story."

I raised my hand in a consoling gesture. "Message received."

Hades glanced between us, clearly unsure whether to talk or not. His sister's stormy face and my closed expression must have dissuaded him.

I sighed and put down my chopsticks. I'd hurt Byssa. Even though I didn't understand her reaction fully—given her love of all things pale folk—she deserved better from me. I reached across and grabbed her hand.

"I'm sorry." I stared at her face until she met my gaze with her bright green eyes. "I didn't realize you felt that strongly about sirening. I promise I won't do it to Jules again."

Byssa searched my face, then she nodded. The tension at the table relaxed, and Hades took a breath. I tried not to smile at his reaction and let go of Byssa's hand.

"But," I said, "I don't promise not to talk to him and tell him about how wonderful you are. Strictly human conversations, of course."

Byssa scowled, but real emotion didn't back the expression. "Butt out."

"Oh, that's rich, coming from you." I raised my eyebrow at Hades. "The unrepentant matchmaker."

Hades chuckled. His laugh turned into a cough. All the blood drained from his face, and his eyes rolled back in his head.

CHAPTER 4

"Byssa," I hissed. "Grab Hades. He's fainting."

Byssa jerked toward her brother and caught his head before it narrowly missed hitting the restaurant table. She patted his cheek to no response, then she turned panicked eyes to me.

"What's wrong with him?" she said in a low tone.

I glanced around the restaurant. No one had noticed Hades's collapse, thanks to the booth seating of the Crispy Prawn. I stared back at Byssa, unsure of what to do. We couldn't take him to a doctor, could we? Exactly how different were pale and dry folk, medically speaking? I'd never been ill enough to worry about the answer to that question.

"Should we get him home?" I suggested. "Has this happened to him before?"

"No." Byssa bit her bottom lip and pushed her brother against the back of the bench. He groaned quietly, and his eyelids fluttered open. Byssa leaned closer. "Hades, can you hear me? How do you feel?"

"Like my head is going to burst," he said in a thick voice. "I don't know, I've never felt like this before."

"You need to visit the doctor." Byssa slung his arm around her shoulders and dragged him to the edge of the bench. I jumped up and helped him to a standing position. He wobbled but held his ground. Together, we limped toward the exit, only stopping long enough at the kitchen for Byssa to make her excuses to the manager.

"My car is back here," Byssa said as we stumbled into

a tight parking lot around the corner from the restaurant. "Come on, get him in the backseat."

"I'm awake, you know," Hades mumbled. "You can talk directly to me."

I yanked open the back door. "Yes, we know. Which is why we know you'll do what's best for you, which is listen to what your sister says."

Without warning, Hades convulsed and vomited on the sidewalk. Byssa and I leaped aside as far as we could while still supporting his weight.

"Are you done?" I asked while Byssa rubbed his back with a queasy expression.

Hades nodded, and we eased him into the backseat. I hopped into the passenger's seat, and Byssa backed out of the parking spot with more speed than care.

"He's fine," I told her. Hades stared out of the window at passing cars, pale but composed. "Don't drive like a maniac."

Byssa released a little pressure on the gas pedal but continued to stare out the windshield with focused intensity.

"What's this doctor, dry or pale folk?" I asked. "Is it safe to visit them? We don't want to give away Hades's true nature."

"Dr. Mazzaella is a siren healer," Byssa said in a clipped tone. "She's also a doctor for humans, but she runs a clinic for pale folk who need it. She's well-known for it."

I pursed my lips. I hadn't heard of Dr. Mazzaella at all, even after being on land for a year. Granted, it wasn't like exiled pale folk gathered for meetings, but still, I was miffed I hadn't heard about her before. My mouth twisted. If I had become ill, I would have gone to Branc, as usual. Who else would know what to do or who to contact? It annoyed me to no end that he would have been my first point of contact. Knowing Branc, he would have charged a hefty fee for a referral to this siren healer.

After a few minutes of driving, Byssa pulled up to a residential house in a pleasant neighborhood lined with leafy trees just starting to turn crispy at the edges with the upcoming autumn. I jumped out when the car stopped and opened the back door. Hades's eyelids fluttered, and his cheeks were bloodless.

"I'll just wait here," he murmured, his head lolling against the headrest.

"No way." I bent down and wrapped his arm around my shoulders. With Byssa's help, I pulled him out of the car, and we staggered down the short driveway. I glanced up at a set of steep steps leading to a covered porch and the front door, and my heart sank.

"It's around here." Byssa pointed at a gravel path that led into the narrow gap between house and slat fence. Carved into a wooden arch over the path was a nautilus shell. I sighed in relief and lugged Hades's resisting weight forward.

A door leading into the house's basement was painted gray-blue and fitted with a translucent window in the top half. A note in Seamount-script etched into the glass read, "Enter, those from the sea who need healing."

"That sounds like us," I said quietly to Byssa.

She nodded and turned the door handle. Together, we tugged Hades over the threshold.

The room was low-ceilinged, but bright and cheery. The walls were a cool, soothing gray, and two long couches rested at right angles to each other, both adorned with brightly colored cushions. Posters on the walls showed underwater scenes of coral reefs and secretive wolf eels.

"Hello?" Byssa called out, not moving toward the couch that Hades was trying to collapse onto. "Dr. Mazzaella?"

Steps clattered down a staircase out of sight beyond a closed door. A moment later, the door opened and a woman entered, wiping her hands on a tea towel. Medical scrubs encased her graceful, willowy limbs, and her white hair was pulled into a severe bun at the nape of her neck. Her warm brown eyes glanced at us, taking in our condition.

"Come right in." Her low voice infused with a hint of calming hum made my shoulders relax. Byssa nodded at me, and we dragged Hades through a different doorway after the healer. She gestured to a tall bench, and we maneuvered our cargo onto the towel-covered surface.

"This is Hades," Byssa said to the woman. "I'm his sister Byssa, and this is our friend Lune. He collapsed at a restaurant half an hour ago. I don't know what's wrong. He was fine yesterday."

Byssa's voice trembled, and I draped my arm over her petite shoulders.

"We'll figure it out," I whispered. "He'll be fine."

"I'll do everything I can," Dr. Mazzaella promised. "I'm both a qualified healer of the Nautilus Academy and a certified doctor of humans. Now, let's examine your brother."

Byssa nodded with a jerky motion, and Dr. Mazzaella bent over Hades. First, she used a strange device that plugged into her ears and connected with a cord to a metal disk she placed on his chest. Then, she took a tiny flashlight on a stick and peered into his mouth, ears and eyes.

"What is she doing?" I whispered to Byssa. My confidence in this so-called healer was diminishing rapidly. "Why isn't she examining him properly?"

"That's how human doctors do it," Byssa replied quietly, her eyes trained on Dr. Mazzaella's movements. "She'll get there."

I pursed my lips but stayed silent. As Byssa had promised, Dr. Mazzaella used a few more inexplicable human instruments on Hades, then she moved onto a proper examination. She placed both hands on his chest and closed her eyes. A faint vibration tickled my feet.

"Finally," I whispered to Byssa. "She's checking for internal damage. I was wondering when she'd get around to that."

After a few more tests that I recognized, Dr. Mazzaella waved us forward.

"If you could help me undress him, we can transfer him to the tub for further evaluation." She pointed at a large basin in the corner of the room that had been hidden behind a curtain. Within its clear waters, small orange fish darted and drifted.

I started with Hades's shoes and socks, and Byssa eased his shirt over his head. He groaned, and Byssa shushed him with a stroke of his hair. The healer and I wriggled his jeans off, not helped by how tight Hades liked to wear them, and when he was down to his boxers, we heaved him into the tub with a gentle splash. Veins in his arms were visible through his pale skin.

"Hold his head up," Dr. Mazzaella instructed Byssa. "I don't want him going through the stress of switching breathing methods."

Byssa cradled Hades's head in the water, and his eyes blinked open.

"This is weird," he murmured.

"Just relax," Dr. Mazzaella told him. "I'm getting the fish to examine you briefly. I'm pretty certain I know what's wrong, but I'd like confirmation."

She stuck her hands in the water and closed her eyes. She must have hummed instructions, because the orange fish immediately flitted to Hades's side and traveled around his body.

"While they're working," Dr. Mazzaella said, "can you tell me anything you've done differently lately?"

"No," he said, his eyes closing as if his eyelids were too heavy for him. "Work, life, the usual."

"And how long have you been on land?"

"We came to land when we were five years old," Byssa said.

"Ah." Dr. Mazzaella nodded then glanced at the fish. They had congregated at Hades's stomach. "Then I have a diagnosis. My best guess is that you have drifting syndrome. I've seen two cases in the past week, so you're not alone."

"What is it?" I'd never heard of drifting syndrome before. Byssa and I shared a worried glance.

"Some sirens develop it after staying many years on land." Dr. Mazzaella turned to a cupboard to rummage for a towel. "It's not the same as land sickness, which is a deficiency of Grace. Instead, the body develops an almost allergic reaction to dry land. Sometimes patients get over it, but often the only cure is to live in the sea fulltime again."

"For how long?" Hades croaked. He stared at Dr. Mazzaella with a crease between his eyebrows.

"The rest of their lives, usually." Dr. Mazzaella folded the towel over her arm. "I'm not certain. Siren physiology isn't widely studied up here, as you can imagine." She chuckled. "And the Nautilus Academy members, as advanced as they'd like to think themselves, are not as focused on scientific inquiry as humans are."

Her attempt at lightheartedness fell flat. Byssa chewed her lip like it was a tough piece of oyster, and Hades's mouth tightened in a grim line.

"But you said he could get over it, right?" I grasped at the lifeline the doctor had thrown us.

"Maybe." She shrugged and handed me the towel, then pulled a wax paper package out of a small fridge under a counter. From the package, she extracted a fingerful of brown paste. She smeared it on the inside of both of Hades's forearms, where it left an unpleasant discoloration. "Give that a few minutes to sink in, and you'll feel much better. Apply this paste every day until either the fainting spells and nausea disappear for good, or they get worse. If they don't improve, get your land affairs in order and move back to the Seamount before you fall into a coma." She passed the package to me and washed her hands in a small sink inset into the counter.

Byssa continued to hold Hades's head out of the water while he recovered. She avoided my eyes, but her turmoil was clear. Would Hades have to leave his twin sister on land? Would they be forever parted because of a cruel twist of fate? The fish swirled around Hades's body while Dr. Mazzaella cleaned up.

"As for you two, make sure you keep healthy in the future." The doctor leaned against the counter and stared at Byssa and me with worry in her eyes. "This clinic won't be an option for much longer. I've had a tough time lately, what with supplies hard to get these days. I'm planning to return to the Seamount. I've been up here for years, and I'm itching to see home again."

"You're leaving, too?" Byssa's face crumpled. As I'd expected, she'd taken Eris's announcement hard, and worry over Hades and Dr. Mazzaella's statement didn't help her peace of mind. "What will we do if we get sick?"

"The closest healer is Dr. Maelstrom in Sechelt. He's too far for emergencies, though." Dr. Mazzaella shrugged. "Stay healthy or move to the Sunshine Coast."

Byssa and Hades glanced at each other. My lips tightened. If Dr. Mazzaella, Eris, and others wanted to go back to the Seamount, fine. They would learn the hard way that the underwater city wasn't all sunbeams and seahorses. I didn't trust these promises of open-armed welcome for half-sirens. I'd only left a year ago, and I knew the real state of things.

CHAPTER 5

After a few minutes, as promised, Hades crawled out of the tub under his own power, dressed, and walked back to the car with a faint hint of his usual cheer. Byssa gave Dr. Mazzaella a gift of Grace then hovered around her brother. He laughed, ruffled her hair, and pushed her away.

When we were all in the car, I mentioned the whale in the cave. "Have you two ever heard of drifting syndrome?"

"No." Byssa released the emergency brake with a stomp of her foot. "Maybe we should go see Dr. Maelstrom while we're at the Lodge. It's close to Sechelt. I'd like a second opinion."

"I'll get over it," Hades reassured us. "People recover. I have no intention of returning to the Seamount. My life is here. Don't get me wrong, it would be nice to see our mother, but I hardly remember the place. I'm not leaving you two, or my job, or Rachel now that she finally agreed to date me. No way."

"What if you don't have a choice?" I said quietly.

Byssa pressed the accelerator with more force than necessary, and the car leaped forward in its lane.

"Let's see Dr. Maelstrom," she said firmly. "Before we travel down the current of what-ifs."

The siblings dropped me off at home, and I played with Squirter until bed. Hades's diagnosis haunted me, and the fact that he wasn't the only one lately made me nervous. What with drifting syndrome, and people voluntarily returning to the Seamount, would there be any of us left on land? Only Byssa and me, by the looks of it. Would they still deliver Grace to sustain us?

In the morning, once I finished dressing in my work uniform, someone knocked on the door of my apartment.

I stared at the entryway, a piece of salted bread and nori halfway to my mouth. No one ever came to my apartment. Even Byssa invited me to hers more than she came here. It was a dismal setting, after all.

Maybe something was wrong with Hades. I strode to the door with urgent footsteps. Although wouldn't Byssa call instead of coming to my place? I wrenched the door open.

The frantic questions for Byssa died on my lips. Branc stood in the dim hallway, the dingy carpet a stark contrast to his polished dress shoes and finely tailored pants, even with his crisp buttoned shirt undone at the collar. Although he owned the apartment block and was technically my landlord, I'd never once seen him on the premises.

"What are you doing here?" I blurted. Then I composed myself. I couldn't afford to be too rude to Branc, not when he controlled my home as well as most other aspects of my life. I tried again. "Hi, Branc. What's up?"

"I have a job for you," he said without greeting. "It will pay well. Grab your things and let's go."

I blinked at him. I never liked to turn down extra pay, but this wasn't how we rolled. Usually, Branc would call me to come down to his club, offer me a job, and I would take it or not. He never made house calls.

My jaw tightened. I was tired of begging for scraps at Branc's feet. After the incident at the Lodge, I'd promised myself that I wouldn't pay off my debt at the expense of living my life.

"I have work," I said. "I'm already running late. Maybe after that."

"This isn't a negotiation."

I stared at him. "No, it's not. I can't do a job right now. You'll have to find someone else."

Branc cursed and grabbed his hair in his hands, glancing around as if to find answers somewhere. I frowned. Branc was always composed. What had riled him up so much?

"You're the best person to do this." He lunged out and grabbed my arm. "You're coming with me now."

Sirening him was a gut reaction, but I would have done it even if I'd had time to consider my actions. Branc had gone too far, and I wouldn't stand for it.

The hum vibrated through my body and up Branc's arm. His grip slackened. He shook his head as if to clear it. Then, his gaze sharpened, and his brows contracted.

"You're sirening me?" He laughed in disbelief. "That is gutsy. I guess you didn't know that it doesn't work on me." He threw down my arm in disgust and stepped back. "But now I can't trust you to do your job properly. And for that, for trying to control me, Grace is going to cost you double. Say goodbye to your freedom."

Branc stalked off, and I stared after him, bewildered and with growing anger. Is that how he'd risen to his current level of power within the land-based siren community, by being immune to compulsion?

"For vents' sake, Branc," I yelled after him. "Double is too much."

He flicked his hand above his shoulder in a dismissive gesture without looking back then disappeared out the front door. I sagged against the doorframe. I already could hardly afford my monthly allotment of Grace. Had standing my ground been worth it now that my freedom was farther away than ever? Yes, but by a very slim margin.

And what had worked Branc up so much that he'd visited me at home, tried to force me to do his bidding, and lashed out against me when I'd disagreed with him? Did it have something to do with the lack of Grace and the mysterious coalition at the Seamount?

I smacked the doorframe with my hand. Branc could keep his secrets. I didn't want anything to do with that vindictive eel. Right now, I would go to work and get back to living the life I'd created for myself.

I stepped onto a ledge then looked up and down the aquarium's back hallway. Tanks burbled, and turquoise light fluttered over the pipe-covered ceiling of the narrow passage. I didn't want anyone to see me drop Squirter off in a tank. My octopus friend would be hard to explain to the humans.

Squirter had wanted to join me on land again after our swim yesterday, and I had no intention of convincing him otherwise. I liked his presence in the apartment because he made it feel like a home instead of only a place to sleep. With what little money I had remaining after food and paying Branc, I'd splurged on a few new toys for him, like a puzzle for toddler bath time which he seemed to enjoy, and a plastic sandcastle mold for him to nap in.

But on workdays, it was aquarium play time for the little cephalopod. Today's adventure would take place in the jellyfish tank, and I couldn't wait to hear what he thought of it tonight. With one last confirmation of my solitude, I tilted my backpack to empty it of water. Squirter poured out along with seawater, and he darted away without a backward glance. He would find a crevasse to hide in while he assessed his new environment for the first hour. Later, he would explore.

A smile flitted across my face as I screwed back on the cap of the backpack insert. It was a fleeting expression, though. Branc's actions this morning pushed to the forefront of my mind, a position they'd occupied during my commute. My stomach churned at the thought of paying double for Grace. It was already taking me too long to pay him back. Stretching out my indentured servitude even longer to pay for necessities felt intolerable.

I sighed. Maybe I should have gone with Branc, done whatever job he'd wanted me to do, got it over with. At least then I wouldn't be worse off. Unless I lost my aquarium job, of course. As tedious as cleaning the tanks could be, it was still a job in my element, which sweetened the deal. And my coworkers were pleasant.

No, I didn't want to risk losing what I had here.

I slung my backpack over one shoulder and walked to the exit. I said I didn't care about what Branc was concerned about. But if he were worried about Grace distribution problems, didn't that also affect Levi? I rubbed my nose, annoyed that I hadn't thought of the connection before.

And it wasn't only the supply of Grace that was drying up. Dr. Mazzaella had mentioned that all substances from the Seamount were harder to come by. What was actually going on down there? And could it hurt the life I'd been so carefully building topside?

When I pushed through the swinging doors that led to the staff room, my coworker Mireille slammed her locker door shut and turned to smile at me.

"Lune, hi. Did you have a good weekend?"

"Not as good as last weekend, when we saw that concert together. That was a good time."

The pulsing bass flowing through the speakers that night had resonated deep in my body in a similar way to a siren call. Connecting with my human friend Mireille had been an added bonus. Predictably, Mireille beamed at me.

"It was, wasn't it? I hear Chordclash is playing at the Underground Lounge in a couple of weeks. Want to try them out?"

"Definitely." I smiled back at Mireille and turned to my own locker. My smile faltered. This was what I would be missing if my life on land were jeopardized. Simple interactions with friends. Normalcy of daily work. Anticipation of fun to come. Was my future really that uncertain? I vowed to call Levi later and ask if he'd heard any new rumors of the secret Seamount coalition.

Another coworker greeted us and opened his locker. Our boss Darryl came out of his office with a clipboard.

"Morning, everyone." He scanned the papers before him. "Mireille, you're helping the marine mammal unit today. Brandon, scrub the inner tanks of the BC Coast exhibits, please. And Lune, it's your turn for food prep."

My mouth twisted. I hated the fiddly task of sorting out the different fish and dietary supplements for each tank. And if I scrubbed algae instead, I could have a visit with Squirter. Surreptitiously, I placed my hand on Brandon's forearm and hummed.

"Brandon was telling me how he wanted more experience learning the requirements for each animal," I said out loud while continuing my hum to my coworker. "Maybe we should switch tasks for today."

"Yeah, that's a good idea," Brandon said. I smiled at him. Clearly, my compulsion was working.

Darryl nodded. "Sure, if that's what you want, Brandon. Okay, folks, let's get to it."

I let go of Brandon and followed Mireille out the door. I didn't want to force anyone to do anything terrible, but this was a task that Brandon knew how to do—indeed, he did it as often as I did—so this little push wasn't a big deal. I probably could have convinced him to switch roles today, with enough time and effort, but sirening was so much easier to get the same outcome. I'd promised myself after the debacle at the Lodge that I would embrace my siren heritage, and today was a perfect example.

The day passed slowly, although diving into the tank where Squirter played was a highlight. I hated the wetsuit that they made me wear to clean the tanks, but asking to avoid it would arouse suspicion, so I suffered through. Squirter played with a hose that sprouted from my mouth, and I chuckled until big bubble puffed out of my regulator.

When I left Squirter for another tank, my mind drifted to Levi. It felt like forever since that intense moment in the dark summer night. My hand scrubbed algae off the glass in automatic circles while I dreamed of his soft lips, his hard chest, and his incredibly touchable hair…

At the end of the day, I entered the staff room and changed into my street clothes. Mireille was nearby, and her head bent over her phone in its sparkly purple case.

"Lune." Mireille waved me over with an urgent flutter of her hand. "My friend just texted me, she's walking to pick me up today. There's some crazy guy wandering around Stanley Park. He's barefoot, totally wet, and scaring people because he only makes clicks and moaning noises. Shirtless, which is a perk given his toned abs. Check it out."

I squinted at the screen, which showed a blurry photo of a man standing at the edge of a tiny lake.

"She's wondering if he's not quite right," Mireille said. "Hit on the head, maybe. The police are trying to calm him down."

"Weird," I said, then my breath caught. My eyes focused on the man's tanned face. He looked bewildered and frightened, but that wasn't why I couldn't breathe.

I knew him.

CHAPTER 6

The sopping-wet man with a shock of white hair at the little lake was Cetus, one of my best friends from the Seamount. We'd grown up together, had fought and stole and escaped punishment together, had cooked and sung and danced together in the Seamount ghetto. We'd even shared our first kiss, although we'd quickly realized that we were better friends than lovers. I'd thought I would never see him again, not after I left the Seamount on suspicion of murder. What was Cetus doing on land?

More to the point, how could I help him escape?

"You said he was in Stanley Park?" I said quickly. "Is that Beaver Lake he's beside?"

"Yeah, I think so."

Mireille continued to text with her friend while I scrambled to pull on my boots. I hoisted Squirter's backpack over my shoulders before Mireille looked up in surprise.

"You're off already?"

"Yeah, a few errands I need to run. See you tomorrow."

I dashed out the door. The Vancouver Aquarium was in the center of Stanley Park, the largest green space in downtown Vancouver. The tiny lake Cetus was currently splashing around in was due north.

I jogged up a wide path, Squirter vibrating grumpily in my backpack. I ignored him. Cetus needed my help. Squirter would have to put up with a little sloshing.

I ignored the curious glances of walkers as I ran by

with my heavy backpack. Before long, a small group of spectators blocked my view going forward. The lake must have been directly ahead.

"Excuse me." I pushed forward despite protests. "I need to get through."

At the front of the group, a uniformed police officer put out her hand. "You need to stay back," she said in a firm tone. Her smooth bun and crisp uniform brooked no arguments. "We are dealing with a situation."

"Please," I said. My eyes flicked to Cetus, standing among the rushes at the edge of the lake, his arms constrained by a police officer behind him. The brown seaweed loincloth he wore hung damply off his hips. He looked bedraggled and scared, and my stomach clenched. I cast around for a suitable lie that would appease the woman. "That's my brother. I need to help him."

The police officer blinked. "That man is your brother?" she repeated. At my nod, she whistled to the officer holding Cetus. "She says he's her brother. Bring him over, will you?"

The other officer nodded and led his captive forward. Cetus's eyes glanced toward us briefly in his scan of the area. Then, they flicked back to me. His jaw dropped.

Lune, he signed at me with a twist of his shoulders. *Help*.

"Looks like they know each other." The cop turned to me. "Is he a danger? Shall we continue to restrain him?"

"No! No, he's fine. Just confused." I gathered my wits to fabricate a story. "He's usually confused. I had him out for a walk, but he wandered away. I've been so worried looking for him. I'm sorry we caused such a fuss."

The officer nodded, her blue eyes compassionate. "I'm happy it resolved for everyone."

Cetus reached us, and I flung my arms around his naked shoulders when the other officer released him. He clung to me like I was the only sane thing in a world of chaos. His hum of relief nearly shook my whole body with its vibrations.

The second cop approached with an emergency blanket, fetched from the pannier of his police bicycle. "For your brother," he said gruffly. "It's a warm day, but I think he was in the ocean. Wouldn't want him to get too cold or succumb to shock."

"Thank you." I wrapped the blanket around Cetus, who gripped the sides with a skeptical glance at the strange material. We didn't have anything similar at the Seamount since our bodies were used to the temperatures. I turned to the female officer whom I'd first spoken to. "Is everything okay? Can we go home now?"

"Yes, if you're sure he doesn't need to visit the hospital." The woman glanced at Cetus, but his calm relief must have convinced her he was fine, because she nodded. "Where do you live? We can have someone drive you there."

I thanked her and told her the address of my apartment. Then I threw my arm around Cetus's shoulders and steered him after the cop. His body vibrated against my arm, and I sent back a welcoming hum.

We sat in the back of a police cruiser that pulled up to the edge of the park minutes later. Two new cops spoke quietly to each other but didn't try to engage me in conversation, which I appreciated. I had too much swirling around in my head to formulate polite chitchat. Cetus tried to speak to me once, but I pressed his hand down with my own.

Later, I hummed. We were sitting close enough that he could feel my song. *When we're alone.*

He nodded and stayed still, watching cars pass out the window. He was remarkably calm about driving around in a vehicle. My first time, I hadn't been nearly this composed. I suppressed a snort at the memory of Byssa shouting soothing words at me as I clawed at the window, Hades wrapping his arms around me from the backseat until I settled.

Cetus had always been adventurous and was good at rolling with whatever waves hit him. His acceptance of the new experiences shouldn't have surprised me.

Cetus's hand crept toward mine and grasped it in a tight grip. Maybe he wasn't as calm as he appeared. I squeezed his hand to let him know I wasn't going anywhere.

The cops dropped us off at the sidewalk in front of my apartment block. After they drove away, I led Cetus by the hand up the cracked pavement and through the dirty glass front door. A prickling on the back of my neck made me turn around and scan the street. Was someone watching me?

I doubted it. My life wasn't particularly interesting. I

shook off the feeling and pulled Cetus forward. Once inside my suite, I closed my door and threw myself into his arms again. We clung to each other for a full minute, our hums of joy and relief harmonizing.

Finally, I pushed back. Cetus touched a tear that traced down my cheek. He looked at the liquid in wonder.

What's happening to your eyes? he asked.

I chuckled and wiped my cheeks. *They're called tears. It happens when we get emotional. Who knew?*

In my closet, I found a baggy pair of shorts and the largest tee shirt I owned. I tossed the clothes to Cetus.

Here, I said. *Something dry to wear. You'll find the humans will worry about you if you're wet.*

He held out the clothes and examined them like they might suddenly bite.

Go on, I urged. *Get changed, and I'll find something to eat. Then you can tell me everything.*

Cetus stripped off his seaweed garment without reservation and gingerly climbed into the clothes I'd thrown at him. I had to help him turn the shirt around to face the correct way. I opened the fridge and pulled out canned tuna and salty crackers from the cupboard, the closest items I had to flavors Cetus would recognize. Once I'd set him up at the tiny kitchen table across from me, I finally asked him my burning questions.

What's the story? I said. *Why are you here? What's happening at the Seamount?*

Cetus brought a cracker to his mouth and carefully placed it on his tongue. His nose twitched, but he chewed the morsel.

I wanted to find you, he said after swallowing. *I found a way past the barrier, just like you must have. They told us that you'd been killed by the upper echelons after killing that pale man, but I never believed it. They didn't give us your body for a send-off, for one. How outrageous was that?*

Did Eelway and Pelagia think I'd died? I bit my lip, thinking of the suffering my foster father and my friend might have endured. If one of them had died under mysterious circumstances, I would have been beside myself.

Everyone did. Cetus scowled. *They thought I was too optimistic, clinging to a false hope. I was tired of no one believing me, and I was tired of life in the ghetto. I wanted more, you know? So I threw my old life to the currents and escaped.* He chewed another piece of cracker. *A ligan nearly snapped my foot off. Then when I got to land, I followed the nautilus shell signs, but the building they pointed to was closed. I've been wandering around all day, on land and along the coastal waters, trying to figure out what to do.*

I stared at Cetus as he ate. I was no stranger to the longings he'd expressed. Life at the bottom of the Seamount was no frolic in the waves. I didn't blame him for wanting more, but I did grieve for Eelway and Pelagia, now bereft of both of us. New sympathy for Eris wanting to see her family welled up in me.

Then I frowned. *Isn't the ghetto cleaned up now? I've heard rumors that people are returning to the Seamount from land. There's an initiative to bring back half-sirens. They've promised the returners housing near the top of the Seamount and no more scrounging for food and Grace.*

Cetus barked a laugh. I'd never heard him laugh on

land before. It was endearing, like a yelping seal, and I would have grinned if I hadn't been so focused on answers to my question.

Yeah, I've seen half-humans who came back. He shook his head. *Right next door. They're not happy about it, either, but what did they expect? Come on, everyone knows how the Seamount treats us. These newcomers have obviously been away too long that they've forgotten the reality of life underwater.*

He took another bite. Before I could reply, he spoke again.

But it's worse than that. The ones who return are chained, kept in their caves until they're taken away to work. Terrible jobs, too, like scraping barnacles off walls until their hands bleed, or acting as training dummies for the mer folk. Cetus put down his cracker with a grimace. *Eelway has been busy patching up our neighbors. They're being punished for ever leaving, I guess. And Grace? They only get a pittance. And I thought our portions were bad enough. I wouldn't go back for anything.*

I took a deep breath, surprised by the fury building in my chest. What Cetus said was no surprise, but the memory of Eris's hope and Dr. Mazzaella's certainty wrenched at my heart. They had been misled, but why? Who was behind this initiative, and what did they want?

Someone was spreading terrible lies. If enough people listened to and left for the hope of a life that would never be, they would only fall into a trap of horrific proportions. What was more, my own life on land was in dire straits. I couldn't follow them, even if I wanted to live as a slave in the ghetto. I was wanted for murder, and death waited for me under the waves. If enough people left, would Grace even be delivered anymore? Would I be fated to die a lingering, painful death from land sickness?

I didn't want Cetus forced back to the Seamount, not when he'd only just escaped, not when it would mean an even worse life than the one he'd left. I wanted him to find his own life on land just as I'd done, although hopefully with more freedom than me. And Byssa couldn't go back even if she considered the sacrifice of freedom worth it because breathing water was as much a death sentence for her as Seamount justice was for me.

Cetus must have seen the fury on my face because he stopped eating and stared at me. *What's wrong?* he asked with a motion of his hand.

Someone is behind this, I said, my gestures sharp and my hums too loud. *They're destroying life on land. I can't let that happen.* Intense anger hardened my resolve, and I gripped the edge of the table as I met Cetus's gaze. *I'm going to stop them.*

CHAPTER 7

I showed Cetus how to use the washroom, remembering vividly the puddle I'd left on Branc's warehouse floor my first day on land. After introducing Cetus to Squirter and giving him a paper and pencil for something to do, I left him with strict instructions to not open the door to anyone. He was practically helpless, and I shuddered to remember my vulnerability when I'd first arrived.

Like it or not, Branc had provided a valuable service for me during a time of uncertainty. I could resent him for hiding the extent of my debt in the beginning, but without him, I could have been locked in a psychiatric ward, tossed in jail, or starved in a ditch. Well, I would have sirened someone for help, but still. Those first few weeks had been bearable, almost enjoyable, compared to the frantic uncertainty I would have been under otherwise. What Branc had provided was a clear way forward.

He still deserved to choke on vent fumes, though.

I hopped off the bus onto a sunlit street and marched toward Branc's club, the Abyss. The bouncer Reef, with his customary pearl stud in one ear, opened the door at my knock, and I slipped past him and strode down the hall. Instead of entering the main club area, where servers prepared for a busy night to come, I veered to the left and knocked sharply on an office door.

I didn't wait for an answer before I burst in. To my surprise, Branc looked almost disheveled. His hair wasn't slicked back in his usual pristine style, and his shirt was unbuttoned in a debonair fashion. Whatever had been bothering him this morning must have been still needling him. I was momentarily speechless.

"What do you want?" Branc said. He pushed papers aside with jerky movements and huffed a sigh. "I'm busy right now, and I don't have any jobs for ungrateful sirens."

"I'm not here for that." My words came back in full force. "I'm here because I just found a new half-siren on our shores. He'd been wandering around all day. Your warehouse was closed when he followed the signs, and so the police nearly took him away." I exhaled sharply. "I may not agree with how you deal with newcomers—in fact, I disagree on most points—but if you provide a service and advertise it, at least follow up on that promise. Cetus was left high and dry in a strange city with no one to help him." I paced, unable to stay still.

Branc watched me, his body entirely motionless. "He arrived this morning?" he said quietly.

"Yes."

Branc was still for another moment, then his fist slammed against the desk. I jumped. Branc was always so collected, annoyingly so, that this display of emotion startled me.

"I was unexpectedly called away on urgent business," he said, his voice thin with strain. "I needed the assistance of all my employees for the day. I thought it was a worthwhile gamble, but now I see that I was wrong." He looked to the side, his breath coming in short bursts. "I know you despise me and my methods, but if I don't capture wandering sirens in my net, they threaten the safety of us all. What would have happened if this Cetus had been taken to hospital? What might the doctors have discovered about our heritage? Could the police have forced him to talk?"

"I'm starting to get it now," I said. "Your methods leave a lot to be desired, but that's not important today. What was the business that called you away? Was that what you came to my apartment for?"

"It doesn't matter."

"Does it have anything to do with the Grace supply issues?" I said with narrowed eyes. Branc might think it wasn't any of my business, but if the delivery of Grace was disrupted, my life on land was in jeopardy.

"Never you mind," Branc said with more force.

"Have you heard the rumors drifting around of people being enticed back to the Seamount? Apparently, it's all lies, but nobody knows that yet."

"I have heard," Branc admitted. "My people are under strict instruction to give me word of these rumors, but so far, none has been approached. Have you been?"

"No. Will you tell me if you find out more?"

"We'll see." Branc shrugged.

I scowled at him. I could sense from experience that I wouldn't get anything else out of him. I'd have to investigate through other means.

"Now that this siren is here, I can take the burden of caring for him off your hands," he said, his voice back to his usual competent tone. "I can get him on his feet."

"Yeah, no." I moved toward the door. "You're not getting anywhere near Cetus. I can handle this myself. He doesn't need your brand of charity."

I threw open the door and stalked out. It felt good to stand up to Branc, even if it were for someone else and not myself.

The short ride home on the bus in the slanting sun of late afternoon only let me stew further. I couldn't believe that Branc had offered to help Cetus—with a straight face—and I gritted my teeth every time his offer passed through my mind. There was no way that I would allow Cetus to get within ten kicks of Branc, not if I could possibly avoid it. I couldn't bear seeing a friend get ensnared in Branc's net.

I sighed and traced a swirl in the bus window's condensation. The annoying thing was, Branc had a point. If he didn't take care of the newcomers, no one else would be picking up the slack. And leaving them to fend for themselves ended badly, as Cetus's lake adventures had illustrated. I closed my eyes and forced myself to breathe deeply. It didn't matter now. I'd alerted Branc of the consequences of his lapse in watchfulness, and I'd rescued Cetus from both the human authorities and Branc. I could only move forward.

I sat up straight and texted Byssa with an idea that had popped into my head. When I jumped off the bus at my stop, I raced down the road past scrubby grass yards and overflowing garbage cans. I only slowed when a prickle touched my neck again like the spines of a sea urchin. My head whipped around. Who was watching me?

A few pedestrians wandered the streets, and cars roared past on the busy road. On the opposite corner of the intersection I was nearest, a dark-haired man stared at me. I was too far away to see his features, and he turned and walked away as soon as I met his gaze.

I shivered. Part of me wanted to run up to him and demand to know what he was doing. Common sense took hold. I was attractive, and he'd noticed. That was all. I didn't need to peer farther into his motives.

I continued to my apartment, determined to push away the memory of the mystery man, and shoved my key into the apartment's lock. I slowed in the hallway and stared at my apartment door that stood ajar.

My heart pounded and I pushed the door open gingerly. Was Cetus all right? He was no better than a baby on land, voiceless and oblivious of the potential dangers that lurked around every corner.

My apartment was still and empty. Squirter was tucked into his plastic sandcastle in the tub, his eyes narrowed in sleep, and I didn't disturb the little cephalopod. I strode into the hall again, my breath coming in short bursts. What should I do now? Start banging on doors and asking my neighbors if they'd seen Cetus? Many were half-sirens themselves and would likely have sympathy for my plight, but I squirmed at the thought of approaching them.

I'd been aloof to any friendly advances they'd made over the past year, not wanting to create ties here when I was so beholden to Branc. Now that I was more willing to reach out and make connections to my fellow exiles, the others were not willing to overlook my previous rudeness.

But Cetus needed me. I straightened my spine and lifted my hand to knock on my neighbor's door. A tiny nautilus shell was scratched into the paint next to the peephole, and I braced myself to greet a half-siren.

The dark-skinned bartender from Branc's club opened the door, and my mouth fell open.

"You live here?" I stammered. "I had no idea. It's Pod, right?"

He stared at me with his piercing gray eyes. When he spoke, his low, smooth voice filled my ears. "I only moved in last week. This apartment is cheaper than the one I had on the top floor, and I'm close to paying off my debt."

I looked him over with new appreciation. He stared back, unimpressed.

"Wow," I finally said. "It's nice to see someone close to escaping Branc's clutches. I'm Lune, by the way."

"Yeah, I know." He left the silence dangling long enough to grow awkward.

I cleared my throat. "Have you seen my friend Cetus wandering around? Tanned skin, long white hair, brown eyes, medium height. He just arrived yesterday, doesn't know English or how land works at all. He was supposed to stay in my apartment, but he's wandered off and I'm worried."

Pod pushed the door open farther. From a ripped couch in the living room, Cetus waved with a cheery smile.

I sagged against the doorframe, my heart galloping

with the release of adrenaline. Then anger kicked in.

How could you? I gestured, striding closer so I could grip his shoulder for my hums to transmit better. *You scared me half to death. You could have been anywhere, and you don't know how land works.*

"New friend," Cetus said clearly. "I'm with new friend."

I stepped back and eyed Cetus, then I glanced at Pod. He shrugged.

"We were working on his English. Honestly, set him up with some television while you're gone, and he'll be ready for land before you know it. You know how fast we pick up languages."

I stared at Pod. It was a good idea, and I wished I'd thought of it first. "I don't have a television. No money for that kind of purchase."

"The apartment has one in the common room for borrowing." He narrowed his eyes at me and crossed his arms. "You really keep to yourself, don't you? I thought everyone knew that."

I tightened my lips. I didn't want to agree with his statement, but his words made me feel stupid and out of place.

"Come on," I said and gestured. "Let's go."

Cetus stood up obediently and followed me to the door. Before we left, I glanced again at Pod. I rarely spoke to other half-sirens, so I wanted to make the most of it.

"Have you been approached by anyone talking about going back to the Seamount?" I asked. "I've heard rumors."

"Not me," Pod said quickly. "But I've heard the same rumors. But I don't want to go back now that I've almost paid off my debts to Branc. Count me out."

"It's all a scam, anyway. Don't fall for it." I jerked my head at Cetus, who was attempting to follow the conversation with a tilted head. "Cetus said the half-sirens who go back are treated like dirt."

Pod's eyes briefly widened, then he reverted to his unflappable self.

"Noted," he said to me, then he placed a hand on Cetus's shoulder to speak to him. "Come back anytime."

Cetus smiled and nodded. I gripped his elbow in my fingers and steered him out the door.

"We're meeting my friend Byssa at a store," I said aloud, taking my cue from Pod and joining my vibrations with speech so that Cetus could learn more quickly. It wouldn't take him long—it was a trait of our race to excel in communication of all types—and I felt stupid for not trying earlier. Then I shook myself. Cetus had only arrived this morning. I couldn't be expected to think of everything. Appreciation for Branc's role in greeting newcomers threatened, but I pushed it down firmly.

"Store?" Cetus repeated out loud while he followed me down the road in a too-small pair of flipflops he'd borrowed earlier.

"Where you buy things that you need." I sighed at having to explain the basics of human interactions to Cetus. Living on land wasn't intuitive to someone from the Seamount. I knew that firsthand. "Humans trade pieces of paper for clothes, food, anything they need." With my free hand, I dug out a five-dollar bill from my pocket and waved it in front of Cetus.

"How do you get the pieces of paper?" he asked in a mix of English and hums. His eyes tracked the blue bill in my hands. We turned the corner onto a busier street lined with shops.

"I trade work for it. Oh, look, Byssa is here already."

With a thankful sigh, I dragged Cetus over to Byssa, who stood at the glass doors of the nearest thrift shop. Her eyes bugged out when she saw Cetus.

"Who is this?" she asked me, looking him over with an appreciative air that collapsed into a blush when Cetus gazed back at her. She pulled me aside and hissed, "You didn't tell me you met someone, not to mention someone hot. Who is he?"

I rolled my eyes at my friend. "For the first and last time, he is not my boyfriend." I pulled her closer to the confused Cetus. "Cetus, this is my friend Byssa. Byssa, this is my friend Cetus. He just arrived today from the Seamount."

Byssa's hand flew to her mouth and covered her gasp. She tentatively put her hand on Cetus's shoulder.

"Oh wow," she said in a mix of English and Seamount language. "Welcome. It's so nice to meet you. I didn't realize you were coming, or that Lune had friends at the Seamount."

Byssa glared at me, and I looked down to avoid her accusing gaze. I rarely mentioned my previous underwater life, despite Byssa's frequent invitations to the contrary. My past wasn't filled with happy memories for the most part, although when I looked at Cetus, I couldn't believe that I'd thrown out the good memories of him and my other friends along with the bad ones of oppression and hunger. I'd had friends who cared about me, although it had been too painful to think about them in the aftermath of my escape. It'd been easier to ignore my past in favor of a fresh start on land.

But I was embracing my siren heritage, and it felt right to remember some of my Seamount times fondly. The Seamount and my friends were a part of what made me who I was. I shouldn't ignore that, nor did I want to, not anymore.

"Let's get you set up," Byssa said to Cetus with a warm smile. She tugged him by his upper arm into the thrift store. "Then you won't have to wear Lune's clothes."

Cetus glanced down at his shirt, whose words, "Whale hello there," stretched over his chest. I swallowed my chuckle and followed the two into the store.

Byssa dragged Cetus into an aisle of shirts and pressed suitable items one by one into his arms. Cetus stared at her in bemusement, and I crossed my arms to watch the master at work. I could have outfitted my old friend in appropriate clothes, but how could I take away Byssa's fun?

When she moved to a rack filled with pants, Cetus's brows drew together.

"What is this?" he stammered out, his words halting but his tone clearly disapproving. "No. I don't like."

He waved at his legs, which were encased in a pair of old sweatpants Hades had passed to me months ago and that I rarely wore. I hated pants as much as Cetus did, and I understood his impulse completely.

"But that's what we wear." Byssa pointed at her own jean-clad legs.

Cetus glanced pointedly at my jean skirt. I took pity on the pair of them and rummaged through the rack. After a moment, I extracted a wrinkled kilt.

"You can wear what you want, Cetus," I said. "But if you don't want to attract much attention, you'll try to fit in. I'd recommend pants, but if you can't stand them, this will be your next best bet."

Cetus's eyes lit up at the tartan garment, and he snatched it from me as if it were a time-limited offer. Byssa sighed and handed him a pair of loose-fitting cotton pants.

"You should have some just in case," she said. "You and Lune, you're just the same."

Cetus grinned at me, and I wrinkled my nose at him.

"Go on," I said. "Try them on in the changeroom."

Byssa showed Cetus where to go, and I browsed the racks for my own purposes. I didn't have much money, and what I did have would go toward Cetus this month, but window-shopping was free. When I saw a tee shirt with a huge wave curling around the words, "The ocean is calling," I bit my lip. It practically had my name on it, but if I waited a month, it would be gone for sure.

I approached the counter with my find. The woman glanced at me through tortoiseshell glasses from under her frizzy orange hair, and I smiled sweetly.

"Could you please set this aside for me?" I asked. "For next month when my paycheck comes in."

"We don't hold items for that long." She folded shirts with brisk efficiency, her front pressing against the counter to support her. "A day, max."

I really wanted that shirt. How could I convince her to change the policy for me? My eyes narrowed. A true siren wouldn't hesitate. Should I? I pressed my hips against the same counter the woman leaned into and hummed. When gentle vibrations of persuasion thrummed into the woman's body, I spoke again.

"I would be so grateful. Write the name 'Lune' on a sticker, put it on the shirt, and tuck the shirt far in the back of the counter. I'll pick it up next month."

The woman stared at me, her hands slowing on her task. My hums were soft enough that she didn't respond to my suggestion right away. Finally, she nodded and held out her hands for my shirt.

"Of course," she said. "I'll tuck it away for you."

I beamed my gratitude and shoved back from the counter, leaving the woman to carry out my orders. That shirt was worth sirening for, and no one was hurt in the process. What was the point of having these powers if I couldn't use them occasionally? They were a part of me, after all. I didn't want to ignore my heritage any longer. I ignored the heaviness in my stomach. There was no need to tell Byssa, though.

"I like ocean clothes better," Cetus grumbled in his mix of English and gestures when he exited the changeroom a few minutes later, a grinning Byssa trailing him. "So dry and scratchy."

I glanced him over with critical eyes. Paired with a well-fitting black tee shirt and leather work boots, the kilt looked like a fashion choice instead of necessity.

"You look good. You fit in better now." I looked at

Byssa. "What do you think? Dye his hair?"

Byssa rubbed her chin as her eyes raked over Cetus's head. "He'd look good as a blond like you," she said finally. "Similar enough to his real hair, but definitely land-worthy."

Cetus raised an eyebrow. "What are you planning?"

"You'll see." I looped my arm through his and propelled him to the exit. "Don't you like surprises?"

CHAPTER 8

Byssa insisted on paying for hair dye from the pharmacy and takeout dinner of pizza. After springing for Cetus's new clothes, it didn't take much for me to swallow my pride and accept her help. It was only mid-month, and my bank account was too lean, especially with my trip to the Lodge rapidly approaching.

On our way out the store, a gasp made us pause.

"Byssa, darling," an older woman said to my friend. Her straight black hair, cut in a severe bob, swayed around her petite face. Luminous gray eyes bored into Byssa's and ignored Cetus and me. "I'm so glad I bumped into you. Just yesterday I met Selo. Has he approached you yet?"

"Hi, Shelley." Byssa frowned. "No, I've never heard of Selo. Who is he?"

"He's a representative from the Seamount." Shelley's large eyes opened even wider with her excitement. Her hair wiggled. "Oh, the pictures he painted of the new lives we could lead, down there in the city! What a marvel." She pressed a hand to her chest. "I knew this day would come, when we'd be welcomed back with open arms to our rightful home."

Byssa smiled tightly. "I'm sure it will be lovely. I can't go, though. Land lung."

"Oh, my poor dear." Shelley placed a consoling hand on Byssa's arm. "I'm so sorry. Well, if Selo speaks to you, maybe he will have a solution." She squeezed Byssa's arm and moved away. "I must run. It was wonderful to see you, darling."

"Wait," I said as Shelley breezed by. "Don't believe this Selo guy. It's all a lie."

"Sorry, didn't catch that," Shelley called over her shoulder. "In a rush. Bye!"

Byssa waved at Shelley's departing back. I stared after her with my mouth agape.

"What did she suppose this Selo could possibly do for land lung?" I placed my hands on my hips, indignant for my friend's sake. "What a callous thing to say."

"It's fine." Byssa shrugged, although she avoided my eyes. "I guess the rumors Eris heard were true."

"She will be surprised," Cetus piped up. "No welcome for half-humans."

"Really?" Byssa's brow wrinkled in her concern.

"They're treated terribly, Cetus says." I looped my arm through hers. "Trust me, you don't need to be jealous of anything. In fact, spread the word to whoever might believe you."

"I can try to talk to Eris," Byssa said. "But she's pretty set on going. I doubt she'd believe me, not without some proof."

I sighed. "As long as you believe me. What are we going to do about Hades and his drifting syndrome, though? Now that we know how bad it is from Cetus?"

Byssa's lips pursed. "We're going to see Dr. Maelstrom right after the grand opening. Hades isn't any worse, so we have time."

"And I can ask him about the rumors," I said. "A doctor will have heard them all. And I can ask around at the Lodge, too. Warn people, if necessary. Come on, let's get back to my place."

We walked the last few blocks to my apartment and entered the musty old building. At my door, a battered old television on a rolling cart sat against the wall. I stared at it for a long while.

"Is that yours?" Byssa asked with curiosity.

"I'm borrowing it," I said and slid my key into the door. My stomach felt odd, like I'd swallowed a live lamprey. The thought of someone looking out for me, someone other than Byssa and Hades, was a novel one. I wasn't sure how I felt about getting friendly with the neighbors. I was hoping to move out as soon as I paid off my debt, after all.

But Pod had left the television for Cetus, not me. With that encouraging thought, I pushed the cart into my living room. Byssa took over coloring the hair of a dubious Cetus, and they ensconced themselves in the bathroom while I brought out plates and cutlery and set up the television. Printed instructions showed me how to plug in something they called rabbit ears, and before the others emerged from the bathroom, I had a staticky talking head on the flickering screen.

My phone pinged, and I glanced at the screen. My stomach leaped around like I'd swallowed a school of herring.

I just thought how much you'd like this dish, Levi had texted, along with a picture of a barbequed salmon on a bed of dried seaweed.

I grinned and replied, *I hope the kitchen doesn't run out of fish before my visit.*

I wouldn't let that happen.

I couldn't keep the smile off my face when Cetus and Byssa entered the living area.

"Look." I waved proudly at the television, then I stared at Cetus. "Wow, you're good at that, Byssa."

Cetus glanced uncertainly at Byssa, who gazed at him with an appraising eye for her handiwork. Cetus's hair was now a short, pale blond, and I had to admit my old friend looked amazing, with his naturally tanned complexion and chocolate brown eyes in an elfin face. Byssa nodded with the satisfaction of a job well done.

"He looks good, doesn't he?" She blushed as the meaning of her words sunk in. "I mean, the hair worked out."

"He looks fully human." I pointed at the table. "And that will help him in the long run. Now, it's time to eat some quintessentially human food, no seafood in sight."

"There are a few shrimp on the top one," Byssa said with a chuckle. "I couldn't resist."

We sat down, but something was missing. I jumped up, grabbed a large glass bowl from the kitchen, then raced to the bathroom. With a careful scooping motion, I collected Squirter and as much water as I could manage into the bowl, then wobbled my way to the table.

"Good idea," Byssa said. She ran her fingers over the glass when I placed the bowl down, then she pressed her hand against the table and hummed a greeting. The little octopus waved an arm at her.

"Shrimp?" Cetus held up a pink curl from the pizza. I nodded, and he dropped it into the bowl. With inquisitive suckers, Squirter touched the shrimp then brought it to his beak and started to munch.

My heart felt too big for my chest. Sitting here with friends old and new, warmth and comfort filled me in a way I'd rarely felt in the past year. I missed those who weren't here, of course, but the joy of having these three with me blunted any pain. I raised a glass of salted water to the others. Byssa followed suit, and Cetus did too after I pointed at his glass.

"To friends," I said in a thick voice.

Byssa repeated my words, then we all sipped our drinks. Byssa reached out and squeezed my hand.

"I'm happy to meet your friend," she said. "And I'm excited for our trip to the Lodge on Saturday. Will Cetus come too?"

I blinked at her. With everything that had happened today, I hadn't considered what to do with Cetus when we left Vancouver for the Lodge's grand re-opening.

"He can come," I said. "We'll bring an extra blanket, and he can sleep on the floor or something. We won't be using up any more space."

"I'm sure Levi won't mind," Byssa said with a knowing grin. "He's happy to please—you, that is."

I kicked Byssa gently under the table then reached out for a slice of pizza. Squirter waved at me, and I dropped another shrimp into his bowl. I caught Cetus's eye, and he held up his slice of pizza with a skeptical glance.

"Food?" he said dubiously.

"Try it, you big grouper," I said, laughing. "You might like it."

A few days later, Cetus squinted in the sunlight on the top deck of the ferry, despite his cheap sunglasses and ballcap. I winced in sympathy. Those early days on land had been brutal for the sheer brightness and garish colors.

"Why don't we swim?" he asked in English, although he gripped my elbow to transmit his more difficult thoughts clearly. "Why this boat?"

"It's a long way," I said, leaning over the railing to gaze at the churning water below. "I wish we could, but I don't have enough time off for that. To even take today off, I had to switch days with Brandon at work. A weekend trip will have to do."

Cetus frowned at my concept of a weekend, and Hades chuckled. He still looked tired and drawn from his drifting syndrome, and the inside of his wrist was stained from repeatedly applying his medicinal paste, but he was in his usual good spirits.

"We work for five days, then relax for two," he said to Cetus. "Then repeat."

I tuned out their discussion and turned to face the dock as the ferry pulled away from shore. A few people stood on a balcony where the foot passengers usually waited to board.

My eyes narrowed. One of the figures, standing apart from the others, looked very familiar. Dark hair, medium build... where had I seen him before? He was too far away to make out features, but he was facing my direction.

A shiver crawled down my spine. It was the man who

had stared at me on the corner near my apartment. I'd brushed off my watched feeling at the time, but seeing him twice can't have been a coincidence. Who was he? Why would someone be following me?

At least he wasn't on the ferry. I could relax my vigilance for a night while I visited the Lodge. I resolutely turned my back on the figure and looked inward to the boat, allowing my mind to think of Levi instead.

Hades and Cetus were still chatting, and Byssa was away buying a drink at the cafeteria, so I idly looked at my fellow passengers. A woman my age stared at Cetus, who was at that moment wildly gesticulating his thoughts to Hades. I narrowed my eyes. Was she attracted to Cetus, or was she eyeing his antics with curiosity?

Either way, I didn't like her interest. Nothing good would come of it. I hesitated, then made up my mind to do something about it since I could. I sidled closer and smiled at her.

"It's a lovely day," I said in my low voice. When she turned to me, I reached out and touched her arm. Before she could jerk away in surprise, I hummed a command of disinterest. Her eyes glossed over Cetus and Hades, then she turned to face the bow.

Satisfied, I released her arm and stepped back. Only then did Byssa's eyes on me register. I glanced at her expression of confusion and concern.

"She was noticing Cetus too much," I said when I walked toward Byssa. My neck prickled with unease. Sirening the woman had been the right thing to do to protect my friend—the best thing to do, as one of the pale folk—but I didn't like the way Byssa was looking at me. "He's too new here to bear much scrutiny."

Byssa looked after the retreating woman and didn't answer me. I pursed my lips and rejoined Cetus and Hades, wondering if my sirening had been necessary after all. A month ago, I would have said no. But a month ago, I'd been determined to ignore my siren side.

"Where do we get Grace?" Cetus rubbed his hands together and his eyes gleamed with longing as he stared at the waves. "I feel empty."

"Better get used to that feeling," I said with a nudge of my elbow into his ribs. "You're on land now. You think you didn't have much at the Seamount, but Grace is expensive and hard to come by up here."

"I brought some," Hades said with a reassuring grin at Cetus. "But it's in the car. I'll give you some when we get to the Lodge if you like."

Byssa pulled into the long driveway of the Lodge, and the car trundled past tall conifers with glints of bright ocean through the trunks. With every tree we passed, my heart grew lighter, and I could barely keep a smile off my face. I'd missed this place more than I cared to admit, even though I'd only spent a few weeks here. The Lodge was where I'd finally discovered a home on land, among my people who understood me, and coming back was like being embraced by an old friend.

I glanced at Cetus and squeezed his arm impulsively. Having him here with me was the seaweed on the fresh mussel, exactly what I needed to make my experience even better. He grinned back at me, not nervous at all entering a strange place. He'd always been the bravest of the four of us. Foolhardy, Eelway had often called it.

"Look, there's William," Byssa said with a wave out the windshield. William, the elderly head gardener in charge of landscape maintenance, leaned against his shovel and waved back at the car. Byssa sighed in happiness and drove the car forward. "It's lovely to be back here. I didn't think we'd get the chance. It's too expensive to stay the night here on a whim, and that job opportunity we had before isn't likely to happen for another year."

"Glad you're friendly with the boss," Hades said with a waggle of his eyebrows when he turned to look at me.

I rolled my own back at him. "Friendly, maybe. But I did save his life. Looks like that's worth a night's stay. Besides, he bought those underwater photos from Byssa for the restaurant wall. How could he not invite her after that?"

Hades opened his mouth to say more—probably further innuendos about Levi and me—but Byssa hushed him. I was grateful. Although I was excited to see where Levi and I might lead, our relationship was too new and fragile to bear much prodding. We'd only chatted a few times over video and text, and had made no promises. I didn't need Hades sticking his foot into the mix.

"I wonder if any people with drifting syndrome come to the Lodge to visit occasionally," Hades said quietly.

Byssa glared at him. "You are not going back to the

Seamount. You are going to get better. Don't even think like that. Do you hear?"

Byssa's furious words didn't inspire a reply, and Hades nodded and looked out the windshield. I held my breath until Byssa sighed and changed the subject.

"Here we are," she said with a flourish of her hand.

The Lodge appeared when the trees opened to a wide expanse of glittering bay. The main building sat in pride of place, its multiple levels perched on a hillside overlooking the water. Its rustic wooden paneling was warm and inviting in a way only dry folk could pull off. I'd been on land for long enough to appreciate the beauty of the reddish wood tones and feel a desire to enter the open door.

"We are here?" Cetus said with a curious gaze out the window. "We will stay here?"

"We sure will," I said.

Hades hopped out of the car when Byssa pulled into an empty spot and took a deep breath of the fresh sea air. "It's good to be back," he said. "Get your stuff out of the trunk, everyone. Let's see where we're sleeping tonight."

I scrambled out of the car and grabbed Squirter's backpack and my duffel from the trunk. Squirter wasn't in his container—I'd sent him swimming north a few days ago to meet us here—but I liked having the option to bring the little cephalopod on land with us. Last time we were here, I'd needed to bring him to the bathtub for his protection when the arsonist had threatened me. It felt good to be prepared.

I led the way to the Lodge's front doors, eager to enter

the familiar territory. Who was I kidding? I was eager to see Levi again. Video calls were fine and well, but nothing beat meeting in person. A flush of warmth traveled through my body at the memory of the moonlit moment we'd shared during my last visit here. Could we pick up where we'd left off?

I wanted to find out.

Sandy the receptionist stood behind the counter as usual, her honey-colored skin contrasting beautifully with her white hair. Her deep brown eyes lit up at the sight of us.

"Lune," she cried, squeezing around the counter to embrace us. "Hades, Byssa. So lovely to see you."

I hugged Sandy back when she reached me, but my breath hitched when my gaze caught on movement behind her.

CHAPTER 9

Levi emerged from the hallway, his blue eyes affixed on mine. He looked just as delectable as he'd always done, and my stomach squirmed with pleasure. His mahogany hair beckoned me, and my fingers ached to run through their waves. The silvery discoloration on his neck glinted in the sunlight streaming through a window. His bright-eyed slow smile when he saw me made my stomach flop again.

I released Sandy and stepped toward Levi.

"Hi," I said less-than-eloquently, my voice low. Should I hug him? Shake his hand? Wave? I settled for nothing, which was just as awkward. Levi hovered, clearly filled with similar uncertainty.

"It's good to see you," he said. When Hades coughed behind me, insufferable as always, Levi's eyes snapped to the others. "Good to see you all. Welcome back to the Lodge."

Byssa and Hades greeted him then returned to speaking with Sandy. Levi's brow creased when he spotted Cetus, and I pulled my friend forward by the hand, then wrapped my arm around his shoulders so I could accompany my English words with vibrations.

"Levi, this is my friend Cetus," I said. "He just arrived from the Seamount last week. Cetus, this is Levi, the manager of the Lodge."

I didn't know how else to introduce Levi—what were we, exactly?—so I settled with the obvious. Levi blinked slowly at Cetus, and his eyes flicked to my torso pressing against Cetus's side.

"Ah," he said after a moment. He cleared his throat. "Right. I see. Welcome to land, Cetus."

I bit my cheek, worried that I was trespassing on Levi's goodwill. He'd given the invitation to the three of us, not Cetus as well. Lodge rooms were expensive, and I didn't want to presume on his generosity.

"He can stay in our room," I said quickly. "And I'll pay for his food and any expenses. I know he wasn't invited, but I couldn't leave him in Vancouver on his own."

"It's fine," Levi said quickly. His smile was gone, and he looked like a serious manager of the Lodge. He swallowed and continued, "If you're willing to share, we'll have enough room. Your party can choose to stay in two land rooms or share one dockside room."

"Dockside?" Byssa gripped my elbow. "That sounds amazing. Really? I'd love to stay in one. We can definitely share. I'll have to stay in the top room, of course—breathing underwater isn't my thing—but I still want to check out the underwater part. Thanks, Levi. This is so great. And the party is tonight? Tell us if you need help with anything."

"It's all taken care of," Levi assured her, his expression calm and collected. Gone was the man excited to see us. When had the light faded from his eyes? All I saw was the manager. "You're here as guests. Enjoy yourselves." His eyes flicked to me briefly then landed on Sandy, as if he couldn't look at me for long. "I'll leave you to get them settled. I have to run."

Levi disappeared, and Sandy didn't give me time to

dwell on the mystery of his change of mood. Maybe he didn't want to appear too eager in front of his staff. He had a presence to maintain, after all, and if he wanted their respect, he probably felt that he had to act a certain way.

I wondered how he was faring with the responsibility, now that he'd been fulltime manager for weeks ever since his parents had given up their posts. He'd been stressed to the limit in his new role the last time I'd stayed at the Lodge. Hopefully he'd found an equilibrium that allowed him to have some fun on the side. I flushed again at the direction my thoughts led me.

"Come on." Byssa tucked an arm through mine and Cetus's until she linked us both. "Let's check out our room. I can guess where Cetus is sleeping tonight. It's a unique opportunity to sleep underwater."

"Underwater?" Cetus's head perked up. "Sleep?"

I chuckled. "I guess we can let him. Although he's been sleeping underwater a lot more than we have lately. Maybe Hades and I should take the underwater room."

Cetus's shoulders drooped, and Byssa nudged him as we walked toward the door that Hades held open for us, keys in his hand.

"Lune is teasing," she said. "Don't worry, I'll fight for your right to sleep underwater."

Byssa released us to get through the door, and I followed her into the warm sunshine with a hint of coolness from the approaching autumn. I was dressed in a tee shirt and jean skirt, as always. Even if it cooled off, I never felt the cold.

We wandered down the grassy slope toward the

docks. On the way, we passed a young woman with bright pink hair lounging on a bench, her legs on the lap of a floppy-haired young man.

"Byssa? Lune?" Kim cried out, leaping up from the bench. "I didn't realize you'd be coming for the grand opening. Are you working?"

"Guests," Byssa said proudly as Kim hugged her and Kim's boyfriend Darren slapped Hades on the shoulder. "Levi invited us."

"Oh, it's like that, is it?" Kim glanced at me, and my traitorous cheeks warmed. "Aren't you lucky. I'm only on my break, then I'll have to get back to the restaurant for a short bit. Well, however you're here, it's great to see you."

Kim hugged me, and a wave of emotion swept over me. I was so used to anonymity in the city, that I'd forgotten how wonderful it felt to be recognized by friends.

We chatted for a few minutes, introducing Cetus to the others and hearing about Darren's plans for university in January, until it occurred to me to ask if they had heard the Seamount rumors.

"Back to the Seamount?" Kim said with astonishment. "Why would I want to do that? My life is here."

"And I was born here," Darren said. "Two half-siren parents."

"Someone named Selo is offering to escort willing people back to the Seamount, give them prime cave dwellings, extra Grace, all that." My shoulders relaxed with relief that the mysterious Selo hadn't reached this far north. Maybe the Lodge was safe from his machinations. "Cetus says it's a lie, though. They're treated worse than scum and punished for leaving the Seamount in the first place. If someone approaches you, don't fall for it."

"Thanks for warning us. I'd hate to give everything up here for a lie." Kim checked her watch and sighed. "I need to get back. Duty calls. But I'll see you all at the party tonight. Maybe earlier for a swim if you're around."

"Wouldn't miss it," said Hades.

We waved the two off and continued our saunter to the dockside rooms. The shell handle was smooth under my hands when I pulled the door open for the others. Inside, cool, moist air wafted into my face, and I breathed deeply. Patterns of blue and green light danced across Cetus's face as he gazed around with a look of contentment.

"This is nice," he said at last. "I like it."

"Wait until you see the room," I said. "Go on, Hades. Show us in."

Hades pushed the key into the second door on the left and swung it open. The walls were textured to look like the gray rock of a cave, and a heavily tinted window shone a dim light on two couches and a large bed covered with a green duvet.

"But the water." Cetus gestured helplessly out the window. "You said…"

I grinned and walked over to a discreet button on the wall. "You want water? Then I'll give you water."

A panel in the floor retracted with a smooth motion and slid away, revealing a square hole with seawater lapping at the edges. With another press of a button, the water illuminated in glowing green. Cetus's eyebrows rose. Immediately, he kicked off his shoes and slid into the water.

"Wait!" I sighed with a shake of my head as my friend disappeared. "Now his clothes are all wet."

Byssa giggled. "He'll get a lesson in laundry today."

"Give the poor guy a break. He's only been here for a few days." Hades threw his bag on the floor and stretched on the couch. His eyes fluttered closed with the tiredness he couldn't hide. "I guess I'm down there tonight, and you two ladies can share the bed up here."

"Thanks." I glanced at the water again, where Cetus's shadowy form was swimming around, checking out the place. "I couldn't tear him away from that room if I wanted to."

Hades rummaged in his bag and extracted a package of Grace that he crinkled between his fingers with glee.

"I knew I'd packed some," he said. "I stocked up last week from Mark the Shark. Man, I hate dealing with that guy, but Grace is Grace, and he's the one who has it. He only let me have a few packages, though, the stingy lamprey. Blamed the shortage, but what do you bet he's skimming off the top? Now, who wants to go for a swim?"

"I thought you'd want a rest," Byssa said with a frown at her brother. "It was a long trip."

"I'm fine," he insisted. "Besides, swimming is relaxing. Are you coming?"

"I want to find Kim again," Byssa said. "She'll be done her shift soon, then I'll swim with her."

"I'll come," I said. The water beckoned with its cool lure, and I relished the ease of entry through our private underwater room. This was luxury, indeed. "I want to see if Squirter made it yet."

Cetus's head popped out of the water, and he rested his forearms on the floor while his body remained afloat. He waved two small packages in his hand.

"Grace," he said with his eyes wide. "I found it here."

"That's what they leave for guests," I said to Hades. "Like chocolates on a pillow."

"I love the Lodge," Hades replied. "But you two can have that stuff. I know you're buying for Cetus as well these days. I have my Grace from Mark."

Gratitude welled in me. I'd never explained to Hades and Byssa the full extent of my financial woes, but they were observant enough to note my frugality and perennial lack of funds. I don't know what they thought, but I was happy to take the Grace without their prying.

"Ready for a swim outside?" I asked Cetus. When his face brightened, I stripped off my tee shirt and skirt, kicked off my sandals, and slid into the water next to Cetus. His leg brushed mine in the tight space. He chewed one of the pieces of Grace and held the other one out of my reach with a mischievous grin.

"Try to get the Grace," he said.

"You lumpsucker," I said with heat, but my laugh gave away my true feelings. I lunged toward him, but he sank below the surface. I gave chase in the room, passing wide kelp fronds for anchoring sleeping bodies and a large stone table near the window. I finally caught Cetus by feinting to the left before grabbing his leg and yanking him toward me until his hand was within reach. I shoved the Grace in my mouth in triumph and chewed.

My eyes closed and my back arched with the overwhelming sensation. When it faded enough for me to swallow and open my eyes again, Cetus was watching me. Unsure what to make of his attention, I peeked into a smaller room in the interior wall to see if housekeeping had given us cleaner fish in the washing room. Three striped fish circled inside a jar on the wall. I closed the hinged door and turned back to my friend.

Breathe underwater? I hummed. Cetus nodded, and together we exhaled. I barely heard Hades enter the water behind us as uncomfortable hacking took my body over. When my lungs had finally expelled all their air and I was breathing calmly once more, I swam over to the outer door and pressed the button to open it. The panel slid sideways, revealing the murky water of the bay.

A blast of pressure flowed from the top of the doorway to reduce the flow of plankton-filled waves into our room's glass-clear waters. Quickly, the three of us exited and I pressed the outer button to close the panel.

Hades led us along familiar paths into deeper water. Cetus brushed his hand against frothy white fronds of plumose anemones, and I sent a loud hum of question to summon Squirter if he were here. It was a long way for a little octopus, but I'd dropped him off days before, so I was hopeful.

Sure enough, once I crested a ridge covered in giant barnacles sweeping their fans through the water, a small figure barreled toward me, noticeable with my Grace-heightened skin sense. I smiled widely as Squirter glommed onto my stomach with all arms suctioned tightly.

You're here, I said with real joy in my hums. *Good.*

Squirter made a wordless hum of contentment, then his slitted eyes glanced at Cetus swimming nearby. *New friend?*

By "new friend", I knew Squirter meant Levi, because that was the epithet I'd given him a few weeks ago. I shook my head.

Old friend, I replied. *New to here.*

Cetus swam over and presented his hand with a hum of greeting. Squirter perked up and reached an arm to wrap around Cetus's finger. He'd played with Cetus in the tub before, but all he'd seen of my friend was a hand and his Seamount-voice. Now that the octopus recognized my friend, he released my stomach and crawled over him with interest.

We played with Squirter and explored the rocky promontory between bays. Once, I thought I felt the same long, sinuous body at the very edge of my skin sense that I'd noticed on my last trip to the Lodge. Before I could mention it to the others, Squirter inked me in the face. I forgot the odd sensation in the distance during my chase of the little octopus. At one point, Hades rubbed his stomach with a twist of his mouth.

Are you okay? I asked him.

He nodded with a shrug. *I'm fine. It will pass.*

I stared at him for a moment longer, but when he straightened with a grimace and swam forward, I followed him without comment. Hades was still in the grips of drifting syndrome, with no sign yet of it fading.

Had it been a bad idea to go for a swim? Maybe he should have been resting.

But the ocean was a restful place for a half-siren, and I couldn't regret getting Hades out here. We could turn around now, though. That would be a reasonable compromise.

But when I swam forward to pull the two others toward our room, Hades curled around his stomach in a jerky motion that looked like a retreating anemone.

I darted toward him. *Hades*, I shouted. *What's wrong?*

He couldn't answer me. Instead, he shook violently, then his mouth opened and vomit shot out. I wrapped my arms around his waist and pulled him away from the cloudy water, back toward the Lodge.

Cetus, I called out. *Help me take Hades back. Something's wrong with him.*

CHAPTER 10

Cetus and Squirter raced back from their position in front, but I wasn't watching them with my eyes, only my skin sense. My focus was on dragging my twitching friend through the water, back to the Lodge. Cetus grabbed one of Hades's arms, I shifted to take the other, and together we swam with intense undulations back the way we came.

I'm worried he's relapsing with his drifting syndrome, I said to Cetus.

Maybe, he replied with a doubtful glance at Hades. *Strange about his veins popping out. Is that a symptom?*

I glanced at Hades's hand. Black veins bulged on the top. I shook my head then propelled myself faster through the water. We needed to get more medicinal paste on him to help his symptoms.

Hades groaned and didn't resist as we drew him closer to the Lodge. Squirter landed on my head, too tired to swim at our speed, and I wore him like a hat. Finally, the pilings of the dockside rooms loomed in my skin sense, and I directed us toward our room.

Once we'd squeezed through the open panel and I'd shut it behind us, I cradled Hades's head in my arms.

How are you feeling? I asked.

His eyes fluttered open. *Like a* ligan *swallowed me and spat me back up again*, he said with a ghost of a grin. *But I'll live.*

Do you want to go upstairs or stay underwater? I ignored Cetus's incredulous look. Hades had lived on land since he was a small child. It stood to reason he'd be more comfortable up there. *If you can manage the transition, that is.*

I can manage, he said. He moved feebly toward the square hole in the ceiling, and I pushed him up to help.

I held Hades steady while he coughed up the water in

his lungs. He hung like a limp rag while I did the same, then I hauled him out of the water with Cetus pushing from underneath. Hades lay panting on the floor when he was up.

"I'm good here," he gasped finally. "Comfort is overrated."

"Hold on, you big lump." I squelched over to the bathroom for towels and found a huge stack of them on a shelf. I grabbed four and proceeded to line the couch with them. While I worked, Hades dragged himself over to me and crawled onto my handiwork. He lay with his eyes closed and his chest rising and falling rapidly. The veins in his hands bulged greenish blue now that we were in better light.

Hades cracked an eye at me and caught me staring at him with a furrowed brow. "I'll be fine," he said in a hoarse voice. "Maybe it's unrelated to my drifting symptoms. I think I threw up whatever it was. It could have been that dodgy burger on the ferry. I'm already feeling better."

"You look terrible," I said baldly, "but you sound fine. If it is food poisoning, then all you can do is wait. I wonder how it got in your burger."

"Restaurant worker ate badly prepared sushi for lunch?" Hades suggested. "Who knows."

"You should probably put on some of that paste Dr. Mazzaella gave you, just in case." I brought Hades's bag closer to him. "What if we're misdiagnosing?"

"Can't hurt." Hades rummaged in his bag and spread the brown paste on his wrist while I took my dry clothes and disappeared into the bathroom to dry off. When I emerged a few minutes later, Hades was asleep and Cetus was still swimming in the room downstairs.

The door to the hallway opened, and Byssa walked in with Kim on her heels. They were laughing at something Kim had said, but they both sobered at the sight of Hades's unconscious, clearly unwell body.

"What happened?" Byssa hissed, whirling toward me with her face taut from fear. "Did he have an episode? I thought the paste was supposed to help."

"He spread some on just in case." I pointed to Hades's hands, hoping to dispel Byssa's concerns, although I was also worried about the potential progression of Hades's illness. "The veins are weird. We think it was something he ate, maybe the ferry food. He's feeling better now, just weak."

Byssa sighed heavily and stared at her brother with worry lines between her eyebrows.

"We could go for a swim later," Kim suggested. "If you wanted to sit with Hades now."

"He's fine," I said. "Honest. Go on, go for a swim. The water's great, as usual. We'll keep an eye on him."

Byssa dithered for a moment longer, but when Hades snorted in his sleep and rolled over, she turned.

"Okay, thanks. I won't be long." She grabbed some Grace from the package Hades had left on the table. "Don't tell him I stole his Grace, especially since I'm taking three whole pieces. He hates it when I do that. I didn't make it to Mark before we left, though, so I'm in a deficit. He's flush."

"Your secret is safe with me," I said.

Byssa and Kim left with towels and Byssa's

underwater camera a few minutes later. I stuck my head in the water to watch Cetus.

I want to go for a walk, I said. Cetus looked up. *Can you stay with Hades, make sure he's okay?*

Sure, he said, and kicked to the surface. I squeezed my hair dry and wiped my face, then threw Cetus a towel once he was sitting on the edge.

"What do I do?" Cetus said. He looked at the sleeping Hades with pursed lips. "He is boring."

I flicked water off my fingers toward Cetus. "You'd be boring too if you were sick. Be nice. Do you want my phone to watch videos? Practice your English?"

When Cetus nodded, I opened a video app on my phone and passed the device to him. He wandered to the bed and sat on the edge, watching a cooking show. I stifled a laugh. At least Byssa would appreciate his new vocabulary.

I fluffed my wet hair with my fingers while I walked down the hall. It was a novelty to stay in these rooms instead of cleaning them. I half expected someone to ask what I was doing there, or to request new towels.

Outside was a shock after the dim, moist atmosphere of the dockside rooms. The sun was jarring and the midday warmth all-encompassing. I breathed deeply and rested my hand against the wall, trying to regain my equilibrium.

Once the brightness wasn't so dazzling and I'd adjusted to the harshness of dry, warm air, I sauntered along the northward path along the sea. My feet took me on a woodchipped trail that meandered through a short stretch of rainforest before leading me to the next bay over.

This one contained a tiny marina of maybe fifteen boats. On the grass above the high tide line, a patio was now accompanied by a white gazebo with ornamented details around the edge. It was a great spot to see the view without being exposed to the harsh sun, and it was currently occupied by three small groups hanging over the railings.

Hammering focused my attention on the dock. I wandered over and greeted a familiar face.

"Hi, Liam," I said to the large, black-haired man wielding the hammer.

He paused and looked up through silver eyes, then his face broke open with a smile. "Lune, you're back. Here for the grand re-opening?"

"You bet. The gazebo looks very picturesque."

Liam grinned at the echo of his own words from weeks ago. "The guests seem to think so."

"I bet." A thought struck me. "Hey, do you know anyone in Vancouver? There are rumors swirling around about efforts to bring people back to the Seamount. Heard anything?"

Liam frowned. "My sister just moved there with my baby nephew. She did mention something on the phone the other day. Laughed it off, mainly, because she would never go back—little Jack can't tolerate cold water, so that's out—but others she knows are considering it. To each their own, I guess. Although I wouldn't mind going back, if only to help my buddy escape. I could sneak him out."

"It's all lies," I said. "A friend of mine just escaped

from the Seamount, and he says those who return are treated worse than ever. Practically slaves."

"Sounds like business as usual at the ghetto for half-sirens."

"Way worse than that, apparently."

Liam raised an eyebrow. "Are you sure your friend isn't exaggerating? Who's running this show, and why would they treat us like that? What's in it for them?"

"Do the upper echelons need an excuse to push us to the depths?" I shrugged. "I believe it, more so than them giving us prime caves and all the Grace we can eat."

"Fair point."

"Tell your sister to warn her friends."

"I will." Liam's jaw tightened. "Why are they doing this?"

"That's what I'm trying to find out. Stay safe and wary until I do." Liam still looked concerned, so I switched the topic to lighten the mood. "Hey, are you coming to the party tonight? Are staff invited?"

"Of course, you know Levi. He wouldn't leave us out." Liam stood and stretched the hammer over his head. "Except for the wait staff, obviously. Hey, Levi," he called out.

An electrified sensation tingled my skin as I realized that Levi was on the other end of the dock, speaking to the head maintenance worker Jess. He was wearing a different colored Lodge shirt from before, and his hair was damp. Had he showered since I'd seen him last? I tried to banish thoughts of him in the shower.

When Levi turned to walk our way, Liam continued, "What's the plan for the party tonight?"

Levi had an easy grin for Liam that slid off his face when he saw me. My stomach shriveled. Why did he look like he'd accidentally swallowed a barnacle? I'd been looking forward to this trip for weeks to see where we might continue what we'd started during my last visit to the Lodge. Why was Levi acting so strange?

"Hi, Lune," he said stiffly then turned to Liam. "Appetizers, drinks, mingling. I have a live band booked, they're setting up right now. For the pale folk guests, there will be complimentary flavored Grace."

"Bacon fusion?" I guessed. Part of the Lodge's stockpile of Grace had been nearly burned during the debacle a few weeks ago. The smoke had infused much of their Grace.

Levi's mouth twitched with the beginning of a smile as he remembered his joking words to me back then. Then he sobered. "Yes, exactly. Speaking of, I'd better go make sure the set-up is going smoothly."

Levi nodded at Liam and strode into the trees toward the Lodge. My heart squeezed with disappointment, and my eyes prickled. I blinked quickly and looked away. Coming here had been a mistake. I'd thought we'd had something, but clearly I'd been wrong. I bit my lip, angry at myself for giving into my feelings.

Maybe it was for the best. Levi was human, after all, and I was only half so. What future did we have, really? I would never be able to share my siren side with him—especially if he refused to swim—and that was a huge part of me. I wasn't willing to forget my recently rediscovered heritage for Levi.

Especially if he didn't even want me.

"I'd better finish these repairs," Liam said, bending to his task. "Can't miss the party."

"I'll see you tonight," I said and stepped off the dock to walk along the beach. Hopefully a few deep breaths would settle the traitorous moistness in my eyes. I shook my head angrily and stomped on the sand. I didn't need Levi. He was an unnecessary complication to my life. And long-distance relationships were too much work, so the Internet told me. I was better off without him. Not that we had anything to start with, apparently.

In my distraction, a splashing sound from the ocean barely registered. It wasn't until a voice called out to me over the waves that my head turned.

"Lune! Help, quick!"

A soaking wet Kim stood in the shallows, holding a limp Byssa under the arms. Kim's terrified face spoke of her panic. I splashed out to help her, mindless of my shoes and skirt.

"She just started throwing up," Kim babbled. "Clutching her stomach, then she passed out. I had to hold her mouth and nose shut so she wouldn't breathe in water—you know she doesn't do that, she always holds her breath—and this was the closest beachfront to bring her. What's wrong with her?"

I bent to sling Byssa's unresponsive arm over my shoulder. Her hand flopped near my face, and the green veins stood out in stark relief against her pale skin.

"Maybe she ate something funny," I said, but my heart sank at the too-familiar symptoms. I didn't want to get into the drifting syndrome diagnosis. What would that mean for Byssa, who couldn't breathe underwater?

I shook my head and pointed toward the Lodge. "Come on, let's get her to our room. Hades had the same thing, and he's already feeling better with rest."

Kim lost the look of panic, and her face grew a determined expression instead. She draped Byssa's arm over her shoulder, and together we dragged my friend out of the water. We were lucky that she was so slight. Byssa groaned after a few steps, and she slowly put one foot in front of the other to help us out.

"We'll get you into bed soon," I promised Byssa. "And figure out what happened."

"Do you think it's poison?" Kim panted when we reached the trail. She winced at the coarse woodchips against her bare feet, but she gamely pushed onward. "Should I go tell Levi?"

"No," I said quickly. Kim referred to the poisoning event at the Lodge during the uproar weeks back, but the sinking feeling in my gut told me a different answer. I searched for a reason to excuse my knee-jerk reaction of not wanting to talk with the Lodge's manager. "No, we haven't eaten anything at the Lodge yet, so it can't be like last time. It would have been the ferry food, I'm guessing. She'll be fine soon."

Kim nodded and we continued toward the dockside rooms. When I pushed open our door from the shifting colors of the hallway, Cetus looked up from my phone.

"What happened to Byssa?" He jumped up and helped us bring her to the bed. Byssa groaned as we laid her down then curled up in a ball. I draped a blanket over her and stepped back with the others.

"I guess I'll get changed," Kim said in a whisper with

a glance at the sleeping Hades and unconscious Byssa. "I'll come back later and see how they're doing. Can I get you anything? Food, medicine, doctor?"

"Thanks, Kim, but I think we'll be okay." I smiled reassuringly at her. "If anything changes, I'll get help."

Kim nodded and left after one last glance at Byssa's small form under the blanket. Once the door closed behind her, I grabbed Cetus's arm to communicate better.

"Byssa's veins are popping out like Hades's are," I said. "And she vomited and passed out. Do you think she has drifting syndrome, too? That would be too cruel, considering she can't breathe underwater. What would she do? Unless the symptoms are unrelated to Hades's condition, and they both ate something funny. But I've never heard of veins like that from food poisoning."

Cetus frowned. "You know what else it looks like? Strolia poisoning. Bryo from a few caves over got nicked once. Same thing happened to him."

My heart squeezed in my chest. The tip of a strolia's horn held a toxin that was unpleasant in tiny doses and deadly in large ones. "How would they be poisoned by a strolia? It doesn't make sense."

"I don't know, it's probably not that. Even if it is, there's nothing we can do except give them rest and let the symptoms pass. They don't look like they got enough of a dose to kill them."

I absently rubbed Byssa's hand between my fingers. "They don't have cuts that I know of. What did they both eat today? What could have been contaminated?"

"Hades had that layered thing on the ferry."

"A hamburger," I corrected him automatically. "And Byssa only had fries, but so did he. Maybe that was it."

"But we both had the fries, too," Cetus reminded me. "And we're fine."

"For now." I tapped my foot on the ground in a nervous twitch. "But why did they get sick at different times? You'd think they would have succumbed similarly. Was there anything else?"

Cetus shrugged. "Just Grace, but you and I had some too."

I stared at him, my mind working frantically. "But we had the Lodge's Grace. Byssa stole some Grace from Hades and ate it later than he did." My mouth dropped as the implications of what I was saying hit me. "He bought that Grace from Mark the Shark, and it's contaminated." I snatched my phone from Cetus's unresisting hand. "Stay here. I need to make a phone call."

I jogged out of the room, my shoes squelching with damp. Cetus called out a question after me, but I ignored him. Blood pounded in my ears as my anger intensified. Mark the Shark was a Grace dealer for Branc.

CHAPTER II

I burst out of the dockside rooms and into the harsh light of the autumn afternoon. A few people were strolling the grounds, so I strode to the privacy of the southern trail. Few people ventured this way. My shaking fingers punched in a phone number, and I held my phone to my face in a tight grip. I leaned against a tree, facing the water, while I waited for Branc to pick up.

"Lune?" Branc's gravelly voice held a hint of question and a dash of promised retribution for interrupting him. I ignored the threat in his tone.

"What the vents are you playing at?" I hissed, my anger overriding any caution I might have felt otherwise. "My friends just ate Grace that your goon Mark sold them yesterday, and now they're vomiting and on death's door." It was a slight exaggeration, but I needed to get my point across. "They show all the signs of strolia poisoning. What are you lacing your product with, and why? What do you gain from poisoning your clients? Vents, Branc. We need Grace. How else are we supposed to get it if we can't trust your supplies?"

When I finished my tirade, silence filled the speaker.

"Answer me," I shouted into the phone. My hands shook from anger, but also from fear. What would we do without Branc's supply of Grace? Sirens on land had very few options. Maybe we could buy some from Levi—he dealt with his own distribution chain for the Sunshine Coast—but my stomach clenched at speaking with Levi right now. With the way he'd been acting today, would he even entertain the idea?

"I," Branc said with slow, deadly enunciation, "did *not* poison your friend's Grace." His breathing grew heavy, which shocked me into calmness. Branc rarely grew upset or showed emotion. His blow-up the other day was the only time I'd seen him upset, and now today. He continued in a louder voice, "I have no reason to contaminate my product. Why would I deliberately lose the trust of my clients? Selling Grace is a large part of my business ventures. Jeopardizing those transactions would be career suicide."

I took a deep breath and released my angst. "If not you, then who?" I said in a more reasonable tone, hoping that Branc wouldn't hold my previous words against me. As he'd shown the other day, it was easy for him to increase my expenses on a whim.

"That's what I need to find out. There have been issues lately." Branc's words sounded carefully chosen to keep me ignorant. "They've been affecting the way I run things, including not being able to greet your friend from the Seamount in the proper way. And now my supply is tainted."

A chilling thought occurred to me. "In small doses, strolia poisoning mimics drifting syndrome. That diagnosis will send people back to the Seamount for their cure."

His breath heaved in and out as if he were trying to calm himself. "Someone wants half-sirens back to the Seamount, and they're using me to achieve their ends. My reputation will be ruined at this rate, and reputation is everything. I will get to the bottom of this, even if I have to track down everyone who bought the tainted Grace and follow the supply back to its source. I'll put all my resources on it."

"I'd be willing to help," I said delicately, "for a price."

I wanted to solve this mystery as much as Branc did, but if I ever wanted to get out from under his thumb, I needed to play his game, but better.

"You're helping," he growled.

"I don't have to," I said, my voice growing bolder. "You can threaten me with expensive Grace, extra fines, whatever you want, but that won't force me to do anything I don't want to do."

I held my breath, hoping against hope that Branc wouldn't call my bluff. I didn't want him to retaliate, but I couldn't roll over and take whatever he wanted to dish out anymore.

The silence rang in my ears, but finally, Branc sighed. "What's your price?" he asked cautiously, his voice holding a hint of warning.

I took the warning and didn't press my luck. "Waiving three months' rent on my apartment for three days of helping you track down the contaminator."

"Five days," he countered, "and two months' rent."

"Four days, and the three months is non-negotiable."

Silence, then, "Done. Come see me tomorrow night when you get back to Vancouver."

He hung up, and I took a moment to dwell on how much Branc knew of my travel plans. I shivered and pushed the phone into my pocket. Branc's omniscience was a fact of life. One day, I'd be free of him.

By the time I returned to our dockside room, both Hades and Byssa were sitting up with as much color as their pale complexions ever had. Cetus was chatting with Hades, and Byssa rubbed the sleepiness out of her eyes.

"You're both awake," I said with real gladness in my voice. As much as I'd believed that they would recover from the strolia poisoning, it was still a relief to see them on the current to recovery.

Byssa smiled at me and patted the bed beside her. I sat and wrapped her in a spontaneous hug.

"How are you feeling?" I asked when I released her.

"Like someone punched my stomach a few times," she said with a grimace, "but better. Whatever the problem was, I definitely got it out of my system. I wonder what we ate. Do you really think it was the Grace?"

"Yes," I said without hesitation. "I'm positive that the Grace supply from Mark the Shark is contaminated. People who take it get the symptoms of drifting syndrome. Why someone would taint the Grace like that, I don't know. I phoned it in, so they're on it now. And nobody at the Lodge gets their Grace from Mark, so they should be safe."

"You called Mark?" Hades said with a raised eyebrow. "That's awfully chummy of you. We're text only."

"Yeah, well, you know me, friendly with a capital F."

Hades chuckled then stared at his sister.

"That means I don't have drifting syndrome," he

whispered. "I don't have to leave."

Byssa was still for a long moment, then she flung herself at Hades.

"I was so worried," she sobbed.

Hades clutched Byssa in his arms with the same relief she showed. When she finally released him with a huff of laughter, wiping her eyes and smiling at me, he winced and held his stomach. I frowned at the two of them.

"I'm glad you're sticking around, but it looks like we're giving the party a miss tonight," I said. With Levi's disinterest, the thought didn't pain me much.

Byssa looked scandalized. "Are you kidding me? I don't care if I have to crawl to the main building, I'm going to that party. I wouldn't miss it for the world. And they're unveiling my photos. How could I not go?"

"You heard her," Hades said with a chuckle. "Besides, I'm starving. They're planning to feed us at this thing, right?"

"Okay." I tried to hide the resignation in my voice. Byssa would only prod into my emotions if I revealed them to her, and I wasn't ready to unpack whatever was going on between Levi and me. Nothing, apparently, and I was having a hard time coming to grips with that. "Then we'd better get ready. I claim the shower first."

I spent too long in the shower, trying to wash away the hurt from Levi's actions and the residual anger from my interactions with Branc. I resolved to make this event about Byssa, since her photography was going to be unveiled in pride of place. This was for her, and it was my job to support my friend. Just because the reveal happened to be taking place in Levi's establishment didn't mean I needed to dwell on the aggravating man. Even if his wavy hair still begged to be touched…

I turned off the water with a growl. If the shower wasn't washing away my frustration, I might as well give it up for Byssa to use. She was spreading out our clothes in the next room, clothes she'd had the whale's share of choosing. At the time, I'd been content to act as Byssa's mannequin and spend the last of my paycheck, imagining the reception I'd get from Levi, but now I wished she hadn't chosen such a form-fitting dress that accentuated my curves. I didn't want to put on a show. I only wanted to blend into the backdrop in a supporting role for Byssa.

I sighed and wrapped a towel around myself to exit the bathroom. Hades and Cetus must have relinquished the room to us, because only Byssa remained. Pale folk might not care about modesty, but male boredom with getting ready for a party appeared to be universal.

"Finally." She pointed at the clothes on the bed. "You took your sweet time. The others will be back in half an hour to get dressed, then we have to go. You should use my hair dryer to speed things up."

I shuddered at the contraption that Byssa held out to me. "It will be dry by then." I shook my tresses out with my fingers. "I can't stand that thing, blowing hot, dry air at me. So unnatural."

Byssa rolled her eyes and disappeared into the bathroom. A minute later, the water started to run. I surveyed the bed with a sinking heart. The slinky, navy-blue dress designed to cling to my waist and hips with sensual ease twinkled with a shimmer of silver threads woven into the fabric. I sighed and dropped my towel. I might as well get this over with. Byssa wouldn't accept anything less than this dress.

By the time Byssa emerged from the bathroom, hair dried and makeup applied, I was doing up the clasp of my silver and crystal necklace. She beamed at me.

"Gorgeous. Just like I thought. The silver and midnight blue combo sets off your hair perfectly."

I ran my hands over my hips and surveyed the low-cut neckline with apprehension. "It's a bit much. I don't know."

"It's gorgeous," Byssa repeated firmly. "I love it, and I bet Levi will, too."

She winked at me, and I managed a strangled half-smile before turning toward the mirror and applying lip gloss to my waiting mouth. Byssa, for once unobservant about my failing love life, turned to her own clothes.

Hades and Cetus came back and made quick work of changing while I avoided the mirror and tried to ignore the silver heels that Byssa had made me buy. They were too similar to the ones I wore during siren night at Branc's club, and I hated heels in the first place. They had seemed like a good idea at the time, but now that I didn't care who saw me, I was tempted to wear my usual boots, or at least a pair of casual sandals. Imagining Byssa's horrified indignation was enough to stop me from carrying through with my plans.

Finally, Byssa and the others were ready. Byssa touched my hair with light fingers.

"It dried," she said with approval. "Good. Now we're all ready. Come on, Hades, your hair looks fine. Stop primping."

Hades took one last look in the mirror and followed his sister out the door. Cetus sidled up to me and offered his arm.

"What movies have you been watching?" I said with a grin. "What a gentleman."

"This is what men do when women wear fancy clothes, yes?" Cetus raised a brow as his eyes traveled down my body. "That is fancy."

"Yes, I suppose it is." I sighed and slid my hand through the crook of his arm. "Let's get this done."

CHAPTER 12

I had to mince in tiptoes over the lawn so my stiletto heels didn't sink into the grass, and I was grateful for Cetus's support. Otherwise, I would have ripped the shoes off, Byssa or no. Thankfully for my friend's tranquility, my heels remained on, and we walked through the front door into the main Lodge building.

The entryway was festooned with garlands of cedar and fir boughs, shells and feathers artfully placed among them. The garlands led us down the hall toward a brightly lit doorway.

Byssa gasped when she entered the restaurant, and when I stepped through a moment later, I realized why. My gaze traveled over walls swathed in billowing sheer fabric in blues and greens, festooned with puffy white paper balls that suggested plumose anemones. A four-piece band played in one corner, and the small dance floor swirled with couples. Tall tables encouraged mingling and light conversation, and each one held a candle in a hurricane glass surrounded by sand and shells. I shuddered at the fires inside a wooden house and resolved to ignore them for the rest of the evening.

A sheet hung over one wall, and I pointed it out to Byssa.

"Are those your photos under there?" I asked. "Looks like there will be a big reveal later."

"Aww, my baby sister is going to be famous," Hades teased.

"We're twins. Two minutes does not make you my big

brother in any practical sense of the word." Byssa stared at the sheet covering her work. "I hope people like them."

"Like what?" Kim joined us and glanced at the covered wall. "What's under there, anyway?"

"A secret," Cetus said at once. I could tell he'd been dying to use that word, with how quickly he'd spat it out.

"Ooo," Kim said. "Love it. It must be the reveal in the schedule. Come over to our table. Some of the staff are hanging out there so we don't have to mingle with the guests." She winked and waved for us to follow her.

Byssa and Hades walked after Kim. Cetus stepped forward and I followed along, still holding his arm. My gaze caught a familiar pair of blue eyes across the room. I hadn't been raised to consider a man in a suit as the height of attractiveness as Byssa had been, but Levi wore his charcoal-gray slacks and midnight-blue shirt like they were his second skin. It didn't escape my notice that we matched, and I almost asked Byssa if she'd had a hand in that. His brow was furrowed, and he looked away as soon as we made eye contact.

What in the sulfurous vents was Levi doing? If he was over me, he was doing a terrible job at showing it. My frustration at his behavior made my fingers clench into Cetus's arm.

"Okay?" he said.

I willed myself to relax. "I'm fine. Let's go mingle."

Kim, Hades, and a young man with a long ponytail named Henry were already chatting with flutes of champagne before them at the standing table. Byssa pushed two flutes toward me.

"I nabbed two for you," she said. "Do you remember Henry?"

"Of course," I said.

Henry laughed. "It's Lune, the strolia secrets pro. Up for a game after this shindig wraps up?"

"I could be convinced to play a round," I said with a smile that soured when I remembered how that game evening had ended: sharing an intense moment with Levi in the moonlit night. I shook away the memory. "Yeah, I'm in."

Byssa introduced Cetus, and the others were welcoming to my friend. He bloomed under the attention, and his broken English grew smoother with practice. After we spoke of Lodge events since we'd last visited, the talk turned to the Seamount.

"Have you heard the rumors from Vancouver?" Henry asked us with a serious expression.

Kim leaned in with a frown on her youthful face, her pink hair darker in the candlelight. "Yes, they were telling me about it earlier. Why, what have you heard?"

"The Seamount wants us to all come home," he said in a whisper. "They're offering an escort back and homes in an elevated section of the Seamount. No more ghetto for the returnees. I've been here for years, but I don't know, it's awfully tempting. A bunch of people I know are seriously considering it. Imagine living without hiding our true selves, and swimming all the time? Not to mention access to Grace. It's been harder and harder to get it here. Who knows how long they'll keep bringing it to land for us?"

"No," Cetus said clearly. "The ghetto is still there. No

fancy homes for half-humans.”

Henry stared at him. Pity bloomed in his eyes.

“Maybe it’s in a part of the city that you never went to,” he said. “And it’s probably only for those who return, not for everyone. I mean, if everyone was moved up, there would still be someone on the bottom, wouldn’t there?”

“And that sits okay with you, does it?” I asked, a hint of heat entering my voice. “You’d be happy with lording it over the half-humans who hadn’t left, just like the full sirens always did to us?”

“Well, no, of course not,” Henry said defensively. “But you can’t deny it sounds plush. And I do worry about our future here if the Grace dries up. What would we do?”

Byssa was silent and twisted a cocktail napkin in her hands. Hades’s mouth was set in a firm line.

“There will always be some half-sirens on land,” he said. “And they won’t cut us off from Grace completely. Have some faith.”

I felt sick thinking about a lack of Grace. Maybe I needed some food to settle my stomach. I hadn’t eaten for hours.

“I’m going to find some appetizers,” I announced to the table. “I’ll be back soon.”

I fled the distressing rumormongering and wandered through the restaurant. The beat of the music throbbed in my ears, but I barely heard it. What would happen to me if Grace stopped coming to land? Would I have to return to the Seamount and live in the outskirts, scavenging for scraps and avoiding the authorities? My gut twisted at the grim prospect.

I straightened. Branc wouldn't let that happen. Presumably he needed Grace as much as the rest of us, and his entire fortune hinged on the half-sirens who lived on land. There was no way he would let Grace distribution slip through his fingers without a fight. As much as I disliked Branc, he and I were on the same side for once.

My resolve didn't waver when I spotted Levi ahead of me. Instead, it grew stronger. I needed to talk to him, clear the air to remove this festering thing between us. If he didn't like me anymore, I wanted to hear it from his lips. Those full, kissable lips that I wanted to taste.

I gritted my teeth and strode toward him. My abominable heels made my hips sway unintentionally with the motion, even though I felt frustrated, not sexy. Levi caught sight of me marching toward him, and his eyebrows lifted. He glanced around as if to find an escape, but I was on him before he could sidle away.

"We need to talk," I said, my voice low but stern. "In private."

"I can't leave the party," he said with an anguished look at the crowd. "The unveiling will happen soon, and I have a speech to give—"

"Two minutes," I said and tugged his elbow toward the exit. I tried to overlook the warmth of his skin through his shirt. "They won't miss you for two minutes."

With a sigh, he stopped resisting and allowed me to steer him into the hall. I dragged him into a side hallway that led to his office, although we didn't enter. The hallway was far enough away from prying ears.

"What's going on?" I demanded, my hands on my hips. "Why are you ignoring me?"

"I'm not ignoring you," he said without looking at me. "It's a busy day. This party had to have all my attention."

"You've been acting weird ever since I arrived. You've hardly said two words to me. I thought—" I swallowed and didn't continue my sentence. *I thought we had something between us. I thought that maybe we had a future. I thought you wanted more.*

"You're here on holiday. I didn't want to disturb you and your friends." Levi gave the slightest emphasis on the word "friends", but I still didn't have a clue what he was going on about.

"I see them all the time. I came here hoping…" I huffed a sigh, frustrated beyond measure. I wanted to press my body against his in this dark hallway where no one could see us, run my hands over his chest and feel his lips on mine, not stand here arguing.

I needed answers, and Levi wasn't forthcoming with any. There was one way to get what I needed. It was for his own good, too. We could clear the air in a moment. I laid my hand on his arm. He stared at it.

"What's going on?" I whispered, infusing my words with the faintest hum of compulsion. It vibrated his arm through my hand with a gentle movement, barely strong enough to feel. I didn't need to force every last secret out of him, only loosen him up enough to tell me what he was really thinking about me, about us. Once the air was cleared, we would both be happier.

Levi met my eyes for the first time since we'd left the

party. Under the influence of my compulsion, they were wide and soulful. The flat blue of his irises bored into my own eyes, filling me with their hopelessness and hurt. What was he going through to make him feel that way?

Levi's mouth opened, slightly, a little more. My own opened in echo, willing him with my hum to speak his mind. Maybe then we could move past this and get to the part where his lips could do something other than speak. My eyes drifted to those lips.

With the lack of eye contact, something snapped in Levi. He ripped his arm away from my hand and stepped back. When I stared at his face again, his expression was slack with horror. Then it twisted with anger.

"You. Sirened. Me," he ground out. His hands balled into fists. "How could you do that? I thought you were different, that half-sirens understood the unfair advantage that siren powers gave others." He stepped back farther, his eyes disbelieving as they searched my face. "Do you think you're better than me, that I'm just a lowly human who needs to be managed? I've dealt with that all my life, but I thought you would have understood. Does it make you feel better about yourself to push me into the mud just like you've had done to you for years?"

His chest was heaving like he'd been running. I brought my hands up in a pleading gesture, then my fist clenched on empty air when Levi stepped back again.

"No," I said frantically. "It's not like that at all. I just—you wouldn't tell me what's wrong, and I…"

I didn't know what to say. My assertions to myself that it was for his own good drifted away like silt in the current. Was there any reason good enough to treat Levi with the same disdain that upper echelon sirens had always treated me with? I remembered the humiliation of their commands, the dreamy unconcern while I was under their power and the sick anger when they released me and I'd realized what had happened.

This wasn't nearly the same—I hadn't made Levi crawl over barnacles until he bled—but if he felt even a fraction of the hurt that I used to, it was too much.

"Levi, I'm sorry," I cried. "I didn't mean to hurt you."

"You don't respect me," he said flatly. His eyes were hard. "That's clear. We're done. You can stay the night, but your room is booked for someone else tomorrow."

He turned on his heel and fled the hallway. I leaned against the wall and sank until I sat on the floor. My eyes stared at the opposite wall, unseeing.

How had I messed this up so badly? I'd only wanted him to tell me the truth, and now I'd ruined any chance we'd had beyond repair. Because Levi was right: I'd treated him the same way the upper echelons had always treated me. At the Seamount, the class structure was clear. Three official layers existed among full sirens—the ruling class, the middle class, and those near the bottom of the Seamount. And then there were the half-sirens, in a class of our own, below all others. The rules were strict for sirening. No sirening above your class, compelling for information only within your class, and anything goes to the classes below. As a member of the very bottom of the pile, most sirening had always been off-limits.

But many at the Seamount saw humans as other, lesser than half-sirens, even. I wasn't one of them, but now Levi thought I was. And was he wrong? I'd sirened him without a second thought, merely to get him to tell me something he clearly hadn't wanted to share. A normal person would have respected his boundaries. I'd charged right through them, with disastrous results.

I was too irate with myself to cry, although tears were near the surface. I blinked a few times until the threatening moisture stayed in place. It was much easier underwater to hide tears from others.

Dimly, I heard Levi's voice from the restaurant, and my whole body cramped with shame over my actions and desire for him. He was announcing the unveiling of Byssa's photos, and I pushed to my feet on wobbly legs. I might be a terrible person, but I couldn't let my friend down. This was her big moment, and I needed to be there.

I slunk into the back of the crowd as they stood facing the sheet-covered wall. A shyly smiling Byssa stood next to Levi, who addressed the crowd with kind words and an expression carved from stone.

"We're happy to support the artists from our local community," he intoned. "Byssa Sweetcurrent is a flourishing photographer who has captured unique moments in our underwater realm, and we are pleased to put her photos in pride of place in the Lodge's restaurant. Without further ado, let me present Byssa's work."

Levi raised his hand, and staff members Jess and Quentin whisked away the sheet with a sweep of their hands. A collective gasp emerged from the crowd, then enthusiastic applause took hold. People surged forward to examine Byssa's handiwork closer—a mélange of sea stars, a threatening-looking king crab advancing on the camera, a close-up of the eye of a shark—and Byssa caught my eye. I gave her a thumbs-up since I couldn't manage a real smile in my current mood, but her beaming face absorbed my gesture with happiness.

She looked away to speak with some of the guests, and I slipped out the door. This evening was done for me. I had no interest in chatting with anyone else. I'd said enough.

At our dockside room, I ripped off my dress, my hated heels, and my crystal necklace. My chest heaved for breath. Quickly, I mashed a button on the wall and the panel leading to the underwater room slid open. Only the sea could calm me now.

I'd been swimming for a less than a minute when a welcome figure jetted toward me. Squirter hovered in front of my face and stroked my cheek with the tip of his arm.

Sad? he asked. My emotions must have been written on my face, or maybe I was giving off vibrations that he could read.

My eyes grew hot with tears, and I cupped the little octopus to my chest.

Sad, I agreed, and Squirter let me hug him against my shuddering chest while I sobbed.

CHAPTER 13

I was in bed when the others finally got back to our room. They were noisy in the way only drunk people trying to be quiet could be, but I steadfastly ignored their antics. I had no interest in answering questions about where I'd been that evening. I'd ask Byssa in the morning how her debut had gone, but not before.

Hades and Cetus splashed into the water and disappeared to sleep in the lower room. Byssa finally crawled into bed beside me and was asleep within seconds. I lay awake for ages after, replaying every expression, every word that Levi had done or said during our confrontation, wondering where I could have fixed things.

In the morning, Byssa groaned next to me.

"It's too bright in here," she grumbled.

"The windows are tinted," I reminded her. "This is literally the dimmest hotel room you will ever stay in."

"It's still too bright." She glared at the offending window. "The sun is a stupid invention."

I couldn't help my chuckle. The sight of Byssa grumpy was so incongruous, I couldn't take her seriously.

"You'll feel better after some water and food," I said.

"Food sounds horrible, but I could use some water." Byssa stretched. "Hey, speaking of food, did you try the cake they brought out at the end? An indulgent fudgy chocolate. I could only eat a few bites because it was so rich. Mmm, so good. Well, I would have added a touch of cardamom, but it was very tasty anyway. Did you get any? I didn't see you most of the night."

"No, I didn't try it." I cast around for an excuse. There was no way I wanted to admit my serious failing to Byssa, who had already been looking at me askance for sirening that woman on the ferry. What would she say if she knew how I'd messed up with Levi? "I wasn't feeling great, so I left early."

"You didn't eat some of that tainted Grace by accident, did you?" Byssa opened her eyes wide, then narrowed them with a grimace at the extra light.

"No, no. I'm fine. Just tired."

Byssa squinted at me, but figuring out my mood must have been too much for her hungover brain, because she yawned and slumped into her pillow. "I guess we'd better pack up. This has been a little window into luxury, but now we have to get back to the real world."

"I sent Squirter home last night." I sat up and put my feet on the floor. The effort to stand felt like too much, but I forced myself upright. The sooner we left the Lodge, the sooner I could put my terrible choices behind me and place Levi in my past, where he clearly wanted to remain. "Let's catch the earlier ferry. I have things I need to do at home."

Byssa frowned at me but didn't question my haste. It was true—I needed to meet with Branc to figure out the contaminated Grace—but that was another thing I didn't want to tell Byssa. Secrets were piling up between us, but I couldn't imagine telling her any of them. I cherished her trust and respect for me, both of which would fly out the window if she found out what I'd been hiding.

Yawning and shuffling, Byssa joined me in packing our things. By the time I'd pulled my hair into a messy ponytail in the bathroom, the others had joined Byssa, dripping on the floor and looking more refreshed than her.

"It's too bad you can't sleep down there," said Hades, rubbing his arms with a towel. "Talk about keeping hydrated. I hardly feel the booze from yesterday, and I wasn't exactly holding back."

"Lucky you," Byssa mumbled with a glare at her refreshed brother.

"I like that stuff." Cetus shook the water from his head. "It's fun. It's like *furod* milk from the Seamount, but without dealing with aching toes the next day."

"You think aching toes are bad?" I said. "You wouldn't say that if you'd slept up here."

"Don't worry, I'm sure he'll learn the hard way one day soon." Hades grinned at Cetus. "Now that he can talk to others, I'll take him out, meet people. What's your pleasure, Cetus? Girls? Guys? Other?"

"Girls," he said quickly with a half-glance at me.

I rolled my eyes at Hades. "If you're quite finished tryouts for the role of Cetus's wingman, let's grab breakfast and get out of here. The housekeeping staff will appreciate us vacating early, trust me."

We ate a quick breakfast in the staff dining hall for old time's sake. Kim and Darren were there, as well as Liam and Quentin, and I managed to pull myself together enough to chat amiably and avoid Byssa's questioning gaze. Once Byssa had finished savoring her kippers and poached egg, I stood.

"If we leave now, we can catch the eleven o'clock ferry to Vancouver," I said.

Byssa frowned at me. "Such a rush? I guess we're ready. Okay, let's find Levi and thank him."

"I'm sure he's really busy," I said quickly. "Let's not bother him right now. We can call him later and say our thanks."

"That seems rude," Byssa said.

"You could even send him a thank-you card," I invented quickly. "Humans do that, don't they? You could put one of your pictures on it. That would be special."

As I'd hoped, the idea mollified Byssa.

"Okay," she said. "That sounds nice. We'd better get moving if we want to catch that ferry. Come on, boys."

I sat in the back with Cetus to avoid speaking much with Byssa. She was too astute to not notice my solemnity, but Hades proved a great distraction as he and Byssa fought over the radio station, and he regaled us with stories from last night's afterparty in the staff dining hall. He and Byssa had fully recovered from their poisoning, which eased my heart. I'd have to let Branc know that the damage wasn't permanent.

On the ferry, Cetus sat next to me on a bench outside while Hades searched for food and Byssa trained her camera on a seagull perched on the railing. He put his arm around me and squeezed in a friendly way.

"Thank you for the nice weekend," he said carefully. "It was fun. I like land."

"I'm glad." I smiled at my old friend with his new blond hair but the same mischievous face underneath.

"It's nice having you here. I missed you and the others so much."

"I missed you, too," he said softly. "The Seamount wasn't right without you. I was so sure you'd found somewhere better to be. I'm glad I was right."

"You're always glad you're right," I said. "It's your favorite state of being."

"True." Cetus flashed a grin at me. "It is a nice feeling. Do you think we could bring Pelagia and Eelway up here? Do you think they would want to come?"

I sighed and leaned against his comforting solidness. His arm squeezed around my shoulders.

"I don't know how to reach them," I said quietly. "I can't go back—not after what happened, if they think I'm alive, that's the end for me—and it's not easy for you, either. Getting past the barrier isn't a swim in a lagoon, you remember."

"I remember." Cetus stared out to sea. "The rumors, about an escort back to the Seamount. I could join it, tell the others that you're alive, and the three of us could escape again."

"And risk being dragged to the depths by the mer folk or worse?" I shivered. "Don't push your luck. Maybe we can send a message with someone who's going, like Byssa's friend Eris."

Cetus opened his mouth to say something, but my phone buzzed in my pocket. I held up my finger to stop his words.

"Hold on." I checked who was calling, and I sighed. "Sorry, I need to take this. I'll be right back."

I stood and Cetus's arm fell off my shoulders. I strode

away so he and the others couldn't hear my conversation and leaned over the railing a dozen strides away.

"Hi, Branc," I said without enthusiasm. "I'm on my way back right now."

"Good," he said without greeting. "Come to the club as soon as you get to town. The plan has changed. You have somewhere you need to be tonight."

"Where?" I said with curiosity. I wasn't annoyed at Branc's presumption—I'd expected to be busy with his business tonight—but I did wonder what I'd be doing.

"I'll tell you when you get here," he said. "I don't trust my people to get out of a sticky situation the way you can, so it has to be you tonight."

"Will I be sirening someone?" My gut squeezed. My last sirening—on Levi—had been a spectacular fail, and I wasn't sure I was interested in repeating it again so soon. The consequences could be more than I wanted to handle.

But if it were for a good cause, if I sirened to stop someone from doing bad things, wasn't that okay? Maybe that was where the line was drawn. Don't siren friends, only enemies.

I breathed deeply. That sounded right. I could live with that guideline. Sirening was part of my heritage, after all, and I shouldn't have to give it up entirely to get by. Used judiciously, for a good cause, sirening could be a good thing. I didn't have to become an upper-echelon type just because I used my siren powers.

"Only if you get caught," Branc said cryptically. "Just get here soon."

He hung up and left me staring at my phone,

wondering what I was getting into tonight.

"Who was that?" Byssa said brightly. She'd recovered from her hangover and now nibbled on fries from the ferry kitchen. Hades was with her, clutching a milkshake.

"Work," I said automatically. Hades stared at me oddly, and I cast around for something else to say. "Just checking that I'm coming in tomorrow, since I traded days with Brandon to get Saturday off."

Hades exchanged a glance with his sister.

"Okay," he said. "Should we head to the car? The ferry will be docking soon."

Hades walked toward Cetus, with Byssa following. I bit my lip. Keeping secrets from my friends hurt, but not as much as their disappointment in me would if they found out about my debt to Branc and how I'd tried to handle Levi. I'd been so stupid, in so many ways, and I couldn't handle them knowing about it.

I settled Cetus at home with food and a key—he was starting to understand land, so I felt better about letting him wander around the neighborhood—then took the bus to Branc's club Abyss. It wasn't open at this hour of the afternoon, but the back door opened when I knocked.

"He's in his office," Reef said when he saw me. "He's in a mood. Good luck."

He left me to find my own way and disappeared into a storage room. I strode down the hall, not excited to meet with Branc but unwilling to put the meeting off any longer. Better to get the information I needed for tonight and get out. Maybe Cetus and I could order Japanese for dinner if we had time.

"Come in," Branc said when I knocked on his office door.

I pushed the lever handle and entered. He waved at me to sit in the chair across from his desk. His collared shirt and pressed pants were impeccable again, and the only sign that the stress of his business's issues affected him was the dark circles under his eyes.

"Have you heard the news today from your friends?" he said once I was seated.

"I don't have many friends," I said with a raised eyebrow. "And the few I have were with me at the Lodge. What should I have heard?"

"It's been spreading like wildfire." Branc grimaced. "A gruesome dry folk analogy, but fitting. It's dangerous and hard to contain."

"You can tell me any day now." At Branc's dangerous look, I said with a hint of repentance, "The sooner I know what tonight is about, the better I can prepare."

"Half-sirens have found advertisements underwater at popular swimming spots. They're etched on bone in runes, clearly Seamount-work. Those who didn't see the ads themselves have heard about them from friends."

"What do they say?"

"They tell people to come to an underwater information session to learn about the escort to the Seamount."

I sat back to digest this information.

"So, we can find out who is organizing these rumors," I said slowly. Branc's eyes didn't leave my face. I frowned. "Why are they doing this? Are enough people finding them? I still don't understand why this faction wants half-sirens back at the Seamount. It's not like they wanted us when we were there in the first place. Do you remember the ghetto?"

"Vaguely."

Branc rubbed the bridge of his nose in a rare sign of weakness. I wondered how old he'd been when he left, and what his story was. I'd never considered it before, and I wasn't sure I wanted to know. I didn't want to soften my opinion of Branc. He was better left as the villain in my life that I needed to escape.

Branc placed a palm on the desk. "We don't know enough, that's the truth of it. I want you to attend this meeting, but from a distance. I don't trust the organizers. They have an ulterior motive, and because I don't know what it is yet, you need to approach with caution. Sneak in and watch from a distance without showing yourself."

My skin prickled with foreboding. Was Branc overly paranoid or rightly cautious?

"Okay," I said. "I can do that."

"Get the identity of the organizers, if you can." Branc drummed his fingers on the desk. "Names would be good. A picture if you have a waterproof camera."

"I don't exactly have the spare cash to throw around on fancy toys," I said with a raised eyebrow.

Branc didn't even have the courtesy to look chastened.

"Fine. Get a sense of their vibrations, then. Some way

to identify them. Whatever you can get is more than we have now. I need to know who we're dealing with." Branc pulled out his phone and showed me a map. "Be at the old anchor off Kitsilano Beach at six o'clock tonight. Don't be late."

"Yes, sir." I saluted him, and he glowered at me.

"Just because I'm trusting you with this doesn't mean you can take the cheek. Don't forget who runs the show here."

"How could I ever forget?" I muttered. Louder, I said, "Six o'clock. I'll be there."

CHAPTER 14

I stepped off the bus a block from the sea with plenty of time to spare. A cool ocean breeze with a smell of rain wafted toward me from between high-rises, and I strolled down the sidewalk toward the sea. My fingers pulled the hood of my raincoat up as I crossed the road to the beach. I didn't want to draw any attention from humans or sirens. This was a clandestine mission, and I intended to keep it that way.

"Lune?"

I cursed and swung around. Byssa's friend Eris walked across the quiet street with a wave for me. I turned my grimace into a smile of greeting.

"Eris, hi."

"Are you going to the meeting?" Eris's face glowed as she fell into step beside me on the sidewalk. "It's such a great opportunity to get our questions answered. Like, what are our new homes like? When does the escort leave? Will our families be able to join us in our new homes?"

"All good questions," I murmured. We skirted a jogger weaving between pedestrians. "Glad to hear you're being critical and prodding further, not taking things at face value."

"What about you?" Eris said. We turned a corner and stepped aside to let a young family with a stroller pass. She continued, "I thought you didn't want to return to the Seamount."

"I believe in getting all my facts to make the best

decisions," I deflected. "Never say never to anything."

Except returning to the Seamount. Unless I had a death wish, the underwater city was strictly off limits.

"I think there's a hidden entry near here." Eris stopped and surveyed the beach below a cement retaining wall with stairs leading to the sand. A few hardy humans sat on driftwood logs enjoying the evening breeze, but most were heading homeward for dinner. Eris pointed to a pier jutting into the water. "There. If we enter under the pier, no human will notice us. Look, there's my friend Aster getting in right now."

A shadowy figure with brilliant red hair undressed in the darkness under the pier. I waved Eris forward.

"Go ahead. I'm waiting for someone. I'll catch you up in the water."

"Okay, if you're sure." Eris nodded at me then walked lightly toward the pier. I slunk into the shadows of a leafy cherry tree and watched until the two slipped silently into the water.

A trickle of half-sirens walked to the pier over the next ten minutes, glanced furtively around, then disappeared under the pier and into the water. It was approaching six o'clock, and I needed to make my move if I wanted to catch the meeting. With a glance around to make sure no humans were watching me, I strolled casually to the pier and sidled underneath.

It smelled strongly of seaweed, and I took a deep breath to enjoy the scent. Quickly, I stripped off my outer clothes and stashed them behind a rock above the high tide line among many other bundles. I tore off a tiny piece of Grace from a package in my skirt pocket and chewed it slowly to savor the rush of sensations. The sand was soft underfoot, and I padded easily into the water.

With Grace sliding through my veins, I dipped underwater as soon as I was waist deep. My skin tingled with sensation and pleasure at being surrounded by my element once again. I exhaled fully, then inhaled to endure the uncomfortable process of transitioning to water-breathing. I had no idea what I would encounter down below, and if I had to remain discreet, I didn't want to attract attention by swimming to the surface for air. Once I'd finished hacking and heaving, I dived along the ocean floor, following it to deeper water. Bryozoans and anemones clung to occasional rocks in the sand, and a lingcod moved lazily out of my way as I passed.

With the setting sun low in the sky, the light was dim, but I didn't need my eyes to feel my surroundings, heightened as they were by the fresh Grace coursing through my system. My body undulated through cool water, and I almost forgot my mission in my enjoyment. I wished Squirter were here to swim with me, but he was still traveling back from the Lodge. It was a long way for a little octopus.

It was probably better he wasn't here. I had no idea what I would encounter at this meeting, and I didn't want to put him in harm's way. He was good in a tight spot, but that didn't mean I wanted to endanger him unnecessarily.

Movement ahead slowed my efforts to a cautious glide. The gathering point where Branc had told me to go was close. I wondered briefly why Branc wasn't down here to catch sight of the organizer himself. He'd been very involved with all this lately—the issues with the Grace and whatever he was hiding were clearly weighing on him—so why not take matters into his own hands?

I guessed it wasn't much of a surprise. Branc liked others to do his dirty work. But still, to hand over a job of this magnitude to me… he either trusted me far too much, or he had some other reason for not coming down here.

I set aside my pondering for another time. Now was the time for stealth, and I needed all my concentration for that.

Sneaking up on a group of sirens, likely amped up on Grace with their skin sense on high alert, was no mean feat. Luckily, I was adept at subterfuge. My lessons in the Seamount's ghetto had taught me well.

My first tool was distraction. This aspect was already covered, as the half-sirens—at least twenty, by my estimation—were chattering excitedly and milling about. They had no interest in scouting out their surroundings with any great attention, which suited my purposes perfectly.

Second, deflection. If someone were watching, maybe keeping an eye out for the organizer of the meeting, I wanted to avoid detection. I waited, pressed against the rocky seafloor, until a large lingcod floated toward me. With the faintest hum, I directed it to swim closer. Then I positioned myself under its body, and together we swam with languid motions closer to the group.

Third, slow movements. I aimed the lingcod toward a rocky outcrop that jutted up from the seafloor. A tiny nook beckoned, perfect for squeezing into and spying. When we hovered over top, I ceased my hum and allowed the fish to glide away through the murk. Channeling my inner Squirter, I clung to the rocks with my stomach pressed against stone. Finger by finger, I inched into the crevasse, squeezing and slithering my body into the darkness. Nothing was waiting for me there—thank Ramu that my skin sense could scout the crack for inhabitants—and by the time I had finally inserted myself into the rock, only my head and pale hair floated above, camouflaged in a cluster of white plumose anemones.

Now that I was safely ensconced in my hiding place, I had a chance to calm my racing heart and survey the group clustered around a massive anchor and broken chain encrusted with anemones. This was a common landmark to visit when swimming in the area. Eris's figure hovered near the edge, and she gestured with energetic movements to her friend from earlier, whose long, red braid floated around her head like a dark rope, the bright color invisible this deep. A nearby older man conversed with what looked to be his wife, by the way they gestured. I recognized Dr. Mazzaella's willowy frame at the edge of the group.

Although the twenty half-sirens surrounding the anchor were of all ages, the majority were either around my age or a generation older, which coincided with the two most recent times of upheaval at the Seamount, the times when mer folk grew distracted and the barrier was weakest. Sirens like my mother tended to use the opportunity to escape and explore dry land. When the politics of the Seamount settled again and security tightened once more, chances to leave the Seamount were far slimmer. Except, of course, for the upper echelons of siren society. I'd learned that from visitors to the Lodge.

Scowling, I looked around again. It was past six o'clock, according to the pull of the moon on my body, that sense that even a year of living on land hadn't taken from me. Where were the organizers of this little shindig? I wanted to get a sense of them, report to Branc, and get back to Cetus and my apartment.

I snorted quietly. Branc had wanted me to bring an underwater camera to take a photo of the organizers. It must have been ages since he'd gone for a proper swim, because there was no way a camera would see anything through the darkness and murk. It was clearer down here, under the plankton layer, but that same layer and the setting sun made using a camera in the low light a ridiculous notion.

I shuddered at the thought of not having swum for so long that I didn't know that simple fact. Surely, there was a simpler explanation for Branc's silly suggestion. A mental slip-up, maybe.

The crowd stilled. My body stiffened, and I strained my skin sense and my eyes to feel and see what was going on.

A single person approached, and I stared in surprise. The man's tawny skin, black hair, and dark brown eyes contrasted against the varied paleness of the half-sirens before him. While he might have passed for a particularly human-looking half-siren, the speckled markings on his naked chest clearly revealed his heritage.

The man was a seal shifter, one of the three human-derived races that dominated the Seamount. Unlike mer folk, seal shifters could come to land, but unlike sirens, rarely did. For the most part, they were content to live at the Seamount and calmly farm Grace with the special abilities and techniques that their physiology was uniquely suited for.

Seal shifters, alone of pale, mer, and shifter folk, were the only race able to draw out the stinging cells of Grace anemones without harming themselves. When shifters brushed against their crops, they gathered the toxins within their own skin and rendered the anemones more palatable to the rest of us. The toxins made the shifters less interesting to larger predators at the Seamount, so everyone except the monsters was happy. Other creatures had their own protection against the Grace anemone toxins—strolia fish digested it without harm, for example—but mer folk and sirens depended on the shifter race for help. I'd stolen some unprepared Grace from a shifter field once. Although the Grace had worked fine, the taste had been awful, and I'd barely been able to eat food for two days after.

Shifters were still influential at the Seamount, even if they rarely exercised their rights. One representative from each race—pale, mer and shifter folk—came together and ruled over the others in the trio known as the Protectorate.

The man stared impassively at the collected group, his large, deep brown eyes giving away nothing of what he was thinking. He was in his human form, which was useful for speaking to sirens, but shifters tended to switch to their seal forms when they wanted speed in the water. When the man's hands rose to speak, I held my breath to listen.

Welcome, he said with a mixture of gestures and clicks. His shifter accent, with its lack of humming, was understandable but clearly distinguished him from pale folk. *I am called Selo of the shifter folk, and I'm here to answer your questions. You made the right decision to come tonight. Returning to the Seamount is the correct path forward.* He waved around the little group. *Separating ourselves from the humans is necessary. You might have some dry folk blood,* a little shiver of distaste crawled over Selo's face before he quickly banished it, *but you are a proud siren of the sea first and foremost. You must embrace that and return to the Seamount where you belong.*

He gazed at the sirens, who stared at him in silence. Eris's brow was wrinkled in a frown, and she shared a glance with her friend. Was this speech not what she had expected? I shuffled my aching foot into a new position and listened harder.

Dry folk must never find out about the Seamount, Selo continued. *We have kept our secrets for thousands of years, but it is more difficult than ever in this age of human inventions. Every half-siren that stays on land is another gap in our barrier between land and sea, and another chance for failure. And spectacular failure is inevitable when sirens live on land. It is your duty to return to the Seamount to keep our home a safe haven for our three folks.*

The crowd fidgeted and looked at each other. They had expected an information session about transportation options and new homes, not a lecture about how their lifestyle was catastrophic to the Seamount. The older woman I'd noticed with her husband pushed herself forward.

What about my daughter on land? she asked with a toss of her head. *I might want to return to my former home, especially with the new caves promised, but she doesn't know anything except land. She has no interest in coming with me to the Seamount, which she barely remembers. And why should she? Land is her home, now, even if she is half pale folk.*

Those who stay on land will face consequences, Selo said with bland menace. I shivered and hunched lower in my crevasse. Branc had been right to warn me to hide. I didn't know what Selo's game was, but he clearly had different motivations than did the hopeful half-sirens before me. The group murmured uneasily to each other, and a few started to swim away.

My skin sensed motion from behind me, and I froze, not breathing. Branc's paranoia now felt like the depth of wisdom, and I flicked my eyes to the side and focused my skin sense in that direction.

The long, sinuous body of a mer woman crawled over the seafloor like a monstrous crab with a tail. Her kelp-brown skin blended with the dark rocks below, and her hair was braided with bones woven into the strands. She clutched a bundle of something brown in her hand.

I didn't move, didn't breathe, didn't blink. My skin sense told me that mer folk ranged in a circle from my position around the group of half-sirens, now shouting questions at the implacable seal shifter. Fifty mer folk rose from their prone positions encircling the group and raised kelp nets, one between each of them.

I had no time to shout out, even if I'd wanted to give away my position. With a twist of limbs, Selo transformed into a seal and swam upward, leaving his ripped swim shorts behind to drift in the current. Cries of confusion from the remaining sirens followed him. The mer folk thrust forward with powerful kicks of their fused tail-legs.

They were on the half-sirens in a heartbeat. Nets flung over the pale folk, who were now pulsing vibrations of distress that hurt me to ignore. Their limbs tangled in the nets. With their capture, the squirming piles of sirens were too easy for the mer folk to contain and subdue, one by one.

A mer man uncoiled a rope from his shoulder and tied together the hands of every half-siren in a long row. Eris stared at her captors with anger and despair, her eye already purpling with a tremendous bruise. I bit my lip so hard it bled.

I wanted to help Eris escape—help all of them escape—but there was nothing I could possibly do. I was one half-siren against fifty mer folk and an influential seal shifter. Even if I had the powers of a full female siren on endless Grace, it wouldn't do me any good. Mer folk weren't susceptible to our powers of compulsion. Shifters were, but Selo was only one small part of this operation. If I tried anything, I would be caught and presumably taken back to the Seamount, either dying in battle here or dying from Seamount justice at my journey's end. Either way, I would be in no position to help Eris and the others.

But if I stayed quiet and brought my findings back to Branc, maybe he and I stood a chance of discovering what all this was about and stopping it. I couldn't leave Eris to complete a forced swim back to the Seamount, where her dreams of a better life would turn to silt in the current. Selo clearly had no intention of setting these expatriates up with plush surrounds. They were destined for the ghetto, I had no doubt, and they would be prevented from escaping to preserve the secrets of our underwater city from dry folk.

Do not resist. Selo had returned and shifted back into his human form. He gazed at the line of twenty half-sirens in varying states of harm with an expression of smug satisfaction. *You will be kept in a secure location until we transport you back to the Seamount once we have collected the rest of your fellows. Take comfort in the fulfillment of your duty to your fellow Seamount folks. You are doing your part to protect us all.*

Selo waved the mer folk northward, then transformed back into a seal and slid gracefully through the water at the head of the train. Sirens along the rope line undulated awkwardly, mostly tugged by mer folk at the front to keep moving in the right direction. The few sirens who refused to participate were dragged by their wrists and prodded with bone spears by accompanying mer folk until they made an effort to swim.

I waited until no trace of the group remained in my skin sense, then I buried my face in my hands. Twenty half-sirens captured and forced to return to the Seamount, including Eris and Dr. Mazzaella. That could have been me, or Byssa, or Hades. Stuck forever in a city that didn't truly want us. It would be a death sentence for

Byssa, who could barely breathe underwater.

My head snapped up, and I bared my teeth. Selo and his mer folk minions thought they'd tidily accomplished their kidnapping and were planning on more. They hadn't counted on me.

CHAPTER 15

I swam back with undulations so strong I jerked through the water like a fish on a hook. When I crawled out of the ocean minutes later, I heaved water out of my lungs as quietly as I could to avoid detection from humans nearby, but it was a task impossible to do silently. Luckily, no one was near enough to hear, or possibly no one was foolish enough to explore the dark underside of the pier where a large cat was hacking up a hairball.

I shook my hair to dry it and picked my way through the rocks to my clothes. My heart squeezed and my newly aired lungs couldn't draw in breath when I saw the clothes of the twenty half-sirens now being dragged to their fate. I slipped into my skirt and shirt, grateful for the absorbent layer that Hades had sewn in for me after we'd noticed the layer that Lodge uniforms all had in them. He'd learned how to sew from his aunt, who'd insisted that he and Byssa both learn.

The bus took a long time to come, and my hair was mostly dry by the time I dropped into a seat near the door. Branc's club was far enough that even the slow bus was faster than me walking there.

The sun had set when I exited the bus, and only the remnants of orange tinted clouds lit the western horizon between city buildings. I ducked my head into my hoodie and marched toward Abyss. A line had already formed for the club's opening hour, and Reef stood patiently at the closed door. When I pushed back my hood and stared at him, he nodded his head.

"Right this way," he said respectfully and opened the door for me.

I thanked him and strode down the hall toward Branc's office. Voices emerged from the partially open door. I knocked and pushed it open fully.

Branc was standing behind his desk with his palms on the top, leaning toward a young human woman I recognized as a server in the club. He glanced at me, and his eyes widened.

"We'll speak later," he said to the slender woman in a tone that somehow managed to be dismissive and menacing at the same time. "Out."

She didn't need to be told twice. She pushed past me and fled down the hall toward the main club room. I entered and pushed the door closed.

"You're back," Branc said. He passed a hand over his forehead, which I would have interpreted as a sign of relief for my safety had he been anyone else. Since it was Branc, he probably suffered from a headache and that was all.

"I'm back." I sat in the chair opposite Branc's desk, grateful for the rest. My adrenaline had worn off, leaving me trembling faintly and slightly queasy thinking of Eris and the others. "You'd better sit down. It's not good news."

Branc continued to stand, but his eyes bored into mine.

"You have twenty fewer customers for Grace sales," I said mockingly, knowing that Branc would likely care the most about that fact. I sighed as the importance of what I was saying aloud hit me again. "It was a set-up, just like you worried about. Once the half-sirens gathered, a seal shifter named Selo came forward. He spoke about the danger half-sirens pose to the Seamount by living on land. He captured everyone there."

Branc hung his head between his palms still resting on the desk. "That old pearl," he murmured to the tabletop. "He's not wrong, but everyone living at the Seamount isn't the answer."

I narrowed my eyes at him. "What do you mean, he's not wrong?"

Branc stared at me with his black eyes. "You really think the Seamount stands a chance at staying a secret in the modern age? The sea is vastly underexplored, but that's changing with every passing year. Satellite imagery, seafloor mapping, more and more shipping lanes—it's a wonder that it's still a secret." He stood straight and shrugged then rubbed his face in tiredness. "But going back to the Seamount isn't an option for many of us, and shouldn't be forced."

I blinked at him. Did he refer to my own situation? What did Branc know of my past? I hadn't told anyone— no one except Levi, who'd promised to keep it in confidence—but if anyone could find out hidden secrets, it was Branc.

Or did he refer to someone else? Maybe even himself?

"No, it shouldn't be forced," I agreed. "None of those captured went peacefully. Fifty mer folk surrounded them and tied them up. Selo said they would take them to a secure location until more half-sirens are captured." I sat up straighter, wanting to show my determination.

"That means we have some time before they're taken back to the Seamount."

"We have to be watchful for their next move," Branc reminded me. "How are they planning to get the rest of us? Mer folk can't come on land, so will they wait underwater and pick off half-sirens one by one as they go for a swim? That would get most of them."

"But when their friends stop coming back from their swims, people would eventually figure something wasn't right." I tapped my fingers on my thigh. "Maybe that seal shifter will come to land. There might be more shifters, you never know."

"But if they come to land, we have the advantage." Branc's jaw tightened. "This is my turf up here. I'd like to see them try grabbing my customers."

I rolled my eyes at Branc. "You're insufferable. Can you at least pretend to show a little compassion for the captured people?" I waved my hand at him. "Never mind, I know a shark can't stop growing teeth. But we need a plan."

"We?" Branc stared at me, his eyes narrowed. "There is no 'we'. You did well tonight, but I will protect my own from here. I'll call you when I need your skills."

"This isn't just about you," I snarled. "I don't want to go back to the Seamount. Just as much as you, apparently. I need to solve this. Trust me, you're the last person I want to team up with, but I need your clout, and you need my abilities. If we don't work together, we risk losing everything. Tell me what you know, what you've been hiding about all this, and we can move forward from there."

"You will be working toward freedom for half-sirens on land," Branc said. "Just under my direction. I don't need to tell you anything for you to do your part. Don't forget—"

"I never forget my debt," I shouted, rising from my chair. "How can I? It looms over me every single day, with every job I do for you, with every coin I spend, with every piece of Grace I eat. But I'm done following your orders like a good little puppet, hoping you'll reward me one day with the freedom I crave. I don't have to do anything. I could sit back and let my debt accumulate. Even better, I could take a trip inland until this all blows over, and when I return, hopefully you'll be gone."

"And so will any Grace you need to survive," he said quietly, his words tinged with threat. "If I go, so does the Grace supply."

We stared at each other. My breath heaved in my chest, but I didn't look away. I couldn't submit to Branc's tyranny, not anymore. This was my chance to stand up for myself, something I'd been subtly trying to do in the past few weeks. I was done dancing to Branc's song. If I didn't stand up to him now and fight for my right to know everything necessary to stop Selo and his plans, I wouldn't get a better chance later. This was it.

The moments crept by while we stared at each other. I wanted to blink but didn't dare break eye contact.

Finally, Branc sighed and sat back in his chair. He steepled his fingers and rested his chin on them while gazing at me. "Fine," he said. "Sit. I'll tell you what's happening."

It took a moment for my brain to catch up with

Branc's words. When I finally understood that I'd won our confrontation, I perched on the edge of my chair gingerly and waited for Branc's explanation.

"But don't think you're getting any debt forgiveness out of this now," he warned. "If you want to be more than a pawn, you don't get paid."

My lips tightened, but this was too important to quibble about. If we all survived Selo's plans to drag us screaming back to the Seamount, I would worry about my debt then.

"Agreed," I said. "Now, tell me what's going on."

"Grace supply has been harder and harder to come by in the past months." Branc picked up a pen from his desk and fiddled with it absentmindedly. "Every shipment has less in it, and they want to charge more. And that's on top of the other distributors trying to squeeze me out of the equation." He scowled, and I recalled Levi talking about "Driftwood" and his shady distribution practices. Did others feel the same way? "My sources tell me that a rogue faction at the Seamount wants to stop shipments altogether, but the Protectorate isn't convinced because selling Grace to land dwellers is lucrative for them. But the rogues are gaining in popularity, especially as they sow fear of exposure to dry folk."

"That makes sense with what I've heard," I said. "But what about the other day when your warehouse didn't greet my friend? And what did you want at the boat party, and why were you so freaked out at my apartment?"

"I was not freaked—" Branc stopped himself and took a deep breath. In a calmer voice, he said, "The man with the boat, the party you went to, he's one of the Grace deliverers. He's dry folk, has no idea what he's shipping, thinks it's some designer drug. We pay him well enough to keep his mouth shut, so it works. He shuttles excess Grace between Canada and the U.S." Branc looked grim. "Someone had convinced him to skip Vancouver that trip. I only heard about it through one of my sources, so I intercepted his boat and took the share he'd promised me, along with inventory notes from the Seamount. I'd hoped they would reveal more intel about the shortage, but no such luck."

"What about the day that my friend turned up?"

"I'd heard that the U.S. distributor was swimming up to speak with the deliverer. I'd hoped to intercept him, but he wasn't where I'd been told to expect him. Now, I wonder if Selo has been sowing rumors to destabilize our supply chain."

"It would be the sort of thing he'd do, by the sounds of it." I stared at Branc, thoughts clicking together in my mind like the shards of a broken shell. "Did you find out who was behind the strolia poisoning?"

"No," Branc said shortly.

"Because I'm certain the poisoning was meant to mimic drifting syndrome." I'd been puzzling over this all morning, and the more I thought about it, the more it made sense. "The only certain cure for drifting syndrome is to live underwater fulltime. Wouldn't it be clever if a tainted batch of Grace did some of Selo's work for him by convincing half-sirens to return to the Seamount?"

Branc stared at me with narrowed eyes. "When I find the mole," he growled, "there will be sulfurous vent fumes to pay.”

“I’ll let you focus on sniffing out the poisoner. We also need to find Selo, prevent any more half-sirens from being kidnapped, and save the ones who are already captured.” I finished ticking the points off my fingers and looked at Branc. “Any ideas?”

“I need to speak with a contact of mine, see what she knows about Selo’s whereabouts.” Branc drummed his fingers on the desk. “Maybe she has some insight.”

“And you’re not going to tell me who this contact is,” I guessed.

He raised his eyebrow. “Just because we’re working together, don’t think you can know everything. That’s not necessary information for you to know. If I find out something of wherever Selo has stashed the captured sirens, I’ll bring you in to mount a rescue mission with my people.”

“Fine.” I bit my lip, thinking. “I’ll spread the word about what happened down there, but I don’t know many half-sirens. Can you give me a list of contacts? Whoever Mark the Shark deals with, for example?”

Branc blew air out through pursed lips. “No,” he said finally. “But I will tell my dealers to spread the word. You talk to whoever you can find through your own network. I’ll call you tomorrow with what I find from my contact, and we will reevaluate our plan then.”

My mouth twisted, but I knew Branc wouldn’t budge from his protective stance. Whoever owned that list of customers would be able to replicate Branc’s Grace sales, provided they had their own supply of Grace.

“Fine.” I stood and moved toward the door. “We’ll

talk tomorrow."

I left Branc in his office, my mind already whirling with plans. I couldn't contact Vancouver's hidden siren community on my own. I needed help from people with far more friends than me.

I dialed Byssa's number on the way back to my apartment. The sky was a deep midnight blue now, and a few of the brighter stars managed to twinkle through the city lights. Byssa would just be getting off work now, thanks to her job as a line cook at the Crispy Prawn, so I wasn't surprised when she answered right away.

"Byssa," I said urgently. "I need your help."

"What's wrong?" she said at once. "What happened?"

"Long story. Can you come to my place now? It would be better in person. Pick up Hades if he's free, too."

"I'll be there as soon as I can," she promised, and hung up.

I replaced my phone in my pocket, relieved beyond measure that my friend was so willing to trust and help me that she would drop everything without question and rush to my side. I hoped she felt the same when she realized how stupid and naïve I'd been about Branc.

When I finally walked through my apartment door, Cetus jumped up.

"You're back," he said. "Finally. It's late. Are you hungry? I have food."

He pointed at the table where a few containers of sushi waited. My stomach grumbled, and I couldn't remember when I'd eaten last. Watching my people being kidnapped had driven such mundane thoughts from my head.

"That looks amazing. Thanks, Cetus. I'm sorry I left you alone for so long."

"It's okay."

I walked over to Cetus and the table and took a sniff of the rice and seaweed flavors. Cetus reached out and brushed a lock of hair back from my forehead.

"It's a little wet," he said in surprise. "Did you go swimming without me?"

"Yes, but it was for an important reason. I promise, I'll tell you about it in a minute."

"It's okay," he said again.

Cetus was being oddly agreeable—his mischievous streak was absent right now—but I couldn't concentrate with the scent of sushi wafting into my nose. I reached out to grab a pair of chopsticks, but Cetus's long fingers touched my chin and gently brought my eyes to face him. I frowned.

"Cetus, what are you…"

He leaned forward with the swiftness of a darting fish and brought his lips to mine.

CHAPTER 16

I froze, my hand awkwardly stuck in midair over my kitchen table in its attempt to reach for chopsticks. Cetus's soft lips on mine pressed firmly. What finally broke the spell was the tip of his searching tongue.

I sprang back.

"What the vents are you doing?" I stared at my friend, who looked startled. "Seriously, what was that?"

"I—" he stammered. "I thought—"

"Since when have we ever been an item?" I leaned against the table with both palms resting on it, trying to calm the whirlwind inside. "We kissed once when we were sixteen, but I thought we'd both agreed that we were better as friends." I looked up at him through my now-dry hair.

His eyes were downcast. "I thought—now that we are on land—everything is different here."

I closed my eyes and took a deep breath. It didn't calm me as much as I'd hoped.

"You feel lonely and out of place," I guessed. When I glanced at Cetus, his startled look told me I'd hit the mark. "And I'm a familiar face. I get it, I really do. But I stand by my earlier decision: we'd make a terrible pair."

Cetus sighed and sank into a chair. I sat next to him and took his hand.

"Maybe," he said to his lap. "You do always steal my food. And you are very grumpy in the morning."

I laughed, partly in relief that we might be able to get past Cetus's blundering courtship. "And you never do your chores. Trust me, that grumpiness would only get worse, especially without Pelagia here to pick up your slack."

At the mention of our mutual friend still at the Seamount, Cetus's face dropped. I rubbed his hand.

"I hope she's okay, too," I said quietly.

We sat for a minute together, both contemplating our life before this strange one we'd escaped to. Finally, the scent of sushi reminded me of my ravenous hunger.

"I don't know about you," I said to Cetus, "but I'm going to devour this takeout."

"I only bought it to impress you," he said with honesty. "Now that you don't want to pledge to me, I might as well eat it all."

I snatched a container of sushi from under his laughing face. "You'll have to fight me for it."

We ate in companiable silence for the first few minutes. My stomach demanded my full attention. When I finally slowed, my mind wandered over Cetus's actions until it hit on a potent detail. I dropped my chopsticks.

"Levi," I gasped.

"My name is Cetus," my friend replied. He picked up a sushi roll with his fingers and popped it in his mouth. "You know this."

"No, Levi. The manager of the Lodge." I stared at Cetus, my breath coming in short bursts. "That's why he was acting so weird. He thought you and I were a couple." I slapped my hand over my mouth. "How could I be so blind?"

"You like this Levi guy?" He frowned. "That's why I did not like him. So dark and human-looking. And weird eyes."

I smacked Cetus's arm. "Stop it. You and I are not getting together, so train your brain to think differently. I'll get Byssa to find you some dates. She loves matchmaking. But seriously, do you think that's what he thought?"

Cetus shrugged and picked up another roll in his fingers. "Maybe. Probably. I would have. I was very clear. Only you didn't notice."

"I need to call him." I jumped up, grabbed my phone from the counter, and raced to my bedroom. "Don't listen in, you big eavesdropper!"

"What is an eavesdropper?" Cetus said before I slammed the door and threw myself on the bed.

I dialed Levi's number, desperately hoping he would pick up, and anxious about what I would say. Was my suspicion correct, or was something else going on with him? Maybe he'd taken one look at me and realized that I wasn't the sort of woman he wanted to be with. Maybe I should have hung up. My stomach cramped. The last time we'd spoken, I'd tried to siren him and he'd freaked out. He wouldn't want to speak to me.

Before I could press the button to end the call, Levi's voice spoke through the speaker.

"Lune?"

"Levi, hi." I swallowed. "Look, I want to tell you something. No, wait, I want to apologize first. I'm so sorry I tried to siren you the other day. It was stupid and disrespectful." I waited for a beat, but when Levi didn't respond, I barreled ahead with the other reason I'd called. "I'm also worried that you might have a mistaken impression. When I came to the Lodge, I brought my friend Cetus, but only because he'd just arrived from the Seamount and I didn't know what else to do with him. We aren't dating, we're just friends." I gulped. "I'm sorry if you got the wrong impression."

The silence on the line billowed for a long moment.

"Levi?" I said tentatively, my stomach writhing like I'd swallowed a live eel. "Say something."

"I did wonder." Levi said slowly. At the sound of his voice, I collapsed onto my side and cradled the phone against my face like someone was threatening to snatch it away. "Thanks for telling me, and for the apology. I don't know if I'm ready to forgive you yet. You crossed the line."

"I realize that now." I swallowed, not sure what else to say to make things right. Could I ever fix this? "Sometimes it's hard to know when to use it and when not to."

"Is it ever okay to use?" he said sharply.

I gripped the phone. "You know what, sometimes it is. If someone threatens me, and that's the only defense I have, yeah, you'd better believe I'm going to protect myself. But on a friend? No, it shouldn't ever be okay, and I went too far. I see that now."

"I just don't know how to trust you," he said quietly.

I closed my eyes and willed the tears not to fall.

"I get that," I said once I'd mastered the tremble in my voice. "And I understand if you can't forgive me. But I could really use your help with a situation here. I'm in over my head, and I need you in your role as a Grace distributor for the region."

"What's going on?" Levi's voice was suddenly strong and sure as he channeled his work persona. My body ached for Levi's warmer side, but at least he was still talking to me.

"I went to a meeting underwater. It was advertised to the local half-siren population. About twenty of us went, but I hid to watch from a distance. A seal shifter named Selo told them they needed to return to the Seamount to protect everyone there from exposure to humans." I paused, remembering the ambush with a sick feeling. "Then about fifty mer folk surrounded the group and trussed them up. They led the half-sirens away to a holding pen, I don't know where. Once they gather up more half-sirens from land, they'll force everyone to swim back to the Seamount for good."

Levi cursed. "Selo, that rings a bell. One of the visitors told me he's part of the rogue coalition protesting the selling of Grace to land. Is that why he's kidnapping people? To get all pale folk to the Seamount and keep all Grace there? I know there have been issues growing the stuff this year, but this seems drastic."

"It's an extremist group, to be sure. Sources tell me that most at the Seamount doesn't mind a sensible amount of Grace distribution to land."

"Sources?" Levi said with suspicion. "What are your sources?"

"I get around," I said vaguely. "Others are searching for where Selo and the mer folk have stashed the captured half-sirens. My goal now is to spread the word among the community about this threat, so nobody trusts any promises of a great life back at the Seamount.

According to Cetus, the ghetto—and worse—is all that awaits them.”

“Definitely worse for you, if you’re captured,” Levi said quietly.

I gulped. So, he did remember my confession of murder that night at the Lodge. Before I could sink into memories, I blurted out, “And if they get Byssa, she won’t survive. She can hardly breathe underwater with her land lung syndrome.”

“This is too big to ignore.” Levi’s words were crisp and focused. “I’ll come help spread the word. I have a few contacts of my own in the city. We need to find these people and make sure no one else is captured. Cornering Selo would be ideal, but I won’t hold my breath for that.”

I sighed in relief. Levi and I might be in turbulent waters, but having him closer felt right in every way.

“Thanks, Levi,” I whispered.

We hung up, and I lay on my bed with my eyes closed for a long, tumultuous moment. When someone knocked on my bedroom door, I squeezed my eyes shut then stood with a groan.

“Byssa,” I said with real gladness when the door swung open and my friend waited on the other side of my bedroom threshold with an expectant look. “You made it. Sit down. I have news.”

“Spit it out,” Hades said from his lounging position on the couch next to Cetus.

“Yes, I want to hear what the urgent news is.” Byssa perched on the edge of a kitchen chair and stared at me with worry in her eyes.

Cetus continued to munch the remainder of our sushi

dinner while he looked at my disheveled hair with a raised eyebrow. I wrinkled my nose at him and sat with Byssa at the table.

"Okay, here's the news."

Briefly, I detailed the underwater meeting. Instead of saying I'd been sent by Branc, I mentioned bumping into Eris then getting nervous and hanging back at the meeting. I could sort out my lies if we got Eris back. *When*, I said to myself fiercely.

Byssa pressed her hand to her chest when she heard about Eris's capture, and tears pooled in her eyes. Hades looked grave.

"What do we do?" he said when I finished my tale. "How do we get them back?"

"That's why I called you here," I said. "We need to contact everyone we know in the city to warn them about Selo and his team of mer folk. I don't know how they'll attack next, but everyone needs to be on their guard. Will they pick us off one by one underwater? Will Selo come to land and find us? I have no idea."

Byssa sat up straight, her moist eyes shining with resolve. "We can do that. Everybody knows someone. Surely we can contact the whole community if everyone passes along a message."

"That's why I wanted you here." I spread my hands helplessly. "My only half-siren friends in the city are in this room. My reach is pretty small."

"Mine is one less, now that Eris is captured." Byssa blinked hard then shook her head. "But there's still Placida from the pool, and a few others I've met over the years."

"And I can call my usual crew," Hades added. "They'll know others, too. We've got this."

"Good." I said. "Warn them, and then ask if anyone has information about Selo. If we can find him, we can cut this issue off at the source."

"How do we help the captured sirens?" Cetus said.

I twisted my hands together. "I know someone who can help. Give me a day to work that angle."

Byssa frowned at me. "Who is it?"

"I'll fill you in tomorrow," I promised her. Hopefully, I could distract Byssa later with good news and she wouldn't follow up with her questions. "Levi said he would come and help, too. He'll arrive tomorrow, I think."

"Are you two on or off?" Hades said. "I couldn't tell if you were chummy or mortal enemies when we visited the Lodge."

"Hades," Byssa scolded, but her eyes didn't leave mine. She wanted to know the answer to Hades's question, too. "She doesn't have to tell you anything."

"Off, currently," I said with a sinking feeling in my stomach. "But he's coming to help, so there's that. Okay, go home and start calling. Give out my phone number so people can call me with information."

The others nodded, and Hades and Byssa said their goodbyes and left. Byssa gave me a swift hug on her way out, and I clung to her like a sea star for a moment of necessity. I wanted to pour everything into her ear, but I couldn't stand to see the look of disappointment on her face when I told her about my sirening of Levi, and none of this mess made sense without that fact. When the door shut behind Byssa and Hades, Cetus crossed his arms and looked at me.

"What did your human say on the phone?" he asked with a half-teasing, half-curious expression on his face.

"I'm not talking to you of all people about it." I threw my hands up and stalked to the kitchen. "I'm having a drink of water then going to bed. This day has been far too long already."

CHAPTER 17

As much as I wanted to take action against Selo and his conniving mer folk, there was nothing I could do. Byssa and Hades had already texted me to let me know that they were spreading the word. Nobody had seen Selo yet, but they were all warned.

With nothing to achieve, I dragged myself to bed. The next morning, I dressed for work. Before I left, I threw Cetus's cotton pants at him as he sleepily watched me from his bed on the couch.

"What are you doing?" he asked, holding the pants up by two fingers with distaste.

"Wear those today. I know they feel weird, but Selo won't be able to pick you out from a crowd of humans with them on. You can go back to your kilt as soon as we deal with the seal shifter. I don't want to see you cooped up in here all day, but I want you to be safe out there."

"I can walk around?" He perked up, and his eyes glanced at me in hope. "Anywhere?"

"Just be safe." I grabbed my coat from a kitchen chair. "I know land is all new, but you're smart and tough. You can handle yourself out there. Just be back before sunset so I don't have to search for you as well as the missing sirens."

Cetus nodded reluctantly, eyeing the pants with annoyance.

"I know," I said with a sigh. "It's a big city, and nobody's probably looking at you twice, but better safe than sorry. And if you get into trouble out there, don't forget you can siren the humans. You're not powerful enough to take down me or any other female siren, but against a human? You'll be able to sneak out of any sticky situation."

"Sticky?" Cetus tilted his head in question.

"Bad," I clarified. "Dangerous. Here, take my spare key. I'll see you after work." I shoved my phone and keys in my raincoat pocket then slipped it on. I pulled out a few bills from my thin wallet and dropped them on the table. "And if you want to buy me dinner again, I won't say no."

Cetus laughed at my wink. "Too much effort if we're not pledged. I saw bread in your kitchen. Bread is fine."

"You're a hagfish," I said. "See you later."

I missed the familiar weight of Squirter's backpack on my shoulders on the bus ride and walk to the aquarium. I wondered if he were back in Vancouver waters yet. I missed the little guy. I could go for a swim tonight and check for him, but what if Selo's mer folk were lying in wait for unsuspecting sirens? I couldn't uncover Selo's nefarious plans if I were captive myself.

The day was exceedingly long. Normally, I didn't mind my work—despite the discomfort of wearing a wetsuit, being immersed in water for half the day while I scrubbed was blissful—but with my mind full of the aftermath of the meeting yesterday, I could hardly keep my focus on my sponge.

I finally made it to my locker at the end of the day. My human friend Mireille waved at me as she passed on her way out, and I returned the motion with a distracted nod. Had Byssa and Hades found out anything? What about Branc?

Two messages waited for me. I unlocked my phone with trembling fingers. The first was from Levi:

I'm in Vancouver now. Staying at a friend's. I have news. Let's meet up.

My heart thundered in my chest. I wanted to see Levi so badly, but the residue of my mistake and his anger still permeated the space between us. Would it be better to see him or to avoid him?

It wasn't about me, I reminded myself firmly. Levi had information that could help us locate Eris and the other half-sirens. We needed to work together to save them, regardless of our personal issues. Too much was at stake.

I quickly changed out of my uniform and into my trusty jean skirt and ankle boots. Just as I was shoving my phone in my raincoat pocket, it rang.

"Hello?" I said to the unidentified number calling.

"Hello, is this Lune Seafields?" said an older man's voice on the line. "My name is Swift. I have news of mer folk sightings. Hades Sweetcurrent told me to call you if I knew anything."

I gripped the phone with whitened knuckles. "Yes, I'm listening. Where did you see the folk?"

"Just off Lighthouse Park in West Van. I didn't see them, but I felt them in the distance. They didn't notice me—their skin sense isn't as good as ours, of course—and I swam in the opposite direction as quickly as I could. Old habits die hard, I suppose. They were always strict at the Seamount barrier, and I ran into trouble with them from time to time when I lived there."

"That's very helpful. I'll investigate. Remember to keep your head down and avoid swimming if you can until this all clears up."

"I'll do my best," he promised. "But when the call of the sea beckons, it's hard to resist."

"I get that. Just be aware, wherever you are."

I disconnected the call then immediately dialed Branc's number. I was borderline annoyed with him for not reaching out with news earlier, since we were supposed to be working together, and I wanted to tell him about this new lead.

"Lune." Branc's voice was flat and measured.

"Branc." I turned around and leaned against my locker. I had the staff room to myself for now, so I concentrated on our conversation. "I just got confirmation of a mer folk sighting off Lighthouse Park yesterday afternoon."

Branc exhaled. "That tracks with what I've found out so far. I have leads on three locations along the Greater Vancouver coastline. That's one of them. My people are busy following up with something else tonight, so I'll get them on it tomorrow morning. I don't want to pull the others off warehouse greeter duty, since we've found out that not having a greeter can be catastrophic."

He was referring to Cetus, and I shuddered at the memory of my friend standing bewildered in Beaver Lake.

"My friends and I can scout out each location," I offered. "Send me the addresses and we'll follow up tonight."

"Don't engage," he said. "I have others for that job."

Branc hung up, and a minute later, I received a text with three sets of coordinates. With quick fingers, I texted Byssa, Hades, and Levi a time and a place to meet. We had work to do.

I arrived at the Crispy Prawn with Cetus at the end of the dinner rush. Patrons were paying for their food and getting up from tables when we squeezed past and slid into our usual booth. Hades joined us a minute later, looking uncharacteristically solemn.

"I've called everyone I know," he said in a low undertone as customers walked by our booth. "Hopefully, the word is getting out."

"It is," I said. "I got a call this afternoon with a mer folk sighting from someone you talked to, but I'll tell you more when the others get here."

A server came with water, and Hades greeted her by name and chatted with her while I twisted my fingers on the table, waiting for Levi. Cetus kicked me gently.

"Your human is here," he whispered.

I sat bolt upright and turned my head. Levi paced across the room, looking as delectable as ever. His hair shifted in dark waves across his head, and his flat blue eyes gazed at our table with intensity. His lips were tight, but he nodded at us as he sat next to Hades.

"Levi, hi," I said in a strangled voice.

"Lune." He jerked his head at me in a stiff motion,

then looked at Cetus with a relaxation of his face muscles. "Nice to see you again, Cetus. You too, Hades."

At least Cetus was forgiven. I gripped my water glass between my two hands, grateful for the cool condensation that trickled through my fingers. I wished I could press it to my pink cheeks to cool their ridiculous hue.

Byssa appeared and bumped my hip with hers until I shuffled closer to Cetus to make room for her.

"I can't stay for long," she said. "I'm on my break. Luckily, it's a quiet night. So, what's the news?"

"Did you have something, Levi?" I jerked my chin at Levi, wanting to give him the floor first.

"A friend of mine was contacted by the seal shifter Selo," Levi said. "He was promised the same stuff that your people heard: new homes, exalted status, and all that. Selo wasn't alone, though. He was accompanied by two other seal shifters. I don't know how many others there might be."

Hades and I glanced at each other with furrowed brows. Byssa leaned forward. "Was Selo threatening at all, or was he still using incentives to draw people back?"

"No threats yet. My friend agreed to think about it. One of the shifters was going to come back tonight to talk more."

"I have a lead on three locations," I said. "All I want tonight is for us to check out each one. Carefully, of course, because we don't want to confront anyone or let them know that we're onto them. I thought we could split up and tackle each location separately."

I showed them the map with coordinates that Branc

had sent me. They all leaned into the center of the table and peered at my phone.

"Who's the blobfish?" Byssa asked, pointing to the label I'd given Branc's phone number.

"It doesn't matter," I said quickly. "Who's going where?"

"I can check out Lighthouse Park," Byssa said. "My friend Phyta lives in West Van, right near there. I'll pop in and see how she's doing."

"Be extra careful there," I warned. "Someone called me with a mer folk sighting near Lighthouse Park."

"I'll check Swishwash Island near the airport," said Hades. "Then you and Cetus can look at the address on the other side of the Lion's Gate Bridge, since it's close to the bus exchange."

"I'll visit my friend again," Levi said. "See if I can get any more information out of his seal shifter visitors. If they turn up, I'll follow them and see where they go, so we can hunt down Selo tomorrow."

"Good." I pulled my phone back and shoved it into my pocket. "That's settled, then."

A familiar lanky figure with floppy brown hair approached our table.

"Sorry to interrupt," he said. "Byssa—"

"Is my break over already?" She jumped up. "Sorry, Jules. I must have lost track of time."

"No, it's not that." He clutched his phone in one hand with a tight grip. "It's my friend Zeb. I have him on the line. He's really not well. Could you talk to him, tell him what you told me about that stuff that could help him?"

<h1 style="text-align:center">CHAPTER 18</h1>

I glanced at Byssa, who didn't seem confused by Jules's words. Instead, she wore an expression of horror and pity.

"Of course. Here, let's take the call outside."

She dashed to the back entrance of the restaurant. Since we were done our meeting—and I didn't think forcing small talk on Levi would be good for either of us—I followed Byssa and Jules out the door.

Jules held the phone up so we could see the screen. I felt the others file out behind us, but my focus was on the man on the phone. He was clearly part-siren—his white hair and pale eyes gave away his heritage— although his skin was a dusky olive. But Jules was right, he looked far from well. Black circles hung under his eyes like he hadn't slept in weeks, and his shoulders trembled. He clutched a small tub of something in his hands.

"Hi," he said in a low voice. "Thanks for talking to me. I'm Zeballos Artino, Zeb for short. Jules said you might know what's wrong with me?"

Byssa was silent for a moment, clearly overwhelmed by the sight of Zeb's deterioration.

"I'm Byssa," she finally choked out. "Why don't you have any Grace?"

Zeb's brown contracted. "I'm usually more graceful than this," he said carefully, waving at his body. "But I'm not feeling great lately."

"He doesn't know what Grace is," I hissed to Byssa. I shivered at the idea of never tasting Grace and my body

162

wasting away like Zeb's clearly was. "Is this what land sickness looks like?"

"Zeb," Byssa said with an attempt at strengthening her voice. "Do you know what you are?"

Zeb stared at her through the screen, his eyes intense. "I've found some clues, but I've never met anyone else like me, not since my mother died when I was a child. Please, if you know anything that could help me, I'm begging you…"

Jules rubbed his face with the hand that wasn't holding his phone. Byssa clutched her chest as if it pained her.

"This is too big to talk about over the phone," she said firmly. "But give Jules an address, and I will courier you something that will make you feel better. Eat it, okay? And as soon as you're feeling better, come to Vancouver and we'll talk properly."

Zeb closed his eyes and took a shuddering breath.

"Just eat whatever it is?" he said with a ghost of a smile. "Sounds simple enough. Thank you, Byssa."

Jules hung up the phone and turned to Byssa, blinking rapidly. "Thank you," he said in a hoarse voice. "I can send whatever it is, if that's easier."

Byssa laid a comforting hand on Jules's arm, and Jules swallowed hard.

"I have some Grace right here," Hades offered. He pulled a package out of his pocket, and I made a face.

"It's not that terrible stuff you got from Mark the Shark, is it? We don't want to poison the poor guy."

Jules blanched, and Byssa smacked my arm. "Don't scare Jules."

"Mark delivered some extra Grace to me, free of charge, after I complained about the bad batch." Hades passed the package to Jules. "Surprising, really. I didn't expect that slimeball to treat me fairly."

"I hope he gave you extra," I said with indignation. "It made you sick, after all. I'll have to talk—"

I shut my mouth, unwilling to mention my connection to Branc. Levi looked at me with narrowed eyes but didn't comment.

"I'll send it right away," Jules promised. "Thank you so much. And it's such a quiet night, I can cover for you if you want to leave early, Byssa."

"What? No, you don't have to do that."

Jules stepped backward through the open door. "It's literally the very least I can do."

He disappeared into the restaurant. Byssa stretched her arms over her head and let out a deep sigh.

"I guess I'm off for the night. Poor Zeb. He looked terrible."

"A shot of Grace will do wonders for him." Hades slung an arm around her shoulder. "He'll be fine, don't worry."

"I wonder how much he'll need," I said. "He looked pretty bad. If he's literally never had Grace before…"

"He will need money," Cetus said, looking pleased with himself at connecting the dots. "Those papers you give stores. Grace costs money, right?"

"Grace isn't cheap." Byssa worried her bottom lip. "I can give him a bit, but I can't support him forever. Jules told me Zeb hasn't been able to work lately because of his land sickness."

"Buying Grace for two eats into your savings." I poked Cetus's arm. "Ask me how I know."

Cetus scowled, but Levi looked thoughtful. "I wonder if he could work at the Lodge. He's part-siren, clearly, and we often have positions available. I pay partly in Grace if the employee wants it. Let's face it, most do."

"That's such a generous offer." Byssa turned a brilliant smile on Levi. "I'll pass it along to Jules."

"How convenient, another reason to seek Jules out," I teased. When Byssa narrowed her eyes at me, I chuckled. "Come on, everyone, let's scout out our locations for the bad guys."

Byssa, Cetus, and I said goodbye to the others at the next intersection. Levi carefully avoided my eyes, and my heart shriveled in my chest. Would the wound I'd inflicted ever heal?

Byssa drove us to West Vancouver, since our location was on her way. Cetus stared open-mouthed as we crossed the huge suspension bridge leading to West Van, and I fought a smile at his interest. Once Byssa dropped us off near our location and drove away, I glanced around the quiet neighborhood road.

"Where do we look?" Cetus asked.

I checked my map again. The coordinates indicated that a small house—more of a shack, really—was ground zero for Branc's suspicions of seal shifter headquarters. It was an anomaly along this well-maintained road lined with expensive waterfront houses. Most of the neighboring dwellings sported manicured lawns and elaborate windows in the double doors of their grand entryways.

This house was destined for the wrecking ball if I could predict anything. Its beige paint was peeling from its clapboard sides, moss grew with abundance on the cheaply shingled roof, and weeds choked out any grass in the tiny front yard.

"That house." I pointed the shack out to Cetus, who stared at it with a dubious expression. "We need to be sneaky, though. Channel your ghetto-self."

Cetus nodded, and as one, we flitted to a large bush at the corner of the neighbor's lawn. We wriggled inside and watched the shack through a veil of leaves for five long minutes. Nothing stirred.

Closer, I signed to Cetus. He nodded and followed me out of the bush once I'd scanned the street for cars and pedestrians. With light feet, I flew across the weedy lawn and pressed myself against the peeling wall of the shack. A second later, Cetus joined me, his eyes bright with excitement. He'd always enjoyed our missions. Too much so, usually. I'd been the one to rein him back when things got dicey.

You look in the front window, I hummed and gestured. *I'll take the side. If it's clear, keep moving around the house.*

Cetus nodded and slunk to the front. I shifted my feet silently on the dry plants underfoot and gingerly raised my head until my eyes peered over the window ledge.

No curtains obstructed my view of the room, empty except for an old wooden chair on its side, missing a leg.

Water stains crept over the ceiling from a leaky roof, and the carpet held furry patches of what looked like mold. I grimaced and moved smoothly to the next window.

This one was for a bathroom, with black grout between cracked tiles and an empty toilet paper roll lying on the grimy counter. I rounded the corner to see Cetus sitting on the sagging back porch steps.

"Nobody," he said. "All clear."

"Not necessarily," I hissed. I glanced at the ocean past a short cement wall that stopped the waves from eating away at the properties here. "Someone could be watching us."

"I forgot. You get, what's the word?" Cetus made a show of thinking. "Yes, paranoid. It's clear."

"We haven't checked the water yet," I said, annoyed at Cetus. He wasn't taking this seriously, as usual. For all we knew, our adversaries could be crouched behind a log on the beach.

But he was probably right. I hopped down the cement wall after a quick glance around. Swift had seen the mer folk where Byssa was visiting tonight. That was the likely location to search. Once Byssa confirmed our suspicions, Branc could send in his people in the morning to take back the captured sirens. At least I didn't have to worry about Byssa giving herself away like Cetus. She was more cautious than I was.

Cetus stripped off his shirt and kicked off his shoes. "Finally," he said with a grin. "A swim. Do you have Grace?"

"No, I need to get more," I said with regret. I wasn't due to meet Mark the Shark until next week. I wondered if I could negotiate some from Branc the next time we talked. Feeding two of us was too much on my sparse supplies. Now that Cetus could speak English well enough, it was time to get him a job. I'd never pay off my debt if I had to support him, too.

"Oh well," he said and turned. "Next time."

"For vent's sake, watch out," I called, but he picked his way over the rocks and splashed in without heeding my words. Scowling, I tore off my own clothes and followed my reckless friend into the lapping waves.

The shore dipped quickly into deep water in a cliff of jagged rock. Hardy creatures like mussels and barnacles clung to the top of the cliff, but anemones and bryozoans grew more numerous the deeper we swam.

I held my breath, unwilling to endure the transition between air and water for our short swim. Cetus had no such compunctions, and after a moment of midwater contortions, he took a deep breath of water with a look of contentment. He'd only been on land for a week after living his whole life breathing water. I remembered my early days among the dry folk, and how blissful returning to the ocean had been.

I closed my eyes and reached out with my skin sense for any indication that we weren't alone. Aside from a school of pile perch and the waving arm of a giant Pacific octopus from a crevasse in the rocky wall, the water column was empty.

The octopus reminded me of Squirter. We weren't far from where I often dipped in, so I sent out a hum of calling for my little friend. I hoped he was back from his long swim to the Sunshine Coast.

Cetus heard my call and joined in, his sounds louder and more distinct since he could open his mouth to amplify them.

We scouted up and down the cliff for a while longer, but it was clear that nobody was stashed in the cracks, and no mer folk floated by. I'd almost given up on Squirter—maybe he was taking a leisurely trip down the coast—when Cetus stiffened.

There he is, he said. *Incoming.*

My closed-mouth smile widened when Squirter appeared in my skin sense. He jetted in a circle around the two of us then squirted a tiny bit of ink in Cetus's face.

Cetus waved a hand in front of his eyes, and I nearly laughed out loud.

He wants you to chase him, I explained. *Play tag.*

Cetus darted toward Squirter without warning, and the little octopus jetted away with a click of delight. I watched the two play for a minute, my smile firmly on my face, until my lungs reminded me to surface for a breath. I undulated toward the sunlight and took a huge gulp of air.

A hand wrapped around my ankle and yanked me down.

CHAPTER 19

I barely had time to hold my breath before my head descended below the waves. Panic flooded my body with adrenaline, and I kicked my leg with furious intention. At the same time, a hum of disorientation exploded from my chest.

The hand let go, and I whirled around to face my attacker. Just before my eyes focused, my skin sense told me the truth. I sagged in the water then darted forward and pushed Cetus's chest in my anger.

For vent's sake, I gestured, my hand movements sharp and jerky. *I thought you were mer folk. You scared the Grace out of me.*

Cetus grinned, unapologetic, but Squirter landed on my shoulder and stroked my cheek with the tip of his arm.

At least someone loves me, I grumbled. *Come on, let's go home.*

Me too, Squirter hummed.

I bit my lip, thinking of how to transport my tiny friend back to my apartment without him drying out. He would last for quite a few minutes without breathing water, but the bus ride would be longer than his limit, and I didn't want to get stranded somewhere without water for him.

The shack sprang to mind, and I gently detached Squirter from my shoulder.

Come to the shore in two minutes, I told Cetus. *I'll go ahead and find something for Squirter.*

Cetus reached out to tickle Squirter's arm, and I swam to the top of the cliff. At the surface, I popped my head above water and quickly scanned the shore for onlookers. Someone sat on their deck a few houses down, but they faced the opposite direction. Besides, it wasn't preposterous to go swimming in these waters for a human, just highly unusual.

I tiptoed across rocks and climbed up the cement wall. At the shack's back porch, I carefully stepped up the creaking stairs and reached for a bucket that lay on its side against the wall. I held my breath and checked it for holes. Miraculously, it was intact, and I raced back to the water as fast as my tender soles would allow me.

Cetus popped his head up when he saw the bottom half of my legs in the water.

"He's coming," Cetus said. He eyed my bucket. "That thing?"

"It will work great," I said. "Why, do you have a better idea?"

Cetus shrugged and crawled out of the sea toward his clothes. Squirter's soft suckers clung to my foot and crawled swiftly up my leg. I chuckled at the ticklish sensation.

"Hold on, buddy," I murmured. I laid the bucket on its side in the gentle waves. Squirter, clever cephalopod that he was, immediately climbed in. I heaved the now-full bucket in my arms and staggered toward my discarded clothes.

With the bucket set carefully on the unstable rocks, I quickly dressed, thankful for the absorbent layer in my clothes. I was doubly grateful when I saw the wet marks seeping into Cetus's pants. I tightened my lips to stop myself laughing at the clear mark of his wet underwear. We'd have to get Hades to sort out Cetus's wardrobe, and soon.

I didn't put my coat on. Instead, I draped it over the bucket. Cetus hauled it in his arms.

"Careful, you'll slosh poor Squirter out," I said, adjusting my coat to cover the bucket better.

"Do you want to carry it?" he huffed.

"Know your place, boy," I said with a ruffle of his hair. "Come on, let's get him home and in the tub."

We waited a few minutes for the bus. When it arrived, the bus driver stared at the strange bundle in Cetus's arms.

"Fare for two," I said brightly, stepping sideways to block the driver's view of my friend. "Here it is. Thanks very much. Have a great evening."

The driver nodded, distracted by my babble, and I ushered Cetus onto the bus.

Once we were seated, Squirter's bucket balanced on Cetus's lap, I texted the others with our lack of discovery. Levi answered with a simple *no luck here*, which made my chest do odd, wriggly things. Hades texted back with his own lack of findings.

Byssa didn't reply, but I assumed she was busy visiting her friend. I would touch base in the morning before work. Byssa always came through.

The next morning, I awoke to a text from Hades.

Has Byssa called you yet? Text me if she has. I'm at work early today.

I frowned and checked my messages while still in bed, but Hades's was the only one I'd received. Quickly, I dialed Byssa's number.

It went straight to voicemail. Was she on a call, or had she turned off her phone?

Call me as soon as you get this, I texted her, then waited a minute before calling again. There was no answer.

She's not answering her phone, I texted Hades. *I'll check up on her.*

A sick feeling was growing in my stomach. It wasn't like Byssa to ignore her friends or not check in with us when we were depending on her to tell us about the location. Had she been seen? Was she in danger? Or had she simply had a good time with her friend and was now sleeping off a hangover?

I couldn't leave this mystery unsolved, not if there were a chance that Byssa wasn't all right. I dialed the number for the aquarium and left a message for my boss saying I was sick, accompanied by a requisite number of coughs. Now that I had the day to myself, I called Levi.

"Hello?" he answered warily.

"Sorry to bother you this early, but we might have a problem. Byssa won't answer her phone, and I haven't heard from her since last night at the restaurant. I'm worried something happened to her at the location she was supposed to scout."

"We'll go there right away," he said without hesitation. My heart melted a little more with his swift agreement to hunt for my friend. "Text me your address and I'll pick you up as soon as I can."

We said our brief goodbyes, then I sent him the address of my apartment. Too many people were visiting this crummy place, and I didn't like others seeing its threadbare carpeting, smelling the musty scent in the hall, and hearing my neighbors through its seaweed-thin walls. But it was the only home I had, and I would just have to grit my teeth and ignore any pitying looks.

Still, I dressed quickly and spent the rest of the wait alternating between nagging at Cetus to get ready, shoving leftover pizza into my mouth, and peering through the window at the street for signs of Levi's truck.

"He's here," I shouted to Cetus when Levi's pickup truck with the Lodge logo on the side pulled in front of my apartment building in the loading zone. "Come on, let's go. I don't want him coming up."

"Why not?" Cetus asked as he followed me out the door. "Too soon to invite him into your cave?"

"No, it's just that it's a dump."

"So was the ghetto, and you were fine there."

I could feel Cetus's confused stare at the back of my head, but I didn't turn around as we clattered down the steps.

"Yeah, I know. I don't know. I just don't want him to come in."

I slammed open the door, unable to explain to Cetus how I didn't want to tarnish Levi's already terrible opinion of me by adding a layer of pity or derision to it. I raced down the sidewalk and flung open the passenger door.

"Thanks for coming," I said breathlessly.

Levi's eyes drifted to my chest, then they flicked up again. His cheeks flushed.

"I like your tee shirt today," he said to the windshield.

I glanced down at today's offering, which showcased a seal's head poking out of the water with the words "that's the sealiest thing I've heard". My mouth twitched at his reaction.

"Thanks." I wanted to say I liked his too, but its only notable feature was how its blue fabric stretched over his biceps, and I couldn't mention that. I pushed back the seat and gestured to Cetus to climb into the tiny space behind. "Go on, you're back there."

Cetus grumbled as he squeezed into the seat with his long legs. I ignored his mutterings and dissatisfied hums and slammed the seat upright before climbing into the truck myself.

"Okay," I said. "Let's find Byssa."

We drove in awkward silence. Everything I thought of to say aloud didn't pass my internal checkpoint, and it was difficult to come up with innocuous comments that didn't reference our shared past, my heritage as a siren, or the Lodge and the time we'd spent there. Cetus in the backseat was another deterrent to casual conversation, so I kept my mouth shut and stared out the window at shops and houses as we passed.

After we turned off a main street, the quieter road ended in a cul-de-sac at a beachside park. No houses lined the waterfront here. Instead, scrubby bushes and waving grasses led to a sandy incline and a high-tide line that was bordered by large driftwood logs. An old boathouse jutted into the water on rotten pilings halfway along the beach to our right. The water was choppier today, with whitecaps cresting in the strait before us and a brisk wind hitting the truck's windshield.

Levi checked his phone. "This is it," he said. "This beach is where the coordinates tell us to go." He looked sideways at me. "Where did you get them, anyway?"

"A trusted source," I said vaguely. "Come on, let's scout around. I don't see Byssa's car, but that doesn't mean she's not here. That old boathouse could be worth checking out."

Cetus was already stripping off his shirt. "I'll look in the water," he said. "See you soon."

"Wait," I said, exasperated, but Cetus had already crawled out from behind my seat and squeezed over my lap to release himself from my door. "Cetus, don't go alone."

"It's fine," he called out from over his shoulder. He ran toward the water and flung himself stomach first once he was thigh-high in the waves. His ash blond hair disappeared underwater, and I heaved a sigh.

"He'd better stay out of sight," I grumbled. "He can be so thoughtless."

"We'd better check out the boathouse," Levi said after a shake of his head at Cetus's antics. "Unless you want to follow Cetus."

A note of longing threaded through his words, and I studied Levi's face as he stared out the windshield at the sea. I still didn't know why Levi wouldn't swim, but we were so far from revealing secrets like that to each other. Even when we were friendly, he had warned me away from asking. He certainly wouldn't divulge today.

"No, Cetus can take care of himself," I said. "If Byssa is being held against her will, it won't be in the ocean. She can't breathe underwater well enough for that."

My fingers twisted, and fear for Byssa ran down my spine. What if they had forced her underwater anyway, and she was gasping for oxygen somewhere below? Why hadn't I check up on my friend last night? I should have known that Byssa wouldn't have left us hanging. She was too responsible for that.

Levi's large hand rested on top of my writhing fingers, and I froze in surprise.

"We'll get her back," he said, his tone the gentlest I'd heard since my sirening at the Lodge last week. "She'll be fine."

I threw him a swift, grateful smile. While I knew he only spoke to comfort me, and we had no guarantee that Byssa was safe, I appreciated him trying to calm me. Maybe he wasn't unreachable.

"Yeah, she will be." I took a deep breath. "Okay, let's check out this boathouse."

I pulled a hat over my too-blond hair, and we walked without speaking toward the boathouse. Levi moved closer to me and slipped a hand in mine. His fingers were warm and fit so well in my own.

"Pretend we're a couple out for a stroll," he whispered to me. "In case someone in the boathouse is looking. This is a public beach, after all. No reason for us not to be here. Assuming they didn't see Cetus jump in the water."

"Okay," I whispered back, my word half-strangled by

my surprise. I gripped his hand with a carefully curated nonchalance, not too loose like I wanted to pull away, but not too tight to seem desperate for his touch. I hoped I was fooling Levi, because I certainly wasn't fooling myself. The sensation of his warm hand surrounding my own was doing odd things inside my gut. I tried to ignore it by focusing my thoughts on Byssa. The notion of her struggling to breathe dampened my ardor considerably.

"Did you hear that?" Levi said with a fake smile plastered to his face. His hand squeezed mine tighter, and he drew me closer to the boathouse as we approached. "I heard voices."

I strained my ears, and they caught a murmur of a female voice.

"Someone's in there," I breathed. My heart quickened past its already heightened state. "Let's get closer."

With quiet footsteps on the damp sand, Levi pulled us toward the entrance of the boathouse that was positioned at the high-tide line. It was a flimsy wooden door, riddled with cracks where the wood had warped and shrunk over years of weathering. Through a gap, light appeared.

"It's open on the other side," Levi whispered.

"Perfect for sirens and shifters working with mer folk," I said. "Listen."

The voices started up again, and I froze to hear. I couldn't understand the female's words, but when a man spoke, Levi's hand tightened in mine.

"How long—" the male voice said with a petulant tone. The rest of his words were drowned out by a crashing wave on the beach.

Levi pressed his mouth to my ear. The tickle of his lips accidentally grazing my earlobe sent a shiver of desire racing across my shoulders.

"That's my brother Austin."

I looked at Levi. His jaw was tight and his eyes hard, but a flicker of pain and worry darted behind his anger. The last we'd seen of Austin, he'd wanted to make amends to Levi, but a siren had compelled him to follow her. Levi hadn't heard from him since. And now he was at the scene of a potential kidnapping scheme? I didn't know what to think.

"It sounds like there's only two of them," I whispered back. If I were being smart, I would back off and call Branc. He would send his people with fighting ability— the muscly bouncer Reef came to my mind—and they would make short work of this, whatever it was.

But Byssa might be in there, and I couldn't stand leaving her a moment longer. By the look of Levi's face, he was just as ready as I was to mount a rescue mission. He glanced around, then let go of my hand to step toward a pile of driftwood. I barely had time to mourn the loss of his warmth when he returned and shoved a stout piece of driftwood in my hand.

"It's the only weapon I could find at short notice," he whispered, brandishing his own log. "Ready?"

I held up the stick in both hands, not sure how I would use it, but happy to have something.

"Ready," I said, and Levi flung the flimsy door open.

CHAPTER 20

We rushed inside the old boathouse, and I instantly processed the scene before me. Austin leaned against a wall, chinks of light surrounding his lean body and dark hair from the warped wood. A pale woman stood with arms crossed in the center of the empty room. And Byssa, my sweet friend, lay trussed up like a fish in a net. Bruises covered her bare arms, and blood trickled down her forehead. Her eyes widened when she saw me.

"Lune," she gasped.

I didn't acknowledge her because I didn't have time. As soon as we burst through the door, the pale woman flung herself toward us with her teeth bared.

"Fight them," she yelled to Austin, who stared at his brother with his jaw hanging. "Now!"

Austin pushed away from the wall and walked with slow steps in our direction. I didn't see what he did next because the siren was on us. Levi swung at her, but she ducked both his driftwood and my next blow with terrifying speed. She launched herself at Levi, and they grappled.

Austin shouted, and I turned to him with my driftwood raised. I saw his surprised face before he fell to the ground. Byssa looked pleased with herself for tripping him with her bound feet. I didn't waste her efforts, and quickly hit him in the side with my stick. When he curled around the blow, I pressed my hand to his shoulder and hummed a swift tone of compulsion.

His limbs drooped, slack, and I turned to Levi's battle.

Levi must have realized the siren's goal—if she had a chance to compel him, the battle was as good as over—because he wriggled and writhed in her grasp with ceaseless movements. His hands pushed at her face to distract her from humming, and he dropped to the ground and rolled to get away long enough to land a blow with his driftwood. The siren was no snail, though, and when she next leaped at him, his arms were trapped by hers for a moment. They teetered on the edge of the open side of the boathouse, silhouetted against the gray sea beyond.

A moment was all she needed. With a hum loud enough to feel from my vantage, she incapacitated Levi. His limbs slackened like his brother's had done, and his fiery eyes grew lifeless.

With a snarl, I raced toward her and threw myself onto the pale woman's back. I screamed a hum of defiance and distraction.

While I was no match for a full-blooded female siren, it took significant composure and concentration to resist the pulse of a sound like mine. The siren jolted, and that was all I needed to pull her hair back with a jerk. Her head followed my yank, and we tumbled to the floor.

Levi woke from his trance, but my motions had unbalanced him. With his mouth open in surprise and horror, he toppled backward and splashed into the water.

"Levi!" Austin shouted, his voice hoarse. He ran to the opening's edge and leaned out.

I wrapped my arm around the siren's neck and squeezed tightly. Not only would she be unable to compel me, but breathing would be impossible. She would last for ten minutes without air, but while she clawed ineffectually at my arm, I whipped my head around to Austin, still staring at the water.

"Are you on our side or theirs?" I demanded. "Tie her legs for me."

Austin didn't respond. His eyes were fixated on the water where his brother had disappeared. Dimly, I realized that Levi hadn't surfaced. Where was he? Fear clutched me tighter than the siren's fingers on my arm. Could he truly not swim?

"Help me out," I begged Austin. "Then I can go search for Levi in the water."

Austin shook his head, hardly seeming to hear my words. Then he looked at the struggling siren in my tiring arms.

"Forget ropes," he snarled. "This will work better."

He swiped Levi's log from the floor. With a swift blow, he hit the siren's temple with one end. The woman wilted in my arms, stunned.

"You earned that," he yelled at the unconscious woman in my grasp. "Manipulative hagfish. You and the rest can sink to the abyss, for all I care."

"Help me—" I started, but Austin turned.

"I have to go," he said. "I can't let them take me again. Tell Levi I'm sorry."

He grabbed a small backpack at the edge of the room and dashed out the door.

I stared after him in disbelief. Did he not care about his brother at all? Levi was drowning, and Austin had only grabbed his things and ran away.

I shook my head at Austin's traitorous tendencies and

crawled with swift movements to Byssa's side.

"I'm so glad to see you," she gasped as I untied her arms. "But go get Levi. I'll tie the siren up with my own ropes."

I didn't need a second invitation. I stripped off my clothes, kicked off my boots, and jumped into the cresting waves below the boathouse.

The water was murky from turbulent wave action, but my skin sense didn't fail me. I darted back and forth over the sandy bottom, intensely searching for a sign of Levi's body. Why couldn't he at least flail to the surface? Had I waited too long to search for him? The waves wouldn't have carried him out to sea yet, surely. But where was he?

With every minute that passed, hopelessness crept over me like a choking oil slick. Humans could only hold their breath for a couple of minutes, couldn't they? It had been far longer than that by now. Was I too late?

My body heaved with the sobs I couldn't release with my held breath. I swam up and surfaced, gulping air and trying to hold myself together.

"Lune!"

Byssa's voice startled me. I turned to the beach, where she was waving frantically to get my attention. Beside her was a tall figure with dripping wet dark hair.

I blinked, my heart filling with wild hope. When I was certain that Levi stood beside Byssa, I cut through the waves with swift strokes of my arms and legs. When sand grazed my fingers, I pushed to my feet and ploughed through the knee-high water toward the other two.

Heedless of my soaking-wet body, I threw myself against Levi and wrapped my arms around his neck. I buried my face in his chest and tried to hold back my sobs of relief. Tentatively, his arms wrapped around me.

"I thought you were dead," I gasped into his shirt. I took a deep, shuddering breath and pushed back, embarrassment finally wriggling past my relief. Levi's arms slowly released me. Was there reluctance when he let me go?

"I swam to shore," he said, his eyes searching my face.

"Your clothes aren't wet." I sniffed and looked at his red and white striped shirt. Except where I'd pressed against him, and the wet fabric clung to his chest in an enticing way, his garments were entirely dry. They were also different from what he'd been wearing before.

"I had spare clothes in the truck," Levi said quickly. "It was cold."

"Right." I surveyed him a moment longer, then belatedly threw my arms around Byssa. She squeezed me back tightly.

"I'm glad you're okay," I said when I released her. "I was so worried."

"Apparently this location is the right one," Byssa said with a ghost of a smile. "They wanted to hold me at the old tugboat shipwreck off Lighthouse Park with the other captives, but I told them I couldn't breathe underwater, so they brought me to the boathouse."

I grimaced at the reminder of Byssa's ordeal. "I need to phone someone to deal with the siren."

"I have your clothes and phone here."

Byssa pointed at the sand, where my things sat in a pile on a driftwood log. I dived for my phone, walked out of hearing of the other two, and dialed Branc's number.

"Come to the old boat house east of Lighthouse Park," I said when he answered. "There's a siren here, tied up. She kidnapped my friend Byssa, but we dealt with her. You need to get her before her friends do."

"I'll be there in fifteen minutes," he said.

"Who was that?" Levi asked when I rejoined them. I dithered on my answer.

"Someone who will help us deal with the siren we tied up," I said. "Don't worry about it. Have you seen your brother? Is he going to be a problem?"

"I don't think so." Levi stared at the waves for a moment. "He didn't want to be with that siren in there, and he hardly put up a fight. Now he's escaped, and I can't imagine he'd waste this opportunity to leave whatever he's tangled up in." Levi kicked some sand down the beach. "I hope he reaches out to me."

For Levi's sake, I hoped so, too. Austin might be a tool who had endangered lives at the Lodge a few weeks ago, but he'd clearly regretted almost harming his brother. With the right encouragement, he could probably be made to see how awful his actions had been.

"Look, I'll deal with the siren," I said suddenly. "Levi, could you please take Byssa home? Cetus and I can find our own way from here."

"Where is Cetus?" Byssa stared at me with wide eyes. My stomach dropped, but Levi pointed out to sea.

"Is that him?

Cetus's head bobbed in the waves as he made his way to the beach. I wilted in relief then picked up a piece of kelp and threw it at Cetus.

"Where have you been?" I shouted over the noise of breaking waves. "You took too long. I thought you'd been captured by mer folk or something."

"You got Byssa!" Cetus beamed at my friend and dripped over to us. "Good. It was a very good swim today."

I swatted his arm. "You're a menace. Did you find out anything?"

"I felt a mer folk." He rubbed his head so that water flung off his short blond hair. "He didn't see me. But I think I know where they have the captured people."

"Okay, good." I climbed into my clothes then looked at Levi with a pointed nod at Byssa, who was swaying on her feet. "Could you take her home, please?"

"Just drop me off at my car," she said. "It's down the road. Come on, Cetus. Let's leave Lune to her secrets."

She narrowed her eyes at me, and I looked away. Hiding from my friends wasn't working anymore, but I didn't even know where to begin unraveling my omissions. Levi opened his mouth, then closed it. He followed Byssa and Cetus back to the truck, and I watched them go with fingers twisting together.

Ten long minutes later, Branc's black sedan purred to a stop in the cul-de-sac. I stomped over to meet him as he approached the boathouse, strangely alone.

"Where are your goons?" I asked when he was near enough to hear. "I thought you'd want to take down this operation."

"That will take careful planning," he said. "You needed a problem dealt with immediately, so here I am."

"Well, good." I wanted to vent at him, but even in my

heightened state of frustration, I knew that antagonizing Branc was never a good idea. "She's in the boathouse."

Branc followed me across the rotten planking and in through the boathouse's open door. The pale woman lay where I'd left her, but her eyes weren't glazed from their blow. Instead, she glared at us and hissed.

"Watch it." I held my arm out to stop Branc. "She can compel us now that she's feeling better."

"Not me," he said. I frowned at him, curious about how he could resist compulsion. Was it an innate ability, something he ate, or what? "I'll grab her."

Branc strode to the woman's side. Despite the hum that emitted from her body so loudly that I could feel the remnants of it through my feet, Branc lifted her over his shoulders in a fireman's carry. He staggered before finding his feet.

"Let's go," he said, his hair mussed from its usual perfection.

I held the door open and followed Branc along the beach to his car. He was panting by the time we reached it.

"Keys are in my left pocket," he forced out. "Open the trunk."

I reached gingerly into the pocket of Branc's pants. This was far too intimate for me, and I snatched his keys as soon as metal bit into my fingers. With a press of a button, the trunk smoothly rose. Branc heaved the woman inside with a grunt and slammed the lid.

"What will you do with her?" I asked, not wanting the answer but needing to know.

"Question her," Branc said shortly. "She'll have

information that will be useful."

"What if she won't talk?"

"She'll talk." Branc dusted his hands and gestured to the car. "I have my ways. Get in, I'll drop you off at home."

The last thing I wanted to do was get into a car with Branc and the trussed-up siren in the trunk, but since Byssa and Levi had already left, it was Branc or the bus. I grimaced and opened the passenger door. Branc turned the key in the ignition, and we roared down the road.

CHAPTER 21

I twisted my wet hair into a loose bun at the nape of my neck and tried to ignore the thumping that had started from the back of the car. Branc turned on the radio to cover it, but the pounding noise was an irregular counter beat to the rhythmic music.

"What's the plan?" I asked. "If the woman tells you where she's hiding the captured half-sirens—which apparently is at the old tugboat wreck—or about the rogue organization's plans? What then?"

Branc tapped his fingers on the steering wheel. He turned a corner sharply before answering.

"I know you want me to storm the castle, but it's not that simple. I don't have enough personnel to subdue fifty mer folk, even with human innovations. I could probably figure something out, but not in the next day or two, and I'm betting we don't have long. And that's assuming the fifty mer folk you saw were the entirety of the guard. We have no confirmation of that fact."

I stared at the side of Branc's face. He glanced at me with a raised eyebrow.

"What if we had more people?" I said slowly, my mind churning with ideas. "What sort of resources could you get us for attacking mer folk? How many people would we need, do you think?"

Branc's eyes narrowed as he internally calculated. "If we were well organized, and the mer folk we saw were all of them, then another twenty people would tilt the scales. Fully swimming folk, that is. We'd need everyone in the water."

"Of course." I huffed a laugh. "We're talking about half-sirens. Everyone swims. Even Byssa does, although she'll need air breaks."

Branc grimaced but continued to drive in silence. I shook my head at his obvious requirements and pondered a little longer.

"I could call a meeting tonight," I said at last. "We have a good contact network now, after the warning message we passed around. Gather everyone together, present them with a plan to get back our people. Most have a vested interest, since so many friends and family members are missing. It won't be hard to mobilize them."

"If you can get twenty more people, we might have a chance." Branc turned onto my street and pulled over in front of my apartment.

"Okay. I'll call you when I have everything sorted. I'll try to get everyone together by the end of the afternoon." I stepped out of the car. The thumping traveled to my ears, and I winced then leaned back into the car. "Don't be too rough with the siren in the back."

Branc stared at me with a blank expression. "I'll do what I need to do."

I stood back, my stomach churning, and Branc roared off. It was dangerous playing with sharks. I hoped I wouldn't get bitten by the end of all this.

I trudged to my apartment door, which was unlocked. Byssa, Levi, and Cetus were inside waiting for me. I wilted a little at Levi seeing my apartment.

"You're back," Byssa said with a frown. "What was all that about? What did you do with the siren?"

"She's taken care of." I didn't meet Byssa's eyes. "She won't be bothering us again today."

"Did you—" Levi paused. "What did you do to her?"

My shock brought my gaze to Levi's. He was the only one who knew of the accidental murder that had forced me topside last year. His eyes searched mine. Did he really think I would kill someone in cold blood on purpose? Is that what he thought I would do, since I was clearly siren enough to compel him against his will?

"She's not dead, if that's what you're implying," I said with bitterness in my voice. "She'll be fine. Can we focus on getting together all the half-sirens we know for a meeting? We know where the captured people are. With enough bodies, we can mount a rescue mission to take them back. But we need to do it now, before Selo forces them back to the Seamount."

"What about the mer folk?" Cetus asked. "They are very strong, and there are lots of them. How do we fight them?"

"I have an idea for that," I said. Branc's narrowed eyes swam in my vision. I didn't like teaming up with him, but I couldn't deny his resources might give us what we needed to win. It would expose our connection to my friends, but I couldn't see any other way around it. "Leave it to me. Just get as many people as you can at the meeting."

"Okay, we can do that." Byssa pulled out her phone. "Where and when are we meeting?"

I bit my lip. If the number of people I hoped for would come, my apartment was too small to house them all. Byssa's, although in better shape, was no larger.

"None of you mind being in the elements," Levi said. "Let's find a park that's easy to get to. What about Stanley Park downtown? Everyone can find that."

"Okay." I turned to Byssa. "Stanley Park by the bus loop at four o'clock. We'll bring weapons for them. If they want to see their friends and family alive again, they will be there."

Byssa nodded, her face set with determination, and started dialing. Levi frowned at me, clearly wanting to pry further about my so-called plans, but I averted my eyes and strode to the kitchen. I was starving, and I'd bet that the others hadn't eaten lunch either.

While I rummaged in the fridge for whatever I could scrounge together, Levi and Byssa made their calls. Cetus disappeared into the bathroom to hang out with Squirter, and I assembled our cobbled-together meal of leftover sushi, bread, and carrots. Byssa and Levi picked at the food absentmindedly when I brought the plate to the table, and I pulled out my own phone to call the few people I knew.

"We have a plan," I told Hades when he picked up.

"What's up?"

"We're going to rescue the captured half-sirens tonight. Come to the Stanley Park bus loop at four o'clock today."

"I'll have to beg off work early, but I'll be there,"

Hades said at once. "But there aren't many of us in Vancouver, and we'll be facing fifty mer folk. How are we going to avoid getting pummeled?"

"I have a plan," I said. "And weapons. Don't worry about that. I'll explain everything at the meeting."

"What did you get yourself into, Lune?" Hades's voice was strained. "We've let you keep your secrets for ages, but at some point you're going to have to let us in. Have you at least told Byssa what you're up to, if you don't trust me?"

My throat closed. I couldn't bear to hear the disappointment in Hades's voice if I told him about my dealings with Branc, but that moment felt like it was hurtling toward me too quickly to avoid.

"It's nothing to do with trust," I said, my low voice husky with emotion. "I just—it's complicated."

"It's never as complicated as you think." Hades sighed. "Fine, be mysterious for a little longer. I'll see you at four."

He signed off, and I held my phone in my hands for a moment. Should I tell the others right now about my debts? Was this the moment? Would I have to also confess my sirening of Levi to Byssa at the same time?

While I dithered, Levi frowned into his phone.

"Selo approached you?" he said. I sat up and stared at Levi. Byssa finished her call then waved at Levi to put his call on speakerphone.

"Yes, he told me all about our new homes that have been prepared for us at the Seamount," a tremulous female voice spoke. "He said my daughter Aster had already left for the Seamount to start her new life, that she'd been offered a position working as a half-siren representative for the Protectorate. Apparently, she was very excited about it. She wants me to join her as soon as I can."

"It's a lie," I said quickly. "Selo will say anything to get you to go back to the Seamount. He's obsessed with getting all of us down there in case we expose our world to the humans."

"But he definitely spoke to my daughter," the woman countered. "He told me that she said to remember to pack my favorite hair comb. No one knows about that except her, so she must have spoken to Selo. What if I don't go and I never see her again? I don't want to miss my chance for an escorted trip back to the Seamount. And what if I help you attack Selo, then they think I'm not worthy to follow my daughter home?"

Byssa and I exchanged worried glances. Selo had already been feeding his lies to the half-sirens left on land. I didn't think for a second that he was telling the truth, but how could we convince her of that?

"He must have forced your daughter to tell her a detail about you that would get you to trust him." Levi rubbed his forehead. "Please believe me when I say that Selo is telling lies. We have a half-siren with us who recently came from the Seamount, and he says that the newcomers are treated worse than they were in the ghetto before they left. As well, one of us saw half-sirens being tied up and led away against their will at the information session the other night."

"What does your daughter look like?" I said. "Any obvious features?"

"She loves to dye her hair," the woman said quietly. "It's bright red at the moment."

I thought back to that night when Selo had snatched the half-sirens away with the help of his mer folk army. A flash of red winked in my mind's eye.

"I saw her," I said. "Getting into the water. Friends with Eris, right? I'm sure she's been captured. Please help us get her back. We need everyone we can get."

Silence lingered on the line. When I opened my mouth to speak, Levi held up his hand for me to wait.

"All right," the woman said through Levi's speaker. "I couldn't bear it if you're telling the truth and I didn't do anything to help my daughter. I'll be there at four o'clock."

She hung up, and I heaved a huge sigh. "Have you heard of more like that?" I asked the others.

"One or two," Byssa said. "They were more suspicious by nature, though, and it wasn't hard to convince them to come and at least check it out today. I think once they see their first mer folk in these waters, they'll come around pretty quickly."

"Selo and his people are everywhere," Levi muttered. He stood and moved toward the door. "I should get going. I'll call more on the way, but I have a few things to do before the meeting. I'll see you there."

"Yeah, me too." Byssa shoved her phone in her pocket and rose. "I'll walk you out. See you later, Lune."

They both left before I could stop them, and I slumped in my chair with a mixture of regret and relief. I had to tell them my secrets soon, but I didn't want to face that decision today.

Cetus wandered out of the bathroom and nibbled on the food I'd left out then made a face.

"Is this it?" he asked.

I glanced at him incredulously. "Oh, I'm sorry my food isn't up to your standards. When are you getting a job, by the way?"

"When Selo is stopped," he said calmly. "He is first. It's okay, I ate an urchin on my swim."

I shook my head at Cetus's brashness, but my phone rang before I could call him out.

"Lune," Branc's voice crawled into my ear. "I know where Selo stays on land. He should be at the West Van address you visited yesterday at dinnertime tonight."

I sat up straight and clutched the phone to my cheek. "Good. I'll go right after the meeting. You're going to be there, right? Four o'clock at the Stanley Park bus loop. Show everyone that you have weapons that can help them defend against mer folk?"

"I'll be there."

I hated the relief I felt at Branc's assurance, but how else would twenty half-sirens ever hope to gain an advantage over the aggressive, powerful mer folk who weren't susceptible to our only weapon, compulsion? We needed more ammunition if we wanted to stand a chance at defeating them.

"How did you find that out?" I asked, not wanting to hear the answer but needing to.

"The siren, of course," Branc said. "How else?"

"Is she still alive?"

"Yes." He paused. "For now. I'll have to decide what to do with her later. I can't let her go, that's for certain."

I said goodbye and hung up, queasy from Branc's words. Sometimes Branc seemed very human—I never saw him swim, his hair and eyes weren't pale, and he fit into the human world so seamlessly—but other times the coldness of the upper echelons filtered through the cracks.

Only one more job, I promised myself. Once we'd freed the captives, I could go back to keeping Branc at an arm's length and choosing the jobs he handed out carefully to keep them within my own moral code.

CHAPTER 22

Cetus and I spent a few tense hours in my apartment. I looked around the place for anything I could bring as a weapon but came up empty-handed. What use would I be under the sea against one of the mer folk? I hoped Branc would bring some worthwhile weapons. I felt vulnerable and helpless without my ability to siren my enemies. What would a human do in this situation? I was equally useless as a siren and as a human. Did that count as embracing both my sides?

I changed into a proper bikini to make sure it was sturdy enough for whatever lay ahead—a racerback would hold firm—and tried to shove a little more food in my roiling stomach. Cetus lounged on the couch and watched videos to improve his English.

"How are you so calm?" I eventually burst out. "We're going to be facing an army of mer folk this evening."

Cetus shrugged. "And we'll figure it out. What does worrying do to help?"

I huffed a sigh, annoyed by his logic and the fact that I couldn't emulate him. Cetus had always been that way. His lack of sense had sometimes wriggled him into trouble at the Seamount, but I envied his calm today.

When it was time, I took my backpack to the bathroom and loaded Squirter into it. He hummed happily, excited to go on a trip, and I tickled his mantle before screwing on the lid. With the backpack slung over my shoulders, I marched into the main room.

"Time to go," I announced.

The bus ride to Stanley Park wasn't long, but my tension made it last forever. Cetus hummed quietly under his breath until I wanted to scream at him to stop. Finally, the bus pulled to the curb at the park and I leaped out, Cetus following slowly behind.

"We're early," I announced to him over my shoulder. My feet took me to the shelter of a stand of trees beside the bus loop. Wind whistled through the branches, and a threatening sky darkened the shadows. "But that's okay. People will be here soon."

Hades was already in the shade of a large fir near the bus loop, and Cetus strode over to join him. I glanced around the open space, but except for a few humans jogging or children pulling their parents' hands toward the aquarium, no other sirens had yet arrived.

A familiar figure walked our way through the thick shade of the path, and my heart squeezed. Levi was here early, too. His blue eyes landed on me, and his face tightened.

My lips pursed. Was he still thinking about what I was hiding from him about dealing with the siren we'd overpowered? He was one to talk. Where had he disappeared to when he'd fallen over the edge of the dock? I'd frantically searched for him, and somehow he'd swam to the shore despite not knowing how to swim, crawled out of the waves, jogged to his truck to change into dry clothes, and come back to wait with Byssa for me to surface? The whole episode felt off to me, and I wanted to know the truth.

"Hi," I said when he approached. "Ready for the

meeting?"

"I guess." He shoved his hands in his pockets and stared at the buses.

I tried to hold back, I really did, but my underlying tension over the whole captives' situation pushed the words out of my mouth.

"What happened at the beach today? You know, when you fell into the ocean?"

Levi stiffened but didn't meet my eyes. "I told you. I managed to make it to shore. I had dry clothes in my truck."

"I thought you couldn't swim," I pressed.

"I said I don't swim. I didn't say I couldn't."

Levi crossed his arms, clearly finished with this conversation, but I was bursting to learn the truth.

"Why don't you swim if you can? Are you just embarrassed by your skills compared to half-sirens? No one who knows you would care. If it's too cold, you can always wear a wetsuit."

Pressure in my chest built up with my desire to know Levi's secret. It would be so easy to get him to tell me what I wanted to know if I sirened him. I couldn't, though, as much as I longed to. The last time I'd tried, it had broken anything Levi and I had had between us. I couldn't risk reopening that wound, even if any relationship potential between us was over.

Levi glanced at me with narrowed eyes. I slapped my hand to my chest, horrified. I'd been thinking so hard about sirening that I'd inadvertently let slip a tiny hum of compulsion without thinking. He must have felt the vibration through his feet.

"I'm sorry," I blurted out. "I didn't mean to do that. It just slipped out."

"Really?" Levi's expression was thunderous. "After last time, you still pull out your siren tricks? I thought I'd made it clear how I felt about that. Do I need to never see you again, and only communicate over text?"

"I'm sorry," I said again, but frustration welled up inside me. "I really didn't mean to. But I can't help what I am. For better or worse, I'm pale folk, and compulsion comes with the territory."

"You can help it," he said through gritted teeth. "Because you're not only a siren. You're also human. You're better when you embrace both sides of yourself. Don't hide behind one side or try too hard to push the other side away. You can be the best parts of both."

He turned and strode away from me toward Hades and Cetus. I fumed inside for a moment, then my better self reflected on what he'd said.

Had I been focusing too hard on embracing my siren side to the detriment of my human side? Byssa's admonishments over my casual compulsions haunted me. Before, I'd been so careful to avoid sirening at all while I tried to live fully on land. Then, I'd thrown myself into my siren heritage once I'd found my people at the Lodge. Had I gone too far? Was it possible to find a healthy balance between my two halves?

But what did that look like? Maybe I needed to set boundaries for myself in a similar way that the Seamount regulated compulsion. As a member of the lowest level of pale folk society, I'd never been allowed to compel anyone. Embracing my siren side without the regulations of the Seamount had meant to me that I could siren who I wanted without repercussions, as long as I followed my own moral code.

Well, my code clearly wasn't working for the people around me, so I needed to rethink it. What boundaries should I set up for myself? What was acceptable?

"Byssa," I said when I spotted her walking toward me. "I need your help."

"Of course," she said. She didn't smile at me, but her face held care and concern in equal measure. "That's what friends are for."

"I don't know when to siren," I said, honesty making my throat constrict. "I've made mistakes lately, but I don't know how to draw the lines. What do you do?"

Byssa gave a little huffing chuckle. "It's simple," she said. "I don't. Siren, that is. Not unless my life or someone else's is on the line. It's far too easy to sink into that abyss. If you start sirening others for something, you do it for everything. And no one should be forced to do things against their will. You lived in the Seamount ghetto for long enough. I thought you'd understand that."

"It's hard to rein it in now that I'm finally allowed to," I muttered. "Never siren. That's your answer?"

"It's the only one I can live with." Byssa wrapped an arm around my shoulder and drew me toward the others, who were being joined by other half-sirens. "Come on, let's free our friends."

We waited another five minutes until our group was twenty-one strong and humans walking on the path glanced at us with curiosity. I waved at everyone to move onto the grass, out of earshot of walkers and joggers. They gathered around me in a tight semi-circle.

"Thank you for coming," I said loudly enough for everyone to hear, but not so loudly that passersby could listen in. "Our friends and families have been captured by the seal shifter Selo and his army of mer folk. I saw them tie everyone up and lead them away forcefully. Selo is waiting to snatch more of us before they make the journey to the Seamount, where our people will be forced to live in the ghetto as prisoners, and you'll never see them again."

CHAPTER 23

Fear and anger creased the half-siren faces staring at me from beside the bus loop.

"You said you saw this?" A woman with a skeptical frown and a mane of frizzy white hair narrowed her eyes at me. "How do we know you're telling the truth? Selo visited me and told me about the homes they've prepared for us at the Seamount. Cave dwellings in the highest positions of the second tier, unlimited Grace, our pick of *yatull* steeds."

A few others nodded at her words. I crossed my arms.

"I don't care what you believe," I said. "I know what I saw, and I saw our friends tied up at spearpoint by fifty mer folk. You don't have to join us today, but I'm planning to rescue them, and it will be much easier with more people."

The tide turned, and those who had nodded at the woman's statement now looked confused and frightened.

"How can we possibly fight fifty mer folk?" A slender man with black hair and pale eyes asked. "I got on the wrong side of one once, and I still have the scars to prove it. They're vicious."

"That's where I come in." Branc had snuck up on our group without me noticing, and he planted his feet firmly on the ground beside me. In his hands he held a metal pole as long as my arm with a sharp point on the end, which I glanced at with curiosity. He gazed impassively at the group. "I have weapons for everyone here. This stinger prod will render a mer folk unconscious almost immediately. I recommend using it in conjunction with a retractable net." Branc held up a small parcel. "That should slow them down enough for you to sting them. The rest of you can take one of my modified spearguns to defend yourselves. We have the advantage of metal on land, so we might as well use it. These weapons will level the playing field against the mer folk. I have more people, so I'll separate everyone into teams and—"

"And who are you?" Levi crossed his arms and glared at Branc. "What gives you the right to barge in here and take over planning? Lune was doing fine on her own."

"Lune is never on her own," Branc said, his eyes narrowing at Levi. The two faced each other, their feet apart and hands clenching.

I didn't know what had set them both off, but the situation needed to be diffused immediately.

"We're all on the same side, here," I said quickly. "Levi, this is Branc. We've known each other since I arrived on land. He has a lot of resources in Vancouver and a vested interest in finding the captives."

Levi stared at Branc, a muscle in his jaw ticking.

"You're Driftwood," he said softly. "The shady Grace distributor. The one who preys on new sirens."

Branc's face was hard. "I don't 'prey' on anyone. I'm the only one bothering to give new arrivals the help they desperately need, and the only one who is organized enough to distribute Grace in the city. If I make a living at it, can you blame me?"

Levi's face darkened, but I stomped my foot.

"Enough," I shouted. "You two have issues, but I

don't care. Right now, we have friends to save, so we need to put aside our differences and work together. We all want the same thing today."

Without breaking eye contact with Branc, Levi nodded. Branc turned and handed me the stinger prod.

"Pointed end into the mer folk," he said shortly. "It's not hard. I have more in the parking lot for when you decide who is going where."

"Thanks, Branc." I ran my hand over the stinger prod, its metal cold and smooth in my hands. "This might make the difference. How many people do you have?"

"Fifteen full swimmers," he said. "And I'll drive my boat. It can hold that many in a pinch."

"Okay." I turned to the group, who had been avidly watching the drama. Byssa's eyes flicked between me and Branc, and I didn't look at her for long. "Here's the plan. Everyone will grab a weapon, then we'll split into three main groups. One group goes with Branc in the boat and comes at the tugboat shipwreck from the ocean side. Another group can leave from the old boathouse at Caufield Park in West Van, and the third from Lighthouse Park. The idea is to converge underwater at the shipwreck and confuse the guards into defending from all angles. Once underwater, our only goal is to free the captives. Use your weapons, look after each other, and stay safe."

"We can do this," Hades said loudly. "We're getting our friends back. Eris, Dr. Mazzaella, Aster, and all the others will be safely on land by sunset tonight."

The group let out a few ragged cheers that grew in strength. I glanced around the group, and my heart squeezed tight. We could do this. We could get our people back and show Selo that he was in the wrong for forcing others to his will. We needed to swim our own currents and make our own choices. None of us should be controlled.

"Follow Branc to the parking lot," I called out over the excited chatter. "We'll split into teams once we have our equipment."

Branc took off without a backward glance, and the crowd followed him. Half strode purposefully, their faces determined. The other half gabbed to their neighbors with manic enthusiasm. This mission was out of most people's comfort zones, but they all wanted their friends back as much as we did. They would pull through, and I was proud that so many had turned up to help.

I moved to follow, but Byssa tugged on my elbow and made me stop. I turned to her with reluctance.

"Is that what happened when you came to land for the first time?" she said, her eyes full of horror and pity. "Like what Eris was saying about being in debt for years?"

I shrugged, uncomfortable with where this conversation was going. "Yeah, I guess."

"So, do you owe Branc a lot of money?"

I shrugged again and tried to walk forward to follow the others. Byssa's hand gripped my elbow with a crab-tight grasp.

"Why didn't you ever tell me?" she whispered. "Why didn't you ask for help?"

I stared into the distance, but all I could see were the

green and brown of thick trees. Finally, I sighed.

"I was ashamed," I said quietly, meeting Byssa's eyes. "I didn't want you to know how stupid I'd been. How naïve. It was my mistake to rectify. And I'm getting there, too, just not quite yet. Branc's not keen on letting me go. I'm too useful to him."

Byssa's mouth twisted. "Bastard," she grated out. "We are going to get you out from under his thumb. I don't care what we have to do. Do you hear me?"

I stared at her petite face filled with fierce protectiveness, and my eyes grew hot. I wasn't alone here. I didn't have to be alone, as long as I didn't mind facing my own idiocy head-on.

"Okay," I whispered.

Byssa threw her arms around me, and I buried my moist eyes in her hair. We clutched each other for a long while, until I finally sniffed and released her.

"But first things first," I said. "We need to free Eris and the others. And, to do that, we need Branc. Come on, let's gear up."

Byssa snaked her arm through mine, and together we followed the path toward the nearest parking lot. Despite the dangers in our evening plans, my elation at Byssa's reaction to my secret shame kept making the corners of my mouth turn up, no matter how hard I tried to maintain a serious face in keeping with our mission.

Branc was at his car with the trunk open. He passed out prods, nets, and spearguns to the group who had followed him. Fifteen half-sirens stood behind him with weapons in their hands. I recognized the bartender Pod from my apartment building, Reef the bouncer with his bald head and pearl stud, and slimy Mark the Shark with his messy ponytail. He winked at me as I passed, and I threw him a withering glance.

I clutched the stinger prod in my hand, my stomach churning uneasily. Would this be enough? At the determined expressions of those around me, my muscles unclenched slightly. It might be difficult, but we could prevail. Eris and the others were counting on us, and we were going to give it our best shot or get captured trying.

"Separate yourselves into three teams," I called over the babble.

"What about Selo?" Branc said to me. "He'll be at his safe house right about now."

"I'll go there first," I said.

"I'll come with you." Levi stood next to me, his hands empty but his solid presence reassuring. He turned to face me. "Since I can't help underwater, this is the best job for me."

Branc's lips thinned, and he turned away to speak to his people. I released a sigh of relief that Levi would be joining me.

"Okay, good," I said. "Branc's information said that Selo would be at the house at dinnertime, and likely on his own. It shouldn't take much to take him down. Mer folk can't come on land, and seal shifters are susceptible to compulsion."

Levi's face twitched, and I bit my tongue in annoyance at myself. I wished I didn't care about what Levi thought of me, but I couldn't help it, and speaking about sirening around him was clearly a sensitive topic.

But did it matter? We didn't have a chance to continue

our relationship, not after what I'd done. He might as well hear my plans. And even Byssa would use her powers of compulsion in this scenario. With captives to save, whatever I did to Selo was fair game.

Hades approached me. "I'm leading the team jumping in off Lighthouse Park, a mix of Branc's people and ours. Byssa's leading our people from the old boathouse, and Cetus is going with Branc and others on the boat."

"I'll join Byssa's group as soon as I'm done with Selo," I assured him. He gave me a tight smile then waved to his group. They dispersed into various cars and vans, and Levi nodded toward his truck.

"Let's move," he said. "Deal with Selo."

I hopped into the passenger's seat and Levi took off through the parking lot and onto the road. After I gave him directions to Selo's house, an uncomfortable silence fell on us. Levi was the first to break it.

"Have you always worked for Driftwood?" he said loudly into the quiet.

I didn't know what Levi wanted to hear, so I settled for the truth. It wasn't as if things could get worse between us.

"Yes. Ever since I came to land and accepted his so-called hospitality. Once I'd buried myself in debt, he had me, hook, line, and sinker."

"I know he makes his debtors do jobs for him. What have you done?"

I glanced at the side of Levi's face, but he kept his eyes resolutely on the road.

"Whatever he asks, within reason." I played with the hem of my skirt. "I compel people to tell me secrets, mainly. Full disclosure, I did it to one of your visitors at the Lodge. But I try to only do jobs that don’t cross the line.” I paused. “Well, the wobbly line that I set for myself. It’s tricky to figure out where the line is when I don’t know what the jobs are for, but I muddle through the best I can. I don’t knowingly hurt people, and I don’t let people use my body.”

Levi made a choked noise. “You’ve been asked to do that?” he ground out.

“On occasion. I have that ‘exotic’ appeal to some humans.” My fingers clung to each other. “But it’s not worth it, not to me. I do the jobs I can, to help pay off my debt.” My voice grew quiet until I didn’t know if Levi could hear me. “I just want to be free.”

I left my explanation there. I didn’t have anything else to add, nothing that wouldn’t be me begging for understanding or forgiveness from Levi, neither of which I felt I had to do. I didn’t regret my choices, only the stupidity that had landed me in trouble in the first place. I’d done what I’d needed to do to get away from Branc, and if Levi didn’t understand, that was on him.

Levi drove in silence until we turned into the neighborhood of our destination. A block away, he turned off the engine.

“Thanks for telling me,” he said in a quiet voice. “About all that.”

“Yeah, well.” I opened my door and stepped out, then leaned back into the truck to meet Levi’s eyes. “I don’t have any more secrets from you. You know everything important about me now.”

“I don’t know your favorite flavor of ice cream.”

I let out a surprised huff of laughter. A smile played at the corners of Levi's mouth.

"Salted caramel," I replied. "I'm a sucker for salty anything. Come on, let's nab this shifter."

I tucked my blond hair under a ballcap, shoved a piece of Grace in my mouth, and held onto the truck's side mirror while sensations coursed through me. I wanted to be at full strength this evening.

We approached the address without looking too closely at it. The old shack that Cetus and I had already visited stuck out like a sea pen from sand among its affluent neighbors. At my next sweeping glance, I spotted movement in the house's large picture window. I clutched Levi's arm, which was pleasantly warm and solid under my fingers.

"He's in there," I hissed. "Don't look now, but I'm sure that's him. Same dark hair, dark skin, build."

"Is he alone?" Levi stole a peek while I pretended to focus on a young couple pushing a stroller across the street. "I can't see anyone else."

"Perfect. Come on, let's sneak around the back and try the door there. If we can get inside, we can corner him without the neighbors calling us in."

Levi led the way while I texted Byssa, Hades, and Branc the news that we were zeroing in on Selo. I received replies from all three of them with varying reports of readiness.

No sign of movement at the boathouse, Byssa wrote. *We're going in. Stay safe!*

Getting my feet wet as I type, said Hades. *See you under the waves.*

Branc's message was succinct. *Good. Team underwater now.*

I took a deep breath of elation. Everything was going according to plan. Once we dealt with Selo, I could join Byssa and the others and take down the mer folk with Branc's weapons. Before long, Eris and the others would join us in land-locked safety once more, and this whole mess would be only a bad dream in our past.

"Ready?" Levi whispered when I joined him at the back door, which led from a rotting deck furnished with an empty flower planter.

I met his gaze, his flat blue eyes intense and determined. "Ready."

Levi reached over to push the door lever down. With a tremendous push, he thrust the door open and leaped inside.

I followed, my heart thundering in my chest and my eyes on high alert. It was times like this that I desperately missed my skin sense on land. I could have known exactly where the seal shifter was and run straight to him.

Luckily, I didn't have to look far. The dark-haired Selo stood facing the stove in the kitchen which we'd burst into.

"It's over, Selo," I said loudly. "You and your abduction scheme are done. Your mer folk are going down, and all the captives will be set free. Give it up."

Slowly, Selo turned. When he faced us, I hissed in a breath, because he wasn't Selo at all.

CHAPTER 24

The unfamiliar seal shifter smiled, his mouth twisted from a scar that ran across his cheek. With a tilt of his head, he studied me.

"Lune Seafields, I presume," he said in a hoarse, barking voice. "We know most of the half-humans in this city, now. I'm sorry Selo isn't here to greet you. Our 'scheme' is not nearly done."

"What do you mean?" Levi said in a hard voice. He stepped closer to the shifter, who held up his hand to stop Levi.

"Selo is planning to take the first batch of deserters to the Seamount tonight. That's why he's not here. My compatriots and I have been left to clean up the mess left on land." He shrugged. "We gave everyone plenty of chances and encouragement to do the right thing. If they chose death instead of repatriation, that was their doing."

"What do you mean by 'clean up'?" I shared a horrified look with Levi. "As in, kill everyone who didn't go with Selo?"

"Yes," he said, nodding like I'd answered a test question brilliantly. "Exactly that. You are all abominations who shouldn't even exist. Selo is too soft for taking some of you back, in my opinion. But he's clever, and he knows that public opinion wouldn't stand for outright culling. No, some examples of bringing back the lost souls to their true home needed to be made. Then no one would question what happens to the rest of you."

"Abominations?" My voice shook with rage. "Judged for something we had no say over? It's bad enough we're treated like the scum of the sea at the Seamount, but to wipe us out entirely for merely existing? That's rich."

"I don't have anything against you, on the whole," he said, surprised. "No, you're fine in the ghetto where you belong. It's when you threaten exposure to the Seamount and our hidden way of life that I take issue. It's only a matter of time before humans discover the Seamount with all their modern tools. We need to preserve what little secrecy we have left, and we can't do that with you making yourselves at home among the dry folk."

"Some of the half-sirens have to be here," Levi said with a shake of his head. "Some can't breathe underwater."

"Doesn't one of the human philosophers say, 'survival of the fittest'?" The shifter nodded sagely. "If they can't survive in their true home, it is kindest to put them down."

I swallowed bitter bile at the fate this monster wanted for my sweet, loving friend Byssa. I remembered her convulsions after eating the tainted Grace, and my breath hitched.

"Your group poisoned a batch of Grace with strolia toxin, didn't you?" I spat out. "To make the sufferers think they had drifting syndrome and needed to return to the Seamount."

The shifter said nothing, but his smug smile was answer enough.

"I don't know how you think you can kill us all," I said with false bravado. "You're a single seal shifter against a huge group of half-sirens. You don't stand a chance."

"Oh, don't I?"

His face melted until his skin loosened and age spots appeared across his sagging neck. He looked forty years older and barely recognizable due to the elastic quality of seal shifter skin. My jaw dropped.

The shifter grinned at me. "Now, how will you see me coming?"

"It's a big city," I said weakly. "You won't ever find us all."

"It is a big city," he agreed. "Luckily, we did our homework. We know who everyone is, thanks to our informant within Driftwood's ranks. Did you know Hades Sweetcurrent lives at Arbutus and Sixteenth, and his twin sister Byssa lives across from a food store on Fourth? Your apartment resides just off Clark Drive." He crossed his arms with a smug expression and allowed his face to morph back to its natural state. "Now, do you still doubt me?"

I shivered at his words. He was too self-satisfied to not be sure of his plans. He knew too much about my friends for comfort. And he wasn't alone, by the sounds of it.

"You won't find our friends tonight," Levi said loudly. "And we can warn them not to go home. Now what are you going to do?"

"Oh, are you trying to rescue everyone tonight?" The shifter plunged his hand in his pocket and brought out a phone.

"What are you doing?" I hissed, lunging forward. Too

quickly, the shifter pressed a few buttons and tossed the phone on the counter.

"Warning my people," he said, sidestepping me. "I have to make sure they know to capture or kill everyone coming their way. Even if you get me, I'm only a small shell in the octopus den. Our noble work will continue without me, and I'll die knowing I'm leaving a safer future for my children at the Seamount."

The shifter scuttled through a doorway into the next room, but Levi dived onto him before he could scurry away. The two landed with a thump in the narrow hallway, and I grabbed the shifter's flailing hands and wrenched them behind his back.

"That was too easy," Levi panted as he struggled with the shifter's wriggling body. He shuffled to pin the shifter's arms with his body so I could find something to tie him up with.

"He was never the problem." I pulled open drawers in the kitchen until I found a length of twine. I dropped to my knees and tied a tight knot around the shifter's wrists behind his back. "The others that he alerted? They're the problem."

Levi and I exchanged a worried look, then I tore off a section of twine and moved to the shifter's twitching legs under Levi's body. Once the shifter was trussed up like a fish in a net, Levi rolled off him and stood.

"What do we do with him now?" he asked. "We can't leave him here to be immediately rescued by his fellow shifters."

"Take him with us, I guess." I worried my bottom lip between my teeth. Levi's eyes tracked the motion before he glanced away quickly. I stood. "Bring the truck closer to the house. I'll find a sheet or something to cover him with, and maybe a stronger rope. We'll take him with us."

Levi nodded and raced out of the room. The front door slammed behind him, and I started my search for stronger bonds. The shifter's pants were held up with a sturdy leather belt, and I affixed that around his ankles.

"Your friends won't get far," the shifter sneered at me, disdain filling his face with unpleasant lines. "What will a bunch of half-humans do against an army of mer folk, the powerful race that defends the Seamount from intruders? You're dreaming if you think you stand a chance."

"You know nothing about us," I said with heat, although my stomach curdled as I thought of Byssa, Hades, and Cetus facing rows of aggressive mer folk. The shifter wasn't wrong. Mer folk were the guardians and law enforcers of the Seamount for a reason. They were quick to anger, speedy to pull their weapons, and unforgiving of transgressions. I tightened the belt another notch, and the shifter winced. "We have our ways. Why am I talking to you, anyway? You're the one tied up on the floor. Shut up while I find something stronger to tie you up with."

I left the shifter on the kitchen floor and stalked through the moldering house. It was sparsely furnished with secondhand items, clearly a way house for these seal shifters to use as a base while on land, not as a permanent residence. No pictures hung on the water-stained walls, and no sense of personality filled the nearly empty rooms. In the bedroom, a chipped night table yielded a lamp cord, which I tore out of the wall and then the lamp base. I stripped the coverlet off the bed and ran back to the kitchen, where I wrapped the cord firmly around the shifter's wrists. I shoved a tea towel hanging on the stove into the shifter's mouth so I didn't have to hear any more of his toxic assertions about my worth or dire predictions of my people's failure.

Once that was done, I picked up my phone and dialed Byssa's number. It rang and rang, until the answering service clicked on. I hung up and frantically called Hades's number, but the same thing happened with his phone. Were they both underwater and on their way to a fully prepared army of opponents? I didn't know how the shifter had communicated with his people—maybe he had someone on the surface who could receive phone signals and send a messenger underwater with the news—but he'd been certain that his message had been received.

I called Branc as a last resort, and to my relief, he answered.

"Did you get Selo?" he asked.

"No, just another shifter. We tied him up, but Selo is under there preparing to take the captives to the Seamount as we speak." I swallowed hard. "And the shifter managed to warn his people via phone before we could stop him. Our people are expected, now."

Branc cursed. "I'll drive as close as I can to the shipwreck," he promised. "And if I see someone acting as surface messenger, I'll deal with them. Get here as soon as you can. We'll need all the help we can get."

"The mer folk might capsize your boat if you get too

close," I warned him. For whatever reason, Branc didn't seem keen to get in the water, and I doubted he wanted his boat to sink to the bottom of the sea.

Branc scoffed. "I'd like to see them try."

He hung up, and Levi burst into the house.

"I brought the truck around," he said.

With a flourish, I threw the blanket over the tied-up shifter to cover him completely.

"Here's the package. Let's get him into your truck bed."

The shifter didn't make carrying him easy, but Levi grabbed him around the torso and I picked up his feet, and together we hauled our squirming bundle out the back door. The driveway led beside the house with a tall fence between us and the neighbors, and since Levi had backed the truck in, no one could see us swing the shifter into the truck bed.

A few seconds after I'd tucked the blanket over the shifter, he kicked free and glared at me. I sighed.

"Can you siren him to be quiet?" Levi said after we contemplated our cargo in silence for a moment. I quickly glanced at Levi, who returned my incredulous look with a somber one of his own.

"I can," I said warily. "Should I?"

"If you don't, someone will call the cops on us for kidnapping." Levi rubbed the back of his neck. "And we'll be stuck at the police station trying to defend ourselves while our friends are risking their lives to save the captives. Lives could be lost because of it. They could really use your help."

"If you think so, I'll do it." I waited another moment

for Levi to object, but he nodded permission for me to approach the shifter. I laid my hand on the shifter's shoulder and hummed a compulsion song of quiet and calmness. The shifter's eyes glazed, and he slumped to the truck bed in a peaceful daze. I stopped my hum and tucked the blanket over him.

"He should be fine until we get to the ocean," I told Levi without looking at him. I didn't want to see any anger or revulsion in his eyes.

His hand turned my chin to face him. "Just because I don't want you controlling me," he said softly, "doesn't mean you can't be you when you need to be. When you're protecting your friends from danger, you need to use whatever skills you have. I wouldn't tie my hands behind my back if a mugger jumped at me for fear of hurting him, and your compulsion ability is no different than my muscles."

"Byssa said something similar earlier." I sighed and leaned into Levi's hand cupping my cheek, then patted it and moved away before I could sink into the pleasure of his touch. "I'll try to figure it out. Come on, we need to get moving. That compulsion won't last forever."

Levi drove as quickly as he could get away with on the busy West Vancouver streets until he pulled onto a quiet road that led to the ocean. At the cul-de-sac, he cut the engine. The boathouse and surrounds were empty except for a half-hidden pile of clothes among the driftwood. Byssa and the others were already underwater and on their way to the shipwreck.

"This is as far as I go," Levi said. His frustration was clear in his voice. "I can't follow you into the water."

I wanted to ask him again why that was, but I desisted. The last time I'd asked, I'd accidentally started to compel him, and I didn't want to touch that sore subject again. Besides, without a wetsuit and scuba diving gear, human Levi wouldn't have been much use. Even with it, he would have been far too cumbersome to battle lithe mer folk.

"You've done lots already," I said. "We've got it from here."

"I hate waiting on the edge, hoping you'll all return," he muttered. He rummaged in a bag on the backseat's floor. When he turned back, he held out a package to me. "Here, this is for you. I meant to give it to you ages ago, but—well, you know."

I did know. With the misunderstanding over Cetus, and my subsequent sirening of Levi, the two of us had been on the outs. I glanced at the package in my hand with curiosity, then my eyes widened.

"A dive knife? For me?"

"It straps onto your calf." Levi helped me open the box and slide the knife out. The sheath was black with a sleek-looking yellow handle. "It's the most streamlined one I could find, so it shouldn't get in the way of your swimming. After the troubles you got into underwater with Austin, I thought it couldn't hurt to be prepared for whatever you met under there. I know it's not like the bone knives you're probably used to from the Seamount, but it should do the job."

I stared at the knife, my throat closing.

"Most girls like to get flowers, I've heard," I said in a husky voice. When Levi stiffened beside me, I met his eye with a watery smile. "I'm not most girls. This is perfect. Thank you."

Levi's smile was like a shaft of sunlight piercing the depths. I basked in it for a moment, then I slipped out of my skirt and strapped the knife to my leg. It hugged my skin tightly. I stripped off my shirt then took a deep, fortifying breath.

"Good luck," Levi said quietly.

"Thanks." I stared at the heaving water. Dark clouds had rolled in, a portent of autumn storms to come, and the ocean was following suit. "I hope I don't need it."

I reached behind my seat and unscrewed the cap of my backpack. With a gentle hand, I pulled Squirter out of his water. He clung to me with squashed, dripping arms, looking forlorn and vulnerable.

"I need to go," I said to Levi, who nodded. I was overcome with a wild desire to kiss his inviting lips, but I desisted with effort. We weren't there yet, and I refused to dignify the threat looming over us with a frantic goodbye kiss. I would come back, and we would have a chance to develop whatever was between us with the time it deserved.

"Stay safe," Levi said.

I swung open the truck door, stepped out, and slammed the door behind me. Asphalt was rough under my feet, and I walked gingerly until I reached sand.

"Come on, little guy," I hummed, clutching Squirter to my chest so he could feel the vibrations. "Into the water."

The cool, stormy sea rose with delicious splashes up my legs, and I ignored the occasional rock underfoot with the beauty of the ocean surrounding me. Once I was waist deep, I submerged myself and released Squirter. With a deep breath out of air and a long breath in of water, I entered the undersea realm.

I followed a happy Squirter deeper along the sandy bottom. My skin sense spread out, but I couldn't sense Byssa or the others. I sped up, spooked by what might lurk in the gloom, and kept vigilant for the sleek shapes of mer folk. I would be able to detect them before they did me, thanks to the heightened skin sense of pale folk, but the advantage wouldn't last me for long. Mer folk were the more powerful swimmers, and they always meant business.

I pressed on, my unerring sense of direction leading me to the coordinates we'd found for the shipwreck, the most likely place that Selo and the mer folk were hiding their captives. I put on an extra burst of speed, and Squirter jetted beside me with gleeful squirts of water.

Movement at the edge of my skin sense made my spine prickle, but the shapes soon sharpened into the figures of the other half-sirens. I undulated faster, and when they noticed me, Byssa halted the others to wait.

You made it, she said warmly when I approached. *Did you find Selo?*

No, I panted. *It was someone else. Selo is down here, and now he and the mer folk know we're coming. They're expecting us, so stay alert.*

Byssa's face twisted into a mask of worry, and the others glanced at each other. The previously skeptical older woman clutched her stinger prod tighter to her chest.

We can't stop now, Byssa said with a firm gesture. *Come*

on, everyone. Let's get in, free our friends, and get out. Keep your weapons at the ready. We're not far now.

We continued forward. Shortly after, Byssa and a lithe redhead girl shot toward the surface to take a breath then rejoined us a minute later. When they returned, something on the edge of my heightened skin sense made me clutch Byssa's elbow.

Do you feel that? I hummed quietly.

The rest of the group froze. When they felt the elongated bodies of mer folk in the distance, they clustered together and brought their weapons up. Byssa's friend Placida shook beside me, although her pale face framed by curly blond hair was resolute.

This was no good. We'd never fend off mer folk clustered into a frightened ball. I swam away and turned, using our precious moments before detection to organize our group.

Those with retractable nets, here and here. I pointed to the edges of the group. *They work better with more space. Those with stinger prods, partner with a net person. The rest, stay in the middle with your backs to each other to cover the others with your spearguns. Go!*

They scurried to follow my directions, seemingly happy to have something productive to do. I joined Byssa and her net with my prod, and we faced the oncoming mer folk swimming our way, still out of sight but not out of sensing.

A ripple of fear crossed our group when we all felt the mer folk take notice of us. As one, the approaching shapes turned in our direction and swam with unerring strokes of their fused legs toward us.

Stay strong, I vibrated through the water at my people. *We can do this. They might be mer folk, but we have weapons and a reason to fight.*

I tasted fear emanating from Byssa. She released an inadvertent vibration of terror, and I brushed against her side to comfort her. She glanced at me and nodded, then gripped her net firmly and spread it in preparation. Squirter landed on my shoulder and suctioned on with strong suckers. I held my own stinger prod aloft, the end with the sharp needle filled with paralytic poison pointed toward the oncoming threat.

Waiting for the mer folk to arrive took forever and yet no time at all. When my eyes finally saw them approach, their kelp-brown faces intent on their prey surrounded by swaying hair of the same color, I shuddered but held firm.

Let's go, I said to Byssa. When I opened my mouth, the sharp tang of fear from my companions drifted over my tongue. The others needed someone to set an example of how to act, and Byssa and I were the leaders, for better or for worse.

Byssa's eyes were huge in her petite face, but she leaped forward with strong kicks and stretched her arms wide. The mer man before us looked perplexed by our aggression. Pale folk rarely fought back.

Byssa stretched out her hand. With a flick of her wrist, the net sailed out and caught the surprised mer man in its grasp.

Byssa's aim hadn't been perfect—it was her first time using the device, after all, but that was why I was here. I thrust myself forward, Squirter clinging to my shoulder, and jammed my stinger prod into the exposed flesh of the writhing mer man's stomach. He lunged toward me, his face contorted with rage at our presumption.

A handspan from me, his face grew curiously slack. He bumped into me, his momentum carrying him forward, but he had no fight left in him. The paralytic poison had done its work. According to Branc, it would keep the mer man quiet for a full hour.

I didn't have time to glory in our success. A mer woman was on us next, her hair braided with bones and teeth above a grim visage predicting doom to us.

While Byssa plucked her net from around the unresponsive mer man, I swung my stinger prod toward the fast-approaching mer woman. She was too quick, and battled the end of my prod away from her stomach. She twisted around and raised her bone spear to skewer me.

A net wrapped around the mer woman's face. She clawed it with her long nails, scratching furiously at her bonds. Byssa yanked harder.

Lune, she screamed. *Now!*

I jabbed my stinger prod toward the mer woman, heedless of where I landed the needle. It pierced her arm. She writhed and twisted, and I didn't swim out of the way of her bone spear's flailing blade. It sliced my calf, and black blood oozed from the burning gash. Byssa held onto the net with grim determination until the mer woman's movements grew slack, and she floated as motionless as her compatriot.

While Byssa untangled her net, I looked around, clutching my wounded leg with a grimace of pain. Battle raged, and I counted ten mer folk including the two we'd incapacitated. The other half-sirens were putting up a good fight, but we weren't clear winners, not by a long shot. Byssa's acquaintance Shelley jabbed at an approaching mer man with her prod, but the nimble swimmer merely dodged. He darted forward and aimed his bone spear at Shelley's torso.

She released a call of distress when the spear scratched her side. Blood pooled from the wound. The mer man's face twisted in satisfaction.

I stabbed my prod into his bare back with force. The mer man turned my way, but his body slackened before his motion could rip my prod out of his flesh.

I swam closer to Shelley, who clutched her side, her face contorted from the pain. Motion alerted my skin sense too late. A mer woman was almost on me, bone blade raised for the blow.

A net sailed across her face, and she reared back.

Lune! Byssa shouted.

I jabbed my prod at the flailing mer woman, who bared her teeth at me with her last conscious movement. I glanced around wildly, on alert for more attacks, but the battle tide had turned. Seven mer folk were down already, and the remaining three fought hard but were outnumbered by stinger prods and harpoon guns. Half-sirens with nets waited on the periphery to entrap any escapees.

By the time Byssa joined me in watching the battle, the remaining mer folk had been subdued. One clutched a bleeding arm while entangled in a net, and the other two floated with glassy eyes.

We did it! Placida crowed, and the communal hum of

victory nearly cracked my heart open with pride. Had I ever felt this powerful against mer folk? They enforced Seamount law with a stone grip, and I couldn't remember a time when I hadn't been wary of them. Now, ten mer folk were under our control.

Prod the bleeding ones, I said. *And tie them all up so they don't float away. Can't have the dry folk coming across them.* I glanced around the group with concern. *Is anyone besides Shelley hurt?*

Three of our people kicked toward me, clutching various bleeding parts of their bodies. I swallowed at the clouds of blood following them.

I'll wrap them up and take them to shore, Byssa said to me. She pointed at my leg, whose blood flow was already slowing. *Are you coming?*

I'm fine, I said with a wave. The wound stung like a jellyfish tentacle, but I'd survive.

Byssa nodded. *Keep going and find Eris and the others.*

Levi can help you, I said. *He's on the beach near the boathouse. He would like to feel helpful, I think.*

She nodded and ushered the injured people back the way we'd come. I watched her disappear into the green gloom and followed her progress with my skin sense even as I focused on the group that was left. Placida had wrapped the ten unconscious mer folk in one of the nets and anchored it to a rock on the sea floor. It was nothing that determined mer folk couldn't fight their way out of, but it would contain them against ocean currents while unconscious.

Good, I said. *Ten down, forty to go. Far less if the others have been as successful. Let's keep going and find our friends.*

The ocean was empty except for passing schools of perch and a long-tentacled jellyfish at the edge of my skin sense. I pressed forward eagerly, wanting to reach the shipwreck soon. Waiting and traveling was hard on my psyche, far harder than the actual battle with mer folk had been. My calf stung with an annoying throb, but I ignored it. Instead, I followed the sloping seafloor below me, sand interspersed with boulders and occasional human debris like a sponge-covered old tire.

Sirens, Placida said beside me. *On our right.*

I focused my attention to the side. Sure enough, a group of sirens swam at the edge of my skin sense. I strained and could make out Hades's familiar figure.

They're ours, I said with relief. *Let's meet up.*

We changed our course to intersect the others, and within a minute, we had converged. Hades gripped my arm.

You're okay, he said. He looked around. *Where's Byssa?*

She's fine, I assured him. *She escorted a few hurt people to the shore.*

Hades nodded somberly. *We lost a few friends along the way from injuries. Not lost-lost, just sliced up and couldn't continue. They headed to Branc's boat.*

We took out ten mer folk already, I said to cheer him up. *What's your count?*

It's a contest, is it? He grinned. *We got twelve, beat that.*

I intend to. I pointed in the direction of the shipwreck. *Come on, slow poke.*

I led the way with Hades close behind me. The others followed, and I pointed our convoy toward our destination.

A current brushed against my skin. I stopped and closed my eyes to feel it better. Something large roamed just at the edge of my skin sense. Squirter gripped my shoulder tighter.

What was that? Hades said beside me. His already pale face grew white.

The current passed again. This time I sensed the immense length of the creature in the distance. My stomach shriveled into a tiny knot of fear and despair.

A *ligan*, the deadly predator of the Seamount—the source of dry folk sea serpent legends—was here.

I whirled around to the others.

Weapons ready, I hummed and gestured with all my strength. *A ligan is coming.*

Should we try to outswim it? Hades said with a glance in the ligan's direction. It was approaching fast.

I shook my head. *We wouldn't make it ten strokes. Brace yourselves and keep away from those teeth. When it's close enough, try to compel it. Maybe if we all work together, we can overpower it.*

I didn't have high hopes for sirening the gigantic sea serpent, but I had to say something to my terrified fellows. Ligans were notoriously difficult to compel, and it usually took at least twenty-five sirens in concert to control one. The mer folk were better at coercion, despite their lack of compulsion ability. Their aggressive use of bone spears worked effectively on ligans.

I started to hum, and soon, everyone joined in. Our concert of vibrations grew in strength as the ligan approached. I kept it up even when the ligan's head emerged in the dimness before my waiting eyes.

It was enormous. Dark green scales, each the size of my outstretched hand, clung to a snake-like body. A huge jaw with prominent teeth stretched from one side of the head to the other, easily as wide as my arm span. Striated yellow and green eyes scanned the water ahead.

The ligan swam slowly toward us. Was it affected by our humming? I poured out all my strength into my vibrations and gripped my stinger prod more tightly. I didn't have high hopes that my weapon would paralyze something as large as a ligan, but it and my voice were the only defenses I had.

It shook its mighty head—once, twice—then lunged forward. Our concerted hums broke as we scattered away from the attack. A sharp tooth sliced the side of my leg, and I yelped in pain. One of Branc's people wasn't as lucky, and a sickening crunch with an accompanying vibration of anguish signaled his defeat.

The ligan shook the man in its massive jaws. It opened its mouth wide and snapped further on its prey. The man didn't stand a chance, and he disappeared down the ligan's throat without a sound.

The rest of us fled from the swallowing ligan, but it wasn't done with us. I didn't know what the creature's head was doing, but vibrations of distress traveled through the water toward me. Hades dragged me along the snaking body of the ligan, which was too wide to wrap my arms around, if I'd felt like embracing the monster. I took the opportunity to stab my stinger prod into its flank, but I might as well have punched the beast with my useless fist for all the notice it took of me. I would have to stab it hundreds of times for enough poison to enter its flesh, if indeed the needle could even pierce deep enough to reach its bloodstream. For all I knew, it had stopped within the scale layer.

Hades tried shooting the animal's side with his speargun, but the small harpoon tip bounced off the ligan's hard scales. He continued to swim toward the beast's tail. My skin sense warned me of approaching danger, and I twisted around.

The ligan had turned in the opposite direction, and now its head was coming toward me while its body slid past. I stared at its yellow and green eyes and the gills fanning out from its head. I was frozen in place from fear of the predator in front of me. My stinger prod was useless, my compulsion ability too weak to make a difference, and I had no other recourse.

I was dead.

CHAPTER 26

I closed my eyes, not wanting to see my death in the shape of a ligan barreling down on me, but nothing stopped my skin sense from feeling the current pushing against my body. Was this it? I wasn't ready to die. I had so much I wanted to do. Why hadn't I kissed Levi before I'd left? What had seemed sensible at the time now felt like foolish bravado. I hummed at Squirter to flee, but he merely gripped my shoulder harder with his strong suction cups.

Another current joined the one caused by the ligan's inexorable progress. My heart sank even lower, which I hadn't realized was possible. Were there two ligans?

That would make my swift death even faster, I reasoned. A manic giggle escaped me at my logic. The new current was from a smaller body, long and slender, but definitely ligan-shaped. My eyes flew open.

A lengthy creature flew past me, heading straight for the ligan's head. I caught a glimpse of silvery-blue scales and a sinuous body before it smacked into the ligan's forehead headfirst. It shot away into the dimness beyond.

The strike had diverted the ligan's attention toward its attacker, and I forced my frozen body to kick away. I didn't know what the creature was, but I couldn't waste the opportunity it had given me.

As I swam, I replayed the scene. Silvery-blue glinted in my mind. What was the creature? I hadn't seen anything like it before. It wasn't from the Seamount, of that I was sure, and I'd swum enough in these waters to know what lurked past the shoreline. Byssa's fascination with documenting underwater wildlife with her camera lens had also familiarized me with the local fauna.

So, what was this lithe, serpent-like creature with the mesmerizing, silvery-blue scales?

A tiny part of me wanted to follow the creature and satisfy my curiosity, but the far larger part was happy to escape with my life. I sensed a cluster of my half-siren fellows in the distance, Hades in the lead, heading directly for the shipwreck. I turned to follow them, but currents from the ligan's battle with the creature paused me.

From what I could tell, the much larger ligan was circling the unknown creature, trapping it in a swirl of body and tail. The creature darted back and forth, but the rapidly tightening loop left it with nowhere to go.

I couldn't leave the creature to suffer, not when it had saved my life. How could I return the favor? I had nothing to hurt the ligan with. I cast my eyes around, and the seafloor's rocky surface beckoned. The start of a plan formed in my mind.

I was a siren, and I could use my voice. If not to compel, then to distract.

Over here! I directed a formless hum of calling toward the ligan. The seafloor wasn't far. I could lunge toward it and tuck myself in the rocks far enough that the ligan's snapping jaws couldn't pry me out.

As I'd hoped, the ligan's head twisted toward me. Would it follow my call?

The unknown creature sunk its teeth into the ligan's

neck. The ligan opened its mouth in a roar of pain. The creature hung on and dug its fangs in deeper. When the ligan shook the creature off, it left a chunk of its neck with the smaller animal.

The vast, mournful cry of the ligan echoed again in my chest. Its ponderous body swirled around as the ligan swam out to sea, away from the sharp teeth of the creature.

I hung limply midwater, too relieved to do anything other than float. The ligan's form ventured further and further away until it was lost to my skin sense.

But when the creature approached, I stiffened and looked up warily, my stinger prod at the ready. I didn't know why the creature had attacked the ligan. Maybe it had wanted a huge ligan snack and would settle for a small half-siren one instead. Would my stinger prod work on the beautiful, silvery-blue scales?

The creature had a wide mouth like the ligan, but its teeth didn't instill the same terror in me. A wide fan around the head fluttered in the current of the creature's passage, and long whisker-like tentacles flowed backward from its snout. It reminded me of pictures I'd seen of mythical Chinese dragons. As if it could sense my nerves, the sea dragon slowed its approach and hung in midwater, staring at me. I gazed into the creature's eyes.

I nearly melted into them. The swirling depths of color were fascinating. Every hue imaginable of blue and green striated the large, soulful eyes and captivated me. I couldn't imagine the dragon ever harming me, not when it could see into my very soul.

But was that what it wanted me to think? I looked

away, confused. Was it, in fact, mesmerizing me so that I would remain helpless before it attacked? Similarly strange creatures lived at the Seamount.

But the dragon has saved me, and it wasn't attacking now. Maybe I was too suspicious, the way Byssa often told me I was. Could the creature simply be a friend, for its own unfathomable reason?

I looked into its gorgeous eyes once more, struck anew by their beauty. The dragon gazed at me for a moment longer, then it glanced at the bleeding wound on my leg. I looked down, surprised at the cloud of blood pooling in the water. With the adrenaline of the ligan attack, the pain hadn't even registered.

Well, it registered now. I winced and looked around for seaweed on the seafloor, but we were too deep for most to grow.

But I couldn't leave my leg to bleed. Sure, it would clot soon, but every second that blood leaked from my body was another second that a shark could catch my scent and trace it back to me. With an open wound, I was a large neon sign screaming dinner. Squirter vibrated with distress from his perch on my shoulder.

The dragon moved forward slightly then paused as if assessing my reaction. When I didn't move, it swam forward a tiny bit more. I held my breath. What was it doing? Oddly, I felt calmed by its strange behavior. I'd seen plenty of predators in my time, and none had ever approached with such caution. The dragon wanted something else, and I was curious enough to let it approach.

The dragon must have seen something of my

resolution in my face because it swam forward at a slow but steady rate. Its head bowed to my bleeding thigh, and I tensed. Was this the moment it attacked? Should I prepare a hum of compulsion to push it away?

The dragon opened its mouth, and I held my breath. A long, wide tongue darted out and licked my wound with a gentle rasp. I winced with the painful contact and jerked my leg away then paused and stared at my leg. Pain didn't grip my thigh any longer. The wound was closing before my eyes. When it had fully, miraculously, healed, leaving only an angry red seam on my pale skin, I glanced at the sea dragon.

It gazed at me. Then it turned its head to the side and propelled its sleek, sinuous body until it disappeared from sight.

Thank you, I called out with a hum, feeling foolish but needing to say something in gratitude. The shape didn't pause, and it quickly vanished from my skin sense.

My solitude snapped me back to my mission. My leg was healed, and we had people to save. Hades and the others were out of sensing range by now, so I undulated quickly to catch up.

It didn't take me long. The group was far smaller than it had been before we'd encountered the ligan, and I swam up to Hades with a questioning expression.

Relief swept across his face, and he gave me a swift hug. *You're okay. I was really worried.*

Where is everyone? I gestured at the group of six with us.

Hades grimaced. *Did you see the one guy who got eaten? The rest were injured and swam up to Branc's boat. We're all that's left in working order.*

That's fine, I said loudly for the benefit of our small group listening in. *We've already conquered plenty of mer folk—and who knows how many Cetus and the others have taken down—as well as made it through a ligan. If we can survive that, we can do anything.*

The others looked heartened. Hades raised an eyebrow at my overly optimistic words but didn't say anything to negate them. The others needed a pep talk, even if I didn't believe my own assertions.

Someone's coming, Pod the bartender said, his dusky skin blending into the darkness of the water. *Mer folk. Hide.*

We dashed to the seafloor, which was liberally sprinkled with boulders and jagged bedrock hiding deep crevasses. Everyone disappeared into the largest crack, and I wriggled in to join the press of bodies between sharp rocks. Squirter climbed higher on my shoulder to avoid being squished.

I had no desire to fight. Despite our victories so far and our weapons, we were only eight against a team of alert mer folk. We might be able to defeat them, but likely with a cost. As my foster-father Eelway had always taught me, it was better to hide than to bleed.

A low hum of calling startled me. It wasn't directed at the mer folk, but instead was pitched at a frequency that best attracted fish predators. I glanced around and saw Placida with a look of concentration on her face.

What are you doing? I said to her.

She ignored me and continued her hum. I left her to it, since she clearly had a plan, and I did not. The call was too low for mer folk to hear, so it didn't really matter.

I closed my eyes and sensed the mer folk getting

closer. I held my breath, and my heartbeat sped up until its thumping was almost painful in my chest. If we could remain undetected until the mer folk passed us, we could carry on toward the shipwreck without engaging them in battle at all.

More figures swam purposefully toward the mer folk, who stiffened and turned to meet the newcomers.

You called sharks? I gestured angrily to Placida. She stopped her hum and glared at me.

What were you doing? she replied. *A whole lot of nothing. Now the sharks can attack, and we can sneak by while the mer folk are busy. You're welcome.*

I grimaced and exchanged a glance with Hades. He shrugged.

She's not wrong, Hades said to me quietly. *It is a good distraction.*

But it was wrong. I'd been down this road before, using my siren ability to compel everything my way. The sharks had no say in what they were doing, and Placida was putting them in harm's way without their consent. I'd promised Byssa, Levi, and myself that I would do better than that, be better than that. Our lives might be in danger, but that wasn't a justification to put other innocent lives on the line.

Placida changed her hum to one of attack, and the sharks darted forward as one. The mer folk cried out, and I felt the movement of their bone spears. Blood oozed into the water.

Stop it, I cried to Placida. When she didn't cease her hum, I made one of my own. I imbued my word with as much power as I could muster. *STOP.*

Placida coughed with wide eyes, and her humming stopped. The carnage above us continued, and I wriggled out of the crevasse to better survey the scene.

The mer folk, true to form, were putting up a good fight. None was hurt, and one of the sharks was already bleeding from a gash on its flank. My heart twisted in guilt and anger.

Leave, I shouted in the wordless vibration that the sharks would understand. *Stop, and leave.*

The three sharks paused mid-attack, one with its mouth open. The mer folk whipped around at the sound of my hum.

As one, the sharks turned and flipped their tails with unhurried motions until they disappeared into the deepening gloom. Now that the sharks were no longer a concern, the mer folk turned toward me with bared teeth. A few had bite marks on their limbs that oozed blood, but they ignored their pain in favor of approaching me with bone spears.

A rush of current poured around me as my fellow half-sirens surrounded me from their hiding place in the rocks. Hades must have urged them forward. He floated beside me now, his usually jovial face grim with resolve.

Put down your weapons, said a mer woman with elaborate twists of bones and shells in her hair. *And we will not harm you. You will be escorted to the Seamount where you belong.*

Thanks, but no thanks, Hades said loudly. *We're not afraid of you. We fended off dozens of mer folk already today. Come get us.*

Only I could feel the tremble of Hades's arm brushing mine, but I glared at the mer folk with as much ferocity as I could muster.

We'd drifted in the current, and at the very edge of my skin sense, a large shape loomed. Was that the shipwreck? Were we that close to Eris and the other captives?

So be it, the mer woman said with satisfied finality. Together, the mer folk pointed their bone spears in our direction. I swallowed hard. Squirter hummed a quiet vibration of courage, and I straightened my shoulders.

Two of our number tossed their nets at the closest mer folk. One became tangled in it, but the other dodged it with swift grace and lunged at the netter, Shelley. She squealed with pain, and her neighbor prodded the mer man with his stinger prod.

I joined the fray with a yell, Hades beside me. Spears flash toward me, but I batted them away with my stinger prod and tried to land a hit. It wasn't easy without Byssa as my netting partner, but Hades was proficient with his speargun, and together we subdued one of the mer folk.

But there were too many, and our little battered team was running low on energy. The mer folk were bursting with vigor, and it showed.

What do we do? I hummed to Hades, our backs to each other. I jabbed at a passing mer woman with my prod, but only succeeded in sideswiping her leg.

Keep fighting, he vibrated back. *It's the only thing we can do.*

A blast of disruption song startled me, and I glanced to the side. Cetus emerged from the murky water, his eyes alight with the heat of victory. A group of our half-sirens followed him.

I nearly melted in relief but kept my wits about me

enough to take advantage of the mer man's distraction in front of me. With a stab of my needle, he fell limp.

Cetus raced toward me and grabbed an approaching mer man around the waist. My friend must have lost his weapon along the way, because he had nothing except his bare hands against an aggressive, fully armed mer man.

Cetus, no! I yelled in horror.

Predictably, the mer man twisted in Cetus's grip and slashed at his stomach with the tip of his sharp spear. Cetus's eyes rolled at the pain, and he released the mer man to clutch his side. The mer man raised his spear to land a killing blow.

No! I screamed, but I was too far away to rush to Cetus's defense.

A series of eerie, high-pitched seal chirps echoed through the water column. The mer folk froze. At another descending row of chirps, they undulated their long bodies and disappeared. Squirter crawled over my torso until his arms wrapped around my neck.

Where did they go? I cried to Hades. *And why?*

I don't know, he said grimly. *But I need to get Cetus to safety. Keep going. I'll take him to Branc's boat and come back when I can.*

Without waiting for a reply, Hades swam toward Cetus, who was curled into the fetal position, black blood blossoming in the water around his side. Hades wrapped an arm around Cetus's chest and tugged him upward.

I hugged myself and looked around. The few half-sirens that were left—maybe ten altogether, including Byssa's acquaintances Placida and Shelley—looked bewildered at our solitude. The call had been from a seal shifter, likely Selo. Why had he called the mer folk off, especially since they had been winning? What did Selo have planned?

And where had Pod gone? He hadn't left with Hades and Cetus. A sinking feeling in my gut pushed me closer to the answer, but I didn't have time to dwell on my conclusions.

The current had pushed us even closer to the shipwreck, and I could feel movement among its moldering wreckage of wood and metal. The ship must have been an old tugboat at one time, but today it was a barnacle encrusted husk of its former self. A familiar figure lurked behind the hulk, and my heart leaped. Eris was there. Selo hadn't taken our friends to the Seamount yet. We weren't too late.

The captives are there, I said to the others. *Let's get them!*

A massive current, like the bow wave on a ship, pushed me sideways. My stomach dropped into my feet, and I looked toward the disturbance.

A huge arm, patterned dark like a bruise and covered with suction cups along the bottom side, reached out of the darkness and pushed aside Shelley like I might flick away a fly on land.

They brought a brigar, Placida said, her eyes wide.

CHAPTER 27

The gigantic octopus moved into view with the slithering ease of Squirter, but on a massive scale. Brigars grew as large as a ship, and this one was no exception. The downed tugboat beside it was dwarfed by the bulk of this monster.

My jaw dropped. There was nothing we could do against a brigar, nothing but run. Around me, everyone's face wore identical expressions of horror.

Swim! I screamed, and my call of distress woke the others from their stupefaction. They scattered toward the seafloor in the hope of finding a crevasse narrow or deep enough that the brigar's arm couldn't follow. Given that even giant octopuses had no bones and could therefore squeeze into unlikely places, it was a fool's hope.

But we had to do something. I darted downward with the same intention, but Squirter's familiar presence on my shoulder disappeared. I twisted with fear, and his tiny body jetted toward the monster now targeting my friends with its grasping, searching arms.

Squirter, I wailed, but the little octopus ignored me. I dropped to the seafloor and peered out from behind a boulder, unable to leave my tiny friend, but too frightened to join him on his suicide quest. My eyes grew hot, and if I'd been on land, tears would have tracked down my face. What was Squirter doing? Why didn't he flee with the rest of us?

I nearly lost sight of Squirter in the mass of enormous,

"

writhing arms and suckers that was the angry brigar. A huge, yellow eye roamed ceaselessly, looking for half-sirens to wrap the tip of its arms around and bring to the hungry beak under its mantle. My skin sense was hardly any use with the chaos of currents made by the octopus.

Finally, Squirter jetted into view. He hovered in front of the brigar, no larger than its angry eye, and waited there. Did he communicate with the brigar in their own cephalopodian way? I had no way of knowing.

One grasping arm groped toward me on the seafloor. I froze behind my boulder, too frightened to move but certain my end was near. It relentlessly searched through every crevasse in the rocks, and mine would soon be next. I clenched my fingernails into my palms.

A kick away from me, the brigar's arms paused. The giant octopus brought the tip of one arm that ended in an almost delicate point and touched Squirter's mantle gently. Then, with a motion that caused tumultuous currents, the giant octopus crawled smoothly along the seafloor toward open ocean.

Squirter jetted back to me, where I sprawled over the boulder, panting with the release of fear. He hummed a satisfied note.

What did you do? I asked breathlessly. *How did you make it stop?*

I know her, Squirter said proudly. *All is good.*

Squirter and the enormous sea monster knew each other? Was there an octopus club at the Seamount I didn't know of? I still didn't understand how he'd stopped the brigar when she had clearly been forced to be here by mer folk, but I didn't argue. We were alive, and that was what mattered.

I rose from my boulder and looked around. My fellow half-sirens were emerging cautiously from their hiding places and clustering together. I started to join them, then my skin sense picked up two signals. One was a line of roped-together people rising from the shipwreck. The other was a group of spear-wielding mer folk from the opposite direction. Since the brigar hadn't killed us, the soldiers were here to finish the job.

But Selo was getting away with Eris and the others. If I stayed to be distracted by the mer folk menace, the captives would be lost to us forever. It took me one agonized second to decide.

Keep the mer folk busy, I shouted at the others. *I'm stopping Selo.*

I didn't wait to see if my order was being followed. I undulated my body as fast as I could, and Squirter jetted along beside me. The shipwreck of the old tugboat loomed out of the darkness, derelict and forbidding, with a bevy of schooling fish hovering around its mussel and anemone-encrusted sides. Behind me, the clash of fighters shifted currents into a chaotic mess that buffeted my sensitive skin. I ignored it and focused my attention forward.

Selo was at the head of the line of trussed up half-sirens. The captives' knees were tied against their chests, so they remained unable to move independently. Selo dragged them through the water with Pod next to him. Rage filled my chest, and I darted straight for the two.

Selo, I shouted. *Stop!*

Pod darted forward, a look of concentration on his

face. He raised his spear gun and pointed it at me, but I flipped to the side and pushed my stinger prod at his stomach. He tried to bat it away, but the tip caught his arm. He stared at me with wide eyes.

Traitor, I said slowly and clearly. *What did he promise you? Don't you know it's all lies?*

Pod's furious face relaxed into blank unconcern as the poison took hold. He drifted away, and I whirled to face the seal shifter.

Selo scowled at me. *Join us, siren scum*, he said in his seal shifter accent, spoken with only gestures and clicks. His chest was bare, exposing the speckles that distinguished him as a seal shifter, but he wore a flimsy pair of swim shorts. *Come back to the Seamount where you belong. It's either that or be killed by the mer folk who understand the stakes.*

The stakes of what? Living on land, the way half-sirens—and some seal shifters—have done for centuries? I shook my head and swam forward. *Everything was working fine until you showed up. We all know to keep our mouths shut around dry folk. Let my friends go. You don't have the right to kidnap them.*

I have every right, Selo snarled. He loosely wrapped the kelp rope that contained the captives to a rocky outcrop beside him. *Those at the top don't seem to care, but someone has to protect our way of life.*

Selo's snarl grew deeper as his body lengthened and transformed. Arms widened into flippers, legs fused, feet flattened, and his svelte body grew rounded and sleek. His thin shorts split and floated away in the water. Within seconds, a seal gazed at me with deep brown eyes that were somehow clearly filled with anger, even without humanoid features.

I braced myself. While seal shifters were generally a peaceful, tranquil race, their sharp teeth and skillful swimming made them formidable foes when pressed. I had my stinger prod, but my best weapon now was my siren song. Shifters weren't immune to compulsion like mer folk were, so I felt confident as Selo approached.

Until I started to hum. When Selo didn't deviate from his target—me—I panicked. Was Selo somehow immune to sirening? If so, I had nothing.

I dodged the seal swimming toward me. He twisted with ruthless efficiency and bit at my arm, which I'd retracted too slowly. I screamed at the pain, the sound lost in the water. My stinger prod fell to the seafloor from limp fingers. With my free fist, I punched the seal in the nose to make him let me go.

His jaw released my arm and he circled away, but not for long. I clutched my bleeding wound and tried to dodge again, but Selo headbutted my stomach then sunk his teeth into my side. I pummeled him with my fist, rage giving me strength. I was fighting for more than the freedom of Eris and the other half-sirens. I was fighting for my right to live where I wanted, for Byssa, for my own life. If Selo took me back to the Seamount, I was dead. If he succeeded in taking all other half-sirens away and cutting off the Grace supply to land, Byssa and I would wither away like Jules's friend Zeb. Either way, if Selo won, I would die.

Selo shook me, still holding onto my side, and I shrieked with pain. Squirter landed on the seal's head and bit down with his beak, but Selo still didn't let go. Dimly through my skin sense, the bodies of the three large sharks Pod had compelled earlier swam at the edge of my sensing. I could reach them with my siren ability. They could rescue me from Selo's vicious embrace.

But then I would be forcing them to put themselves in harm's way for my benefit. I would be no better than Selo, who wanted to control all the land-based half-sirens for his own convictions. I couldn't force the sharks to follow my will if I couldn't guarantee they wouldn't be hurt. I'd be no better than Selo.

But without my sirening ability, I had nothing else to fight Selo off with. His teeth sank deeper into my flesh, and I gasped with pain. I tried wrestling him off me, but his smooth skin gave me no purchase. He closed his eyes to protect himself from my scratching fingernails, and kicking was futile from my angle. Hums of distress from the watching captives filtered through my haze of pain, but I had little attention to spare from the shaking seal clamped to my side, teeth inexorably sinking deeper into my flesh. My only saving grace was that he'd clamped onto the very edge of my waist. If he adjusted his bite, he would likely puncture an organ.

I kicked again—because I had to do something—and the water rushing over my leg was impeded. My eyes widened.

The dive knife Levi had given me was strapped to my calf. I'd forgotten about it until this moment. My siren ability was useless, but I could still fight like a human. I was half-human, after all, as much as Selo despised that fact. It was time to act like it.

I twisted my leg toward my hand, gasping from the pain. Selo's teeth shifted their grip. Before he could clamp down with force, I slid the knife out of its sheath and plunged the blade into the shifter's chest.

He jerked, his teeth digging into my side tighter, then he released me. I pulled the knife free and stabbed him again in a different spot. Bile rose in my throat as the sharp blade pushed without resistance into Selo's flesh. His suffering at my hand wasn't my aim, despite his treatment of me, but it was important that plenty of blood leaked out of him.

After one last plunge of my knife into the twitching shifter, I kicked away, my hand pressing into my side. With a blast of desperate humming, I summoned the sharks drifting at the edge of my range.

Food.

Despite using my sirening ability, I wasn't forcing the sharks to do anything. All I was doing was alerting them to the clouds of blood that they would have discovered on their own eventually.

Selo's gasping breaths were frenzied, but I clenched my jaw and kicked with limping strokes toward the line of captives. We needed to get away from the copiously bleeding shifter before the sharks arrived. I was bleeding, too, and I wanted the sharks to focus on Selo, not me.

Squirter jetted toward me and clamped himself over my wounds. He wasn't quite large enough to cover all the teeth punctures and tears, but he sealed enough with his little body to reduce the flow. The pain was still vicious, but at least I wasn't a shark signpost.

Thanks, I hummed. Squirter tickled my stomach with a free arm then sealed another puncture hole with his suckers.

Swiftly, I untied the captives. They all hummed notes of gratitude, and Eris threw her arms around me when I released her.

Thank you, she said with a sob. *I thought I was lost to land forever.*

I patted her on the back, happy she was safe but in too much pain to fully appreciate her sentiment. Others I'd freed released the remainder of the captives, and Eris towed me away from the bleeding Selo as sharks arrived. I shuddered at the terrible scene that unfolded in my skin sense, even as I averted my eyes.

The half-sirens quickly found Placida and the others, who looked battered and bruised but all alive. A brief frenzy of greeting between those who knew each other ensued, but I couldn't join in. The pain under Squirter's body was overwhelming, but motion near us also captured my attention.

The mer folk that my fellows had subdued while I was dealing with Selo floated in a paralyzed stupor. A pale woman, long white hair floating in the current, tied their unresponsive wrists to a long kelp rope. She clearly wanted to tug the group away before we noticed her, but she must have sensed my gaze, because she stared straight at me.

I sucked in a breath. It was the woman who I'd encountered immediately after accidentally murdering the man at the Seamount. Her name was Marina Highcave, and she was the daughter of the siren-Protector. She'd known who I was and had chased me out of the city, even going as far as following me onto a fishing boat before I'd faked my own death to escape her. That was the only reason I was still alive and not facing Seamount justice.

But now she'd seen me. After a moment of blank staring, shocked recognition flared in her eyes.

CHAPTER 28

I twisted and chivvied the others away from Marina and the unconscious row of mer folk. When I glanced back, she wasn't following, but neither had she moved from her place. Had she been involved in Selo's plan to return all half-sirens to the sea? Did she know me? Did I need to watch my back for Seamount justice?

Those were all questions I wouldn't find answers to right now. Marina and her mer folk were in no shape to follow us—and we were too many for her to easily compel all at once—but neither were we in fighting condition to attack. The battle was over, the captives saved, and the others needed my help. Placida put her arm around me and led the others to the surface.

When my head crested the waves, a roar alerted me to the motorboat coming our way. Branc pulled up close by, and Hades threw a ladder over the side. I ushered the others into the boat. Before I joined them, I ducked my head under to answer Squirter's gentle tapping on my skin.

I want to come, his hum clearly stated. He crawled along my injured side to hug my stomach.

I tickled his mantle. *Go to the beach. I'll meet you there.*

Content, he jetted away. I resurfaced and climbed the ladder with wincing steps, blood oozing from my wounds. Hades wrapped me in a tight hug.

"You're back," he said, his voice gruff with emotion.

I grinned then pointed at my mouth. When Hades laughed, I leaned over the side of the rocking motorboat and breathed the water out of my lungs. Several hacking coughs later, I straightened with a wince.

"Always an elegant maneuver." I wiped seawater off my face and turned to face the interior of the open-roofed boat, my hand on my bleeding side. Thirty-two of us were crammed into the tight quarters, some even clinging to the gunwale of the boat with legs dangling in the water. Now that we were all squished aboard, Branc revved the engine. He turned us slowly toward the beach and to the abandoned boathouse.

"You're hurt," Hades said with concern. He bent across three jammed-together people and pulled an old cloth out of a side pouch of the motorboat. They'd clearly been earmarked as rags for checking the engine, but I wasn't in any shape to question their purpose. I pressed the rag to my puncture wounds, hissing at the contact.

Cetus pushed through the crowd and lunged at me with arms outstretched. His motions were stiff with pain, but his injured side had mostly stopped bleeding. His hum of gratitude and relief vibrated my body.

"I'm glad you're okay, too," I said. I pushed him back and examined his stomach, which was covered in a blood-soaked rag. "You're going to survive?"

He nodded, and we hung on to the railing, shoulders bumping familiarly while Branc drove us across choppy waves to the beach.

A group of people clustered on the shore. When someone spotted our boat approaching, a slight figure with black hair disengaged from the crowd of half-sirens and splashed into the water to meet it. Byssa clambered into the boat before it crunched against sand and threw herself at Hades then me, tears streaming down her face.

"You're okay," she sobbed. "That was horrible. But you got everyone." She whirled around to find Eris and hugged her tightly. "I can't believe you almost left."

"Thank you so much for rescuing me," Eris said, her grip on Byssa as tight as she received. "If that's how they treat us, I never want to go back to the Seamount."

The captives and others climbed out of the boat with shaky legs, helped by enthusiastic and weeping friends and family on shore. Tearful reunions seemed the order of the day. I helped everyone out until only Branc and I remained.

"It worked," I said to him. "We did it. My friends are back, and you still have clients."

"We won a battle." Branc stared at the chattering group on the sand with narrowed eyes. "But war against land-dwellers continues. The rogue faction still wants to stop any Grace from leaving the Seamount. Until we stop them, our lives on land are in jeopardy."

I sighed and glanced at the rolling waves tilting the motorboat in the wash. Branc was right. We'd saved the captives, and Selo was dead, but he hadn't worked alone. We needed Grace to survive, and we needed the Seamount's cooperation for it to be delivered to land.

"I saw Marina Highcave underwater," I said, my eyes still on the waves. Branc stiffened. "She took away the mer folk. She saw me." I swallowed. I'd never told Branc why that was a bad thing, but I'd often wondered if he knew my secret.

"She's the current siren-Protector's daughter." Branc

drummed his fingers on the motorboat's steering wheel. "If she's heading the rogue faction, this runs deeper than I'd feared. I'll have to talk to my contacts with this new information."

I sighed again, wanting to celebrate with the others on the beach, but weighed down by Branc's dire predictions. I brought my eyes to his face.

"Why didn't you come down with us to help?" I asked.

"That's why I hire people," he said, not meeting my gaze. "To do the dirty work. Besides, someone had to drive the boat."

Branc was skirting some truth he didn't want to share. I shrugged and left it alone. If he wanted to hide something, what did I care?

"I'll expect you at the club tomorrow night," Branc said, his voice growing hard. His eyes flicked to my rag-covered stomach. "Injury or no. I have a job for you. Don't forget, I still own you."

My lips pursed with distaste. Trust Branc to remind me of my debt at the culmination of our victory. Was it a reaction to my questioning?

"How could I forget?" I carefully climbed over the bulwark and dropped into the surf, desperate to get away from Branc despite the pain movement caused me. "Later, Driftwood."

I turned my back on my creditor and waded to the shore. Levi was among the half-sirens now with a large first aid kit beside him and Cetus's bandaged leg in front. When he finished with Cetus, Placida took his place.

I walked to his side and crouched down. "Can I

help?" I said in a quiet voice.

Levi jumped, then his face split in a relieved smile. He twitched like he wanted to hug me but refrained. My heart squeezed at the omission.

"You're okay. I've been hearing the wildest stories." He glanced at my stomach, and his brow contracted. "We need to fix that up."

"Do Placida first," I said firmly. "That wound looks terrible. I'll live. Here, I'll hold the bandage for you."

Levi didn't look convinced, but he cleaned Placida's wound when I shoved a sterile wipe at him. I looked at him closely.

"Levi, why is your hair wet?"

Levi didn't look at me, instead focusing intently on his task of cleaning the wound.

"It rained while you were underwater," he said finally. "I didn't bring a jacket."

I glanced at the sand, which showed no sign of rain despite the stormy skies, then I shrugged. Too many people needed our help for me to dwell on Levi's mysteries.

After we bandaged Placida's wounds, Levi's gentle hands peeled away the rag on my stomach. His breath hissed, but he carefully dabbed at the punctures with a sterile wipe and cut a large pad of gauze to tape over the area. Together, we patched up those who urgently needed help, Dr. Mazzaella joining Levi and me once she'd finished greeting her friends.

Branc's people got into the motorboat, and Branc drove away without any further comment to those of us on shore. I was glad. We'd teamed up for the sake of the captives, but I could never forget his hold over me. Branc didn't have an altruistic bone in his body, and it was best to keep him at arm's length.

In twos and threes, the others drifted away to cars after thanking me. Byssa approached me.

"I'm going to take the others home." She waved at Hades, Cetus, and Eris huddled together on the shore. Eris had her arm over Cetus's shoulder as he supported her wobbly frame despite his own wound. "Are you ready?"

"I can take her," Levi cut in. He glanced at me. "If you want."

"Thanks." I wasn't quite ready to leave him yet, especially if he wanted the contact. I hugged Byssa. "I'm glad this all turned out."

Byssa gave me a radiant smile. "It sure did. We're a ligan-brigar-mer folk fighting machine." Her face fell. "Except for that man that Driftwood brought. The one that the ligan ate, Hades told me. I think his name was Jet."

Levi closed his eyes and swallowed as Byssa left. I sighed deeply, trying not to remember the crunching of Jet's body between the ligan's teeth. I hoped he was now with the goddess Ramu in the peace of her endless sea. To distract myself, I changed the topic.

"Whatever terrible stories you heard of our trials underwater are all true," I said to Levi, teasing him now that the danger was past. "I thought I was a goner until the mystery creature arrived."

Levi stilled. "What mystery creature?" he said carefully. "It helped you? What was it, do you know?"

"No idea. It was long, obviously not ligan length, but snake-like. Honestly, it reminded me of a Chinese dragon, you know, with the whiskers and head shape. I've never heard of anything like it at the Seamount or elsewhere."

"Weird." Levi busied himself with packing up the first aid kit. "It helped you though, right?"

"It did. I don't think I'd be alive today if it weren't for that sea dragon." I breathed in, remembering another detail from that chaotic time. "It licked my wound—I thought it was going in for the kill, tasting my blood first or something—and afterward, the gash healed. Look." I pushed my leg in front of Levi's face. He glanced at the healed scar, then his eyes traveled up my thigh until he brought them back to his first aid kit. His cheeks tinged a faint pink, and I smiled to myself. Maybe we weren't totally over yet.

"I need to grab Squirter," I said to relieve the tension of the moment. We could talk about the strange sea dragon another time. "Give me a sec."

I waded into the water, sent out a hum, and waited. Before long, tiny suction cups gripped my ankles. I bent down, carefully lifted my little friend, and cradled him against my chest.

Levi was already walking toward the truck, and I jogged with limping strides to catch up. Levi looked at Squirter curiously.

"I guess you've never met him properly before," I said. "He's not at his best here, all squishy and wilted. Too bad you can't visit underwater sometime."

"Yeah, it's too bad," Levi echoed and turned his face

away. "Here, let me get the door and his backpack."

Once Squirter was safely ensconced in his special backpack container, Levi handed me a towel and I dried off before slipping into my skirt and tee shirt. Today's read "captain" with a stylized anchor drawing.

"You were certainly a competent captain today," Levi said with a nod to my shirt.

I shrugged and crossed my arms over my chest. "Except for Jet. I wish I could have stopped that."

"I'm impressed there weren't more casualties, to be honest." Levi gave me a searching glance. "You were all amazing down there."

I tried to smile, but the expression didn't sit right on my face. Instead, I glanced in the back of Levi's truck. Something was missing.

"Where's the seal shifter we had tied up in here?" I asked.

Levi's head whipped around. "I don't know. Did he escape?"

The blanket and ropes were gone, which told me that someone had taken the shifter instead of him freeing himself of his bonds and escaping. It could have been one of his friends, but my money was on Branc and his people. I shivered at the thought of what he had planned for the shifter.

"Yeah, I guess he escaped," I said with a shrug. "Oh well, we don't have to deal with him now. Silver linings."

I climbed into the cab and slammed the door shut. When Levi was also inside, he took a deep breath, turned to me, and grabbed my hand. I let him, too shocked to move.

"I'm so glad you're okay," he said in a hoarse voice. "It was horrible waiting on land. I couldn't stand it."

I squeezed his hand back, moved by his emotion. "I'm glad too." I laughed lightly. "Obviously. I won't lie, it was touch and go down there for a while."

I sighed, and Levi released my hand as if embarrassed by his display. He fumbled for his keys.

"It's not over yet, though," I said, unwilling to break the mood but needing Levi to understand. He was a Grace distributor, after all, as well as the manager of a business that depended on siren clientele. "The rogue faction is still out there, wanting to stop Grace from coming to land. They'll just try another tactic next time."

"And we'll meet it when they do." Levi started the engine with a roar and backed out of the parking space with a grim expression. He flashed a brief smile at me as he turned back to the road. "As today showed, we're not going down without a fight."

I leaned back in my seat, comforted by those words. The relief I felt at having friends at my back, ones I trusted and who knew me and trusted me in turn, was indescribable.

I couldn't put any of that into words, so I let a comfortable silence fall over us like a blanket of marine snow.

"Hold on, I need some gas." Levi pulled into a gas station and wheeled into a spot. "Can you pass me my credit card? The red one. My wallet's in the glove compartment."

I opened the compartment and grabbed Levi's black leather wallet. When I flipped it open, a red credit card was in the front slot. I passed it to Levi, who pushed his door open and stepped out of the truck.

Idly, I glanced at the wallet still in my hands. What else could I glean about Levi from it? Did he have a photo in there? What sort of cards did the Lodge manager tuck into his wallet?

Levi's driver's license was behind the windowed section. I did a double take, then unbuckled and carefully leaned over the driver's seat to speak out of the open door.

"Levi is short for Leviathan? Your full name is Leviathan Storm?"

Levi's cheeks colored again in that understated, delicious way they had.

"You can see why I go by Levi."

I chuckled. "Your adoptive siren mother must have named you."

He smiled tightly. "How can you tell? She said she thought it was funny."

"Named after a legendary sea monster? Bit of a cruel joke for the human in the family, especially if you don't swim."

I slid back to my seat, and my dive knife caught on the console. My fingers reached to the buckle to unstrap the weapon.

"Oh, I meant to say thank you." I held up the dive knife when Levi entered the truck again. "This saved the day. If you hadn't given it to me, I'd be dead right now."

Levi swallowed and glanced at me with fear in his eyes. "Good present?" he said hoarsely.

"Best present ever. I hate to admit it, but you were

right. I needed both my siren and human sides to win this battle." I sighed and wiggled into the corner of my seat and the door, trying to get comfortable despite my aching injury. "But it's hard to know where to draw the line, sometimes. You know, when I'm exercising my siren side." I glanced at him sidelong. "I could use someone to keep me accountable."

Levi caught my eye. His slow smile was a beautiful thing, like an unfurling anemone on a reef.

"I'd be happy to help."

CHAPTER 29

A few days later, I walked out of the aquarium and took a deep breath. The autumn air was warm from sun, but an undercurrent of crispness highlighted the coming winter. I didn't mind. The cold didn't bother me, and the ocean was always clearer without summer algae creating a murky mess in the surface waters. The wounds in my side were stiff but the skin had healed over already. It was time for a swim.

Hades was waiting for me at his motorbike. He passed me his spare helmet.

"You finally made it," he said. "Come on, I'm dying for a swim. Just because you spend half of your working life underwater doesn't mean the rest of us do."

"It's hardly half," I said. "And scrubbing algae off windows is not exactly a good time. Also, wetsuits."

I shuddered my distaste, and Hades nodded.

"Point. Wetsuits are the worst."

"Hey, Hades." I stopped him from putting on his helmet. I'd been wanting to ask someone I trusted my question, but Byssa had been frantically busy at the restaurant and her pool job since the rescue mission. "I wanted to ask, did you see the creature that saved us from the ligan?"

"Not with my eyes. I felt some sort of long body. I figured it was a baby ligan that distracted the big one, but it was such a mess down there, I couldn't tell."

"I saw it." I chewed my lip. "It wasn't a ligan. I'd never seen an animal like it before, not at the Seamount, not anywhere. I don't know how to find out what it was."

"Well, you're asking the wrong guy." He grinned at me. "I left the Seamount as a kid, remember? But if you want sea lore, you should talk to Marea. She lives on the Sunshine coast, past the Lodge. She's a story singer, the only one I know of on land. If anyone will have answers, it's her."

I turned the helmet in my hands, then shoved it on my head. A story singer sounded perfect. They were the knowledge keepers of our people, since although we had written words, memory and songs were far less clumsy. This Marea would know about the creature that saved my life, the one I'd felt such a connection to. I wished now that I'd tried to speak with it. As a siren, I could communicate with any creature. The quality of conversation depended on the animal's intelligence, but from the way the sea dragon had acted, I was willing to bet on a decent exchange.

It was too late now. The best I could do was to look up this story singer and find out what had helped me and why. I fastened my helmet under my chin and mounted the motorbike. Hades kicked the engine to life, and we roared down the road toward our friends.

At our destination, we climbed down a long flight of stairs and finally arrived at Wreck Beach. Byssa, Cetus, and Eris were waiting for us on the rocks, towels in hand.

"I'm so looking forward to a swim," Byssa said to us when we were close enough not to shout. She clutched her underwater camera in one hand. "It's been nuts the past few days at work."

"It's because you have three jobs," Hades said with a

shake of his head. "Swim teacher, chef, and teaching assistant at the culinary school. You're insane."

"How could I give up any of them, though?" Byssa shrugged helplessly with a sweet smile. "I wouldn't know how to choose."

I caught Eris glancing nervously at the ocean. "It will be okay," I said soothingly. "We'll be on the lookout. No one is going to sneak up on you with all of us nearby."

"That reminds me." Hades pulled out three packages from his backpack and handed one each to Byssa, Cetus, and Eris. "Lune and I already have them."

"Good idea," Byssa said, holding her new dive knife aloft. "Now I can stop borrowing yours."

"Exactly," Hades agreed.

"Thank you, Hades," Eris said with a heartfelt smile. "I'll feel better with this on. I need to get over this fear because I can't not swim. The knife will help."

"Does it work on oysters?" Cetus touched the blade with a bare finger, then yelped when blood welled on its tip.

I chuckled. "I think it will."

Eris slipped her shorts off and strapped the knife to her leg. She reached to the sky in a stretch. "I can't believe how close I was to being dragged back to the Seamount. I miss my mother and sister, but there was a reason I left. I don't want to go back to the ghetto and scrape to survive, or worse."

"I'm glad you're here, too." Byssa gave Eris a hug. Cetus eyed the two as if wanting to join in. He refrained, and I chuckled at his restraint.

"Are you ready to swim?" Cetus asked Eris when she

and Byssa parted. "The water looks good."

Eris nodded, and the two of them stripped off the rest of their outer clothes and waded into the low surf. Was Cetus interested in Eris? I hid my smile in my shirt as I pulled it off.

"Lune," Byssa said. She glanced at her brother, who nodded with encouragement. "Hades and I were brainstorming ways to help you pay off your debt. What do you think of a bake sale? Or I could sell some of my photos as postcards."

I stared at my friend, whose earnest face evaluated mine for my reaction. My chest grew tight. Why hadn't I swallowed my pride earlier, if this was the result of divulging my shameful secret? My friends rallying around me filled my heart with emotion. Byssa's ideas likely wouldn't work—a bake sale wouldn't earn nearly enough cash, and I had no intention of taking money that Byssa could make from her art—but the sheer fact that they were trying was enough.

"Thanks," I said once I'd swallowed past the lump in my throat. "Both of you. Thanks for sticking with me."

"Of course we're here, guppy." Hades punched my shoulder lightly. "Where else would we be? Now, pass me Squirter so I can get him in the water. Poor guy must be unscrewing his own cap by now."

I pointed at my backpack, and Hades opened the container and carefully extracted Squirter. The octopus hung limply in Hades's hands until he waded into the sea and released the little cephalopod to his home.

"So maybe a bake sale wouldn't work," Byssa said, continuing her train of thought. "I don't know how much you owe. You don't have to tell me if you don't want to, that's fine. But what about asking Levi for another short-term job at the Lodge? The pay was amazing when we went in the summer."

"I don't know if I'm ready to ask him for a favor like that." I twisted my shirt in my hands.

"You two seemed a little off," Byssa conceded. She glanced at me sidelong. "Anything you want to share?"

"I sirened him," I said in a rush, the secret draining from me like poison from a wound. "He wouldn't open up, so I tried to make him. The compulsion broke before he could say anything." I shuddered. "He was so angry."

Byssa didn't say anything for a long while. We stared out past the gentle surf to the blue vastness of the ocean.

"I regret it, obviously," I said finally. "I wanted to embrace my siren side, but I went too far. Now I'm trying to find the right balance. It's hard, but I want to get it right."

"I wondered if something like that had happened." Byssa turned to me. "Don't forget that Levi is a human raised by pale folk. I doubt it's the first time he's been on the wrong end of compulsion. It's probably a sore point with him."

"I hadn't thought about that." My mouth twisted as I considered Levi growing up at the Lodge. Had his brother forced him into things when their parents weren't looking? Knowing Austin, I wouldn't have put it past him. I continued, "Anyway, we're on speaking terms now, but asking for a job feels like overstepping at this point. Did he say anything to you while you were waiting on the beach during the battle?"

"Levi wasn't there. He only turned up with the first aid kit after you'd surfaced." Byssa shimmied out of her shorts and kicked off her shoes, then walked toward the water. "Come on, let's go for a swim."

I narrowed my eyes at Byssa's retreating form. Where had he been while the rest of us were underwater? What secret was Levi Storm hiding from me?

ALSO BY EMMA SHELFORD

Depths of Magic
Sea Fire
Sea Song
Sea Dragon

Nautilus Legends
Free Dive
Caught
Surfacing
Hooked
Riptide

Magical Morgan
Daughters of Dusk
Mothers of Mist
Elders of Ether

Immortal Merlin
Ignition
Winded
Floodgates
Buried
Possessed
Unleashed
Worshiped
Unraveled

Forest Fae
Mark of the Breenan
Garden of Last Hope
Realm of the Forgotten

ACKNOWLEDGEMENTS

Firstly, I'd like to mention my wonderful Kickstarter backers who helped make this project come to life. You are all amazing! Especially:

Heidi Moone
Thordis
Deborah Hedges
Rohkon
Collin Bartley
Lea Robertson

I'd also like to thank those who read through initial drafts of the manuscript and helped me polish it like a pearl: Anna McCluskey, Steven Shelford, Nadene, Bettina, and Lynda. Vincentas Saladis created the enchanting interior illustrations.

ABOUT THE AUTHOR

Emma Shelford feels that life is only complete with healthy doses of magic, history, and science. Since these aren't often found in the same place, she creates her own worlds where they happily coexist. If you catch her in person, she will eagerly discuss Lord of the Rings ad nauseam, why the ancient Sumerians are so cool, and the important role of phytoplankton in the ocean.

Emma is the author of multiple urban fantasy series, including Depths of Magic, Nautilus Legends, Magical Morgan, Immortal Merlin, and Forest Fae.